EROS
ISLAND

EROS ISLAND

Lucinda Betts
Dawn Thompson
Devyn Quinn

APHRODISIA

KENSINGTON BOOKS

http://www.kensingtonbooks.com

APHRODISIA BOOKS are published by

Kensington Publishing Corp.
850 Third Avenue
New York, NY 10022

All Kensington Titles, Imprints, and Distributed Lines are available at special quantity discounts for bulk purchases for sales promotions, premiums, fund-raising, and educational or institutional use.

Special book excerpts or customized printings can also be created to fit specific needs. For details, write or phone the office of the Kensington special sales manager: Kensington Publishing Corp., 850 Third Avenue, New York, NY 10022, attn: Special Sales Department, Phone: 1-800-221-2647.

Aphrodisia and the A logo Reg. U.S. Pat & TM Off.

ISBN-13: 978-0-7582-2214-5
ISBN-10: 0-7582-2214-9

First Kensington Trade Paperback Printing: February 2008

10 9 8 7 6 5 4 3 2 1

Printed in the United States of America

CONTENTS

CENTAUR HEART

Lucinda Betts

To SKK and WTT

1

The King of the Centaurs stood in my palace courtyard, thick equine legs stubbornly spread, muscular arms crossing the planes of his chest.

Despite the arrow I had aimed at his throat, Chiron did not look afraid.

"Take one more step toward me, Lord Centaur," I said, "and I'll loose this arrow." And I would, too, regardless of the wicked glint in his wide gray eyes.

"Akantha," he said, his voice melting over each syllable. "Do not allow Lycurgus to be your Champion."

"The Mother Rite is slated, centaur," I said, trying not to let his flicking tail distract me. Chiron looked dangerous. If I took my eyes from him for a moment, he could lunge. "And Lycurgus will triumph."

"Akantha," he said again, stepping toward me with a placating gesture. "He lies. He'll forgo the Mother Goddess in favor of Earth Shaker. You'll lose your rule. The island will become a patriarchy."

Coolly, I tensed my sinew bowstring, and he stopped.

Which showed intelligence. I'd hit any target in my sight. "I've heard other tales, too," I said with heavy sarcasm. "The Tears of Eternity have been found, and your greatest wish is about to be granted."

"I tell you no child's fable," he said, his animal hooves clicking on the flagstone. "I can prove I'm right—allow centaurs in the Mother Rite tourney, and I'll best Lycurgus at any weapon of your choosing."

I didn't know whether to laugh or shoot the beast for his effrontery. Aside from the fact that centaurfolk and humans rarely mixed, how could a centaur be a Queen's Champion? He had the phallus of a horse.

"I'd be mad to let a centaur into the Mother Rite," I said calmly. "Your folk are more animal than people. They're drunkards and debauchers."

The muscle of his broad jaw tightened, and his wide eyes narrowed at my words.

And I had to admit—he looked like a man, not a beast. At least in that moment.

"You don't know what you're talking about," he said. "Have you ever befriended a centaur?"

"I don't have to befriend a leopard to know I don't want it on Crete," I said. "Or in my bed."

"There are no leopards on Crete," he said, walking around a bench sitting in the shade of an acacia tree. "There are, however, centaurs aplenty."

I pulled my bowstring back again. "There'll be one less if you don't leave."

"You'll not shoot me."

I let an arrow fly.

On target, the sharp blade on my arrowhead grazed his brawny arm. Blood beaded along the thick muscle of his bicep, but he didn't flinch.

"The next one strikes your heart," I said. "I'll not be the first

Knossos Princess since the beginning of time to allow a centaur into the Mother Rite." I pulled another arrow from my quiver. "Especially since you've no evidence against Lycurgus—King Lycurgus."

Chiron stood as still as a rock. He looked about as solid as one, too. "Palace Phaistos fell, Princess."

Chiron maddened me. Did he think me ignorant of the facts? "From an earthquake," I said.

"Which is Earth Shaker's tool," he said, as if I weren't too intelligent.

"A coincidence only."

A wicked smile lit his features. Which might have been . . . attractive, if it'd been on a human. "Let me take part in the tourney," he challenged. "If I lose, you'll know you're correct."

"Not unless Earth Shaker himself walks into the courtyard."

His hooves clattered over the flagstone, and powerful haunches launched him through the air as he leaped toward me then. Thick arms snaked around me, disarming me, and my bow rattled to the ground.

"May Earth Shaker take you," I cursed, struggling in his arms. I tried to slam an elbow in his stomach, but it was no use. As easily as he might lift a newborn lamb, he swung me around until we faced each other.

Then he pulled me toward him.

"The Lapith King cannot become your Champion," he said, his face inches from mine. My nipples, crushed against his brawny chest, hardened. "Lycurgus is evil incarnate."

I looked into his face, unhindered by the sight of his equine back, his hooves and tail. With his high cheekbones and aquiline nose, his face was breathtaking. Thick hair the color of polished bronze hung in his eyes. His gaze was piercing, almost otherworldly, and his eyes reminded me of the summer sky just before a storm. If he had feet rather than hooves, I would have thought him from one of the noble lines.

But no one could do this to me—not and get away with it.

"You," I said. "Are evil incarnate." Then, with all my strength, I jerked up my knee, slamming right into his balls. Or that's what I would have done if he'd had human anatomy.

Chiron laughed, a surprisingly warm sound, and said, "See? For a moment you thought me human."

I growled something incoherent as his breath warmed my cheek.

"You progress," he said. And with that feral grin, he released me and stepped back. I stood a moment, staring at him. My knees felt as if the Mother Goddess had replaced bone with octopus tentacles. I—

A roaring filled the air, and the earth began to shake, making dust rise around us. The courtyard walls wobbled, and plaster chips from the fresco rained to the ground.

I stepped away from the walls into the open, but Chiron jerked an arrow from the quiver slung across his back. Nocking the arrow into his massive bow, he eyed the entryway.

Did he think to slay an earthquake? But Chiron didn't strike me as stupid, not at all. I retrieved and armed my bow, too.

"Hello, Princess."

"Lycurgus," I said with a smile.

The Lapith King sauntered into my courtyard exuding the sexual energy of a bull. His black hair hung in ringlets to his shoulders, and his lidded gaze examined Chiron, then me. "Is that any way to greet your future husband?" he asked, nodding at my bow, which I quickly relaxed.

"Husband?" I asked.

"Champion," he corrected himself. Apparently unconcerned, Lycurgus reached behind him and shook the dust from his cloak. As the dust cleared, I saw a beautiful fur of a type I didn't recognize. Jet-black circles swirled over a sea of honeys and ambers.

"You like it?" Lycurgus asked, seeing the focus of my attention.

"It's beautiful," I said.

"Like you," Lycurgus said. He unhooked the clasp around his neck and removed the lustrous thing. Shaking it out, he hooked it around my neck, enveloping me in his pungent scent.

"It's from the Egyptian pharaohs," Lycurgus said. "And I present it to you in honor of our betrothal."

But there was no betrothal—only the Mother Rite. Theoretically, any man could prevail, any man who could best Lycurgus.

"That is the pelt of a leopard," Chiron said, interrupting our private moment. "Like the kind you said you'd never want to meet."

"Then I'm glad it's dead," I said.

"This human should be dead," Chiron said, pointing his bow at Lycurgus. "He is no mortal."

"Chiron," I said. "Leave now. I've had enough of this discussion."

But the King of the Centaurs didn't move.

"Begone, centaur," Lycurgus said, coming to my aid. Menace laced his voice as he reached for the sword at his hip.

"He's not what he seems, Princess," Chiron said to me.

"You!" Lycurgus turned on Chiron with a shocking viciousness. His sword glittered beneath Chiron's chin, but the centaur didn't blink. "You abomination. The gods were drunk when they decided to mix hooves with brains."

"And yet, look at you," Chiron said. "You lack both—no hooves, no brains."

A warning sound escaped Lycurgus.

"I wonder what else you lack?" the centaur challenged.

But I didn't need schoolboys bickering in my courtyard. For the second time that morning, I let my arrow fly—this grazed Chiron's other bicep. The reverberating sound filled the air as the arrow buried itself in the wall, and for a moment none of us said anything.

"You've provoked us enough, King Chiron," I said. "I'll not ask again. Leave."

But then I saw something I likely should have recognized when I'd first found Chiron in my courtyard—he was mad. As cold as a winter wind, he loosed an arrow of his own.

I gauged its flight. It flew true, aimed for Lycurgus's heart.

But the ground trembled, and the world lurched beneath my feet. "Consort's balls," I swore as I fell hard against the stone bench.

Chiron remained steady on his feet, and he let three more arrows fly, one after another. Thick dust roiled into the air as the tremors ceased. Each hit exactly where Lycurgus stood.

"Lycurgus!" I shouted, waving my hand in front of my face. "Lycurgus!"

But the dust was too thick and I couldn't see. I couldn't find him. Taking my dagger from my hip, I searched the dust for the body of the Lapith King. I'd kill Chiron if I found him first.

But what I saw as the dust settled hurt my brain. Four arrows, fletched in centaur reds, stood side by side in the ground where Lycurgus should have fallen.

But Lycurgus was gone.

Across the courtyard Chiron looked at me with an expression I couldn't read. Was it trepidation?

"What've you done with him?" I shouted, vaulting over the bench. I landed with my dagger extended, a handspan from his chest. "Arm yourself."

But my words were redundant; his blade glittered in the meager sunlight penetrating the churned dust.

"You won't win this, Princess," he said. "I'm the best there is."

"I'll win," I said, lunging toward him fast. I hit the hilt of his blade and heard him grunt in surprise. I knew I'd numbed his blade hand. "I always do."

Chiron stepped back quickly, trying to regain the offensive, but I feinted and parried so quickly he didn't have a chance.

"I didn't kill him," he said, fighting off a flurry of blades as I yanked my second dagger from my ankle strap.

"I suppose he evaporated into the ether, then." Metallic clanging bounced off the walls, mixing with the noise of Chiron's hooves on the flagstone.

"You needed to see he couldn't die," Chiron said. He was breathing heavily now as I leaped to his off side. The courtyard was too small for him to maneuver. As he checked his balance I nicked his horse coat and grinned as a trickle of blood laced his sorrel fur.

"I'll find his body in the entryway or hall," I said, parrying a blow that made up for in strength what it lacked in speed.

"If that's so," he said, stumbling away from me, "then why did you find four arrows?"

The truth of that shocked me, and I blinked. If Chiron had hit Lycurgus—killed him—then shouldn't an arrow be missing?

But none were.

Chiron took advantage of my inattention and struck, hitting the handle of my dagger and making it fly from my hand.

It landed right next to his crimson-fletched arrows.

"Perhaps you set five arrows free. Where is he?" I asked.

Chiron shrugged, making the sheen of sweat on his chest glimmer. "Look," he commanded. "Inspect the area."

And I did.

But I found no corpse in the adjacent garden, none in the cool entryway. I found nothing in the back hall. But I didn't believe Lycurgus was alive. I knew those arrows flew true. I'd seen it with my own eyes, and centaur arrows always hit their marks. Therefore, Lycurgus had to be dead. Chiron played some black jest on me for his own dark purpose.

Suddenly terrible anger swept over me. I turned toward the centaur with deliberate calm. "Do you know what you've done?" I asked. "My alliance with the Lapiths would've ended a generation of bickering between Palace Malia and Palace Knossos. We could've brought Kato Zakros to heel." I threw up my hands in exasperation. "And now we have nothing but warfare in our future."

"He'll be at the Mother Rite."

The way in which Chiron said those words chilled me. His tone exuded certainty and strength, and I decided the next course of action right then.

"If he is, King Centaur," I said. "You and you alone will fight him."

2

"Akantha!" my servant said, bursting into my chamber. I was selecting the formal dress for the tourney where I'd take my Champion before all the land's nobility.

"What?" I asked. "Have you found Lycurgus?" *Or his body?* That thought filled me with dread.

"The King of the Centaurs is in the hall—looking for you!"

"What?" Bronze bangles dangled from my fingertips. I'd permitted him to enter the melee. What more could he want?

"Hello, Princess." For a moment I saw fire burning in his gaze—but then I realized it was the sun shining over his shoulder.

"You don't appear to be a dumb beast," I said, trying to irritate him. I suddenly felt very conscious of my tight bustier, which pushed my bared breasts up and forward. I hadn't donned my robe yet, and my nipples tingled. "And yet you're here—uninvited in my chamber—and that just might provoke me to change my mind."

"You won't change your mind." Chiron stood in my doorway, hip cocked against the frame. The amber light of the sun silhouetted him, lighting a blazing halo behind him. His red cloak magnified the effect.

"Your confidence astounds me." I straightened and took my asp from his soft woven basket. Unwinding Kleio, I let him coil around my neck and breasts.

"You need to come with me," Chiron said.

I laughed at that. "So I'm not in the palace when they find the corpse of Lycurgus?"

"There'll be no corpse found."

"Have you thrown it into the Aegean, then?" I swallowed. Lycurgus deserved better than that.

"I'm going to take you to the Mistress's Sacred Glade." I heard no question in his voice—only assurance.

"My ears must be deceiving me," I said, ignoring the audacious words. "After arresting you for murder, I must greet the folk traveling from Palace Malia and console the folk from Palace Phaistos." *And have my men comb the palace ground for any sign of the dead man.* "I've no time for a trip to the Glade."

"The summer solstice is upon us, and we must attend the Glade," he continued as if I'd said nothing. "We'll return to Palace Knossos for the Mother Rite—where I'll combat Lycurgus one-on-one."

"No," I said with exaggerated patience, trying not to admire his muscular arms. How could an army of mere humans stand a chance against him? Even Earth Shaker himself would pale in comparison. "I need to organize the tourney."

"I cannot conquer him—Lycurgus—without your help. We must go to the Sacred Glade."

I'd had enough. Chiron had lost his mind. "Get out," I said. "And leave me be." I shooed him with my hand, wishing I had another arrow with which to convince him—the man was as stubborn as an ass.

He stepped toward me, and I shouted, "Inis! Get the guard!"

"I apologize, Princess Akantha." He fully entered my chamber, but I heard the guards rushing over the flagstone. "Truly."

With that, he snatched me up in his powerful arms, spun on his massive haunches, and bolted down the hall—away from the palace guards.

"Chiron," I said as his hooves pounded rhythmically over the stone, "I'll kill you the first moment I get."

He simply grunted. In the convoluted passage system, he skidded around a corner, and I threw my hands around his neck so I wouldn't fall. Then he swept past a series of entryways that led nowhere only to slide left at the only corridor leading out of the palace. Aghast, I realized—he knew our labyrinth.

"How do you know our maze?" I demanded as my naked breast registered the heave of his brawny chest. Guards clattered behind us.

"Who do you think built it?" he said, not even panting as we left the palace proper and entered the grounds.

Despite my captive state, I scoffed. "King Centaur, this palace predates your birth by at least seven generations." The sound of the guards' feet fell farther behind us, but I felt no discouragement.

"You know nothing, Princess."

Chiron passed the bull-leaping arena and the barn when a figure appeared before us. Though Chiron's gait and grip jostled me, I saw the figure bore a mighty sword, and my heart leaped.

"Lycurgus!" I shouted. "He lives!"

"By the tits of the Mother," Chiron swore.

"Help!" I started kicking and pushing now, but Chiron's grip tightened around my waist. "Lycurgus, help!"

I heard the earth rumble and I groaned. Another tremor. But the ground shrieked this time, and Chiron's gallop lost its smooth rhythm. My body wrenched in his arms.

"Let me go!" I shouted, clawing at his eyes. Chiron simply tucked me under his arm like I was a hen bought at market.

The tremor escalated into an earthquake. Beneath us, the ground screeched and rattled, and a strange odor filled the air. It smelled like sulfur and burning hair.

Still Chiron ran straight toward Lycurgus. With me under one arm, he reached for his sword in his belt. The sound of metal on metal added to the noise of ripping earth.

Then I saw it. A huge chasm had opened in the ground between Chiron and Lycurgus. Other chasms opened all around us.

For the first time since I'd met Chiron, the iron taste of fear filled my mouth. "Oh please, Chiron," I pleaded. "Just stop. Don't jump."

But he did.

The power of his haunches collecting beneath him rippled through his body, and I closed my eyes. For a moment, we flew through the air like a pair of hawks—or more like a hawk with a mouse caught in its beak. And we landed with a thud so close to Lycurgus I could see the red veins in his eyes.

And then I jerked my body with all my strength. He fought my release hard, gripping me with bruising fingers. But I had the strength born of desperation.

I landed with a thud in the dust at Lycurgus's feet, and the quake stopped.

The Lapith King jerked me to my feet, sword following Chiron as he loped a wide circle around us. "That abducting murderer must be stopped," Lycurgus said.

But he didn't attack Chiron as the centaur galloped back toward us, his long tail flowing behind him. He attacked me— with his lips.

Lycurgus brutally pulled my face toward his and kissed me. In the few private moments we'd shared before now, he'd been formal. He'd never behaved thus.

But now—but now spider legs of fear crept up my spine. His touch was not at all like I'd imagined. He pressed hard and he demanded. I tried to yield, but my mouth refused to obey.

"She's mine, centaur!" Lycurgus shouted, ripping his lips from mine.

I tried to step back, but his grip on my waist kept me at his side.

"I belong to no one, King Lycurgus," I said. "And should you win the Mother Rite, *you* will belong to *me*."

I thought he was going to slap me, but instead he kissed me again. Cruel lips pressed against mine, and he sucked hard. His lips pushed against my tender flesh so insistently I tasted blood.

Then Lycurgus bent and flicked his cold tongue over my bared nipple, which hardened despite myself.

His hand made to grab my other breast then, but Lycurgus came face-to-face with Kleio's opened mouth, his loud hiss, and he pushed me away. Many folk are cautious around serpents, but the Lapith king jumped back, keeping a cruel grip on my arm.

I wiped his saliva from my breast. "What are you doing?"

But his eyes were tracking the centaur and I understood—he baited Chiron with his actions.

Chiron deliberately sheathed his sword, and he pulled his bow from his shoulders. His eyes, locked on Lycurgus, were calculating variables all archers needed: the speed and direction of the wind, distance.

"If you miss, centaur," Lycurgus said. "You'll hit the Princess." His voice didn't waver.

"I never miss," Chiron said.

I heard Chiron's arrow leave its bow just as I heard the earth's fissure tear in my direction. The ground started shaking, shredding beneath my feet.

Suddenly solid ground fell away and Lycurgus's grip on my arm was gone. Flailing frantically, I fell into a hole as dark as the underworld. My feet sought purchase to no avail; my knees scraped along earth and stone. But my fingers found hold, sinking desperately into the ground above my head. The strength of my ten fingertips held my entire weight. Gasping for breath, I tried to pull myself up, but dirt crumbled into my face, between my bare breasts.

"Lycurgus!" I shouted, fighting a growing panic. "I'm down here!"

Nothing.

More dirt fell into my face; the loamy scent filled my nose.

"Lycurgus!" I tried again. "Please help me!"

Still nothing.

And then the heat of his hand grasped my forearm. Relief washed through me, and nothing ever felt so good. Whatever evil I'd thought of him, I vowed to erase from my mind.

He pulled, and my feet found the side of the fissure. In a moment, my face met the sunlight, blinding me after the jet-black hole.

"Thank you," I said, throwing my arms around him and closing my eyes against the bright sunshine. I kissed him then. He deserved at least that much from his future queen. His lips covered mine. Giving myself to the moment, I collapsed in his arms, yielding to the warmth of his mouth.

The liquid glide of his tongue sent my mind spiraling. He awakened a hunger in me I hadn't imagined in all our meetings concerning the Mother Rite and the unification of his lands with mine.

And the brutal cruelty was gone—along with the threat from Lord Chiron.

With my hand in his, he ran my palm over his chest. The intimacy of the moment made breathing difficult. As he showed me exactly what he wanted, my fingers drank in the muscled planes of his pectorals and his abdomen, the tightly muscled curve of his waist, the thick sinews of his arms.

My body curved toward his. I longed to press into him until his skin couldn't be discerned from mine. I longed to lay claim to him—all of him. After this kiss, I knew I'd never look at another man.

When I finally opened my eyes, I saw him. His eyes were closed, and his face was turned toward the sun as if he savored the pleasure of the moment. Then he opened his eyes, and I saw—not lidded green eyes but smoky gray.

"Chiron!" I stepped back, horrified.

Then I slapped him. Hard.

He blinked, stunned. Then his gray eyes narrowed, erasing the dreamy quality of his expression.

I was . . . sorry to see it gone.

"You are a cold woman, Princess Akantha," he said. "But we must go to the Sacred Glade—now more than ever."

I stepped back from him, reaching for the blade at my ankle. But my foot found the lip of the fissure, and I stumbled.

His arm caught me, and he whipped me onto his back. "Hold on or fall to your death," he said. Then he bounded over first one fissure, then another. My knees clamped his sides, but when he landed, my face knocked into the back of his head, making my teeth click together hard.

"By the Mother herself, Chiron," I said. "I'm coming to truly loathe you."

"Hold hard to my waist, and you won't bounce," he said.

And I wondered if his words referred to horsemanship or some other sport.

3

His body pounded beneath my thighs as he galloped over the grassy plains. Chiron ran so fast that rocks and trees passed in a blur. With my hands around the hard muscles of his waist, I held tight, grateful that his quiver of arrows kept my bared breasts from pressing against him.

Something about him made me very aware of my sexuality.

"Chiron," I shouted over the wind rushing over my face. "I won't try to escape. Please, slow yourself." A bull-leaper could have jumped from the speeding beast, but I'd trained as a priestess, not a tumbler.

"We've no time," he said. "Not if we're to return to Knossos for the Mother Rite—and we must hold the tourney as planned."

"Why?" I said archly. "To save the world?"

"Yes."

Of course, I thought with exasperation.

But my mind churned. How could Chiron be correct? Lycurgus was not Earth Shaker. I'd known him my entire life, had fostered in his palace.

Still I had to agree with Chiron on one point—the earth-quakes seemed peculiar. Every time one might suit Lycurgus, a tremor would appear.

Coincidence. It could be.

Chiron's gait became choppy and I looked up. A thick veil of mist rose from the grass before us, and Chiron slowed to a trot, then a walk.

"We're here," he said. But I didn't release his waist.

"I don't—" I knew the Sacred Glade, but I didn't recognize this place, not with the fog.

"You must go into the mist alone," he said.

"This is strange magic." I swallowed as he helped me from his broad back. "The Mother's power is so thick."

"Today is her day, and she's requested you."

I looked at him, his intelligent gray eyes and strong jaw. "I don't understand," I said. "How did she request me?"

"Through Pholus's augury."

As a priestess, I knew—Pholus was renowned for her ability to scry the Mother's desires, but the Glade made my skin creep. Tendrils of fog formed long, silvery fingers, fingers that curled around each other. They crooked and they beckoned.

"And if I go in there," I asked, "I'll return before the tourney?" *If I go in there, I'll live?*

"You're to leave your weapons and take only your asp," Chiron said. The concerned expression on his face didn't comfort me. "I'll hold them for you."

"No, I'm keeping my daggers."

"Unless you have the Tears of Eternity, blood cannot be spilled in the Glade, not on the solstice."

"The Tears," I scoffed. "Would you go anywhere unarmed?" But by the look of his rippling muscles, I realized Chiron was never defenseless.

"Even a drop of spilled blood robs the Mother of power on her day." He held out his hand for my daggers.

I looked south, toward my palace. "What if we simply go home, forgo the trip to the Glade?"

"I've never heard Princess Akantha described as a coward," he challenged with an impudent expression lighting his stormy eyes. "Perhaps folk won't believe me when I tell them."

I sighed. "You can't goad me into anything, Lord Centaur."

"Are you certain?"

"If you give me your word the Mother Goddess herself requested my presence, I'll go."

"I give you my word." The teasing glint was gone.

Resigned, I unbuckled my quiver and unhooked my ankle straps. Then I noticed the fingers of fog had coalesced, almost solidified.

And fear danced through me.

"Wish me fortune."

For a moment, I thought he'd kiss me. But he didn't.

Praise the Mother.

I walked toward the Glade without looking back. I didn't want to see warmth or . . . anything, not on the face of the beast who brought havoc to my life.

Striding boldly into a wall of curling fingers would take more courage than I had, although I'd have admitted that to no one. So I closed my eyes and touched my asp, who twisted without apparent concern about my neck and breasts. I took a deep breath—and ran.

I'd thought the long gray digits menacing. I'd thought hands would grab at my ankles and trip me, or shred my clothing. I'd thought they'd yank me hard and snag my wrists.

But the fingers of fog had other interests.

Gently they guided me to a thick bed of moss, and there, they bade me to rest. They lay me down and pressed my eyelids closed. When I tried to open them, they pushed with quiet insistence. *Stay closed*, they said, and I obeyed.

The enforced blindness brought an unexpected comfort. In the purple blackness behind my eyes, silvery stars danced. Strange visions of wide gray eyes flickered just beyond reach.

The misty tendrils were surprisingly warm as they massaged away the ache of my wild ride on Chiron's back. They kneaded deep into my thighs, unlocking tension, forcing me to relax. The arch of my foot received the same attention, as did my calves and hands.

A fog hand wrapped around my wrist and pulled, using muscle-soothing pressure. At the same time, another tendril captured my other wrist; both my hands were above my head. Fingers worked away knots in my arms even as another hand grabbed an ankle and stretched that firmly. My legs were spread, and I couldn't close them.

An ethereal lethargy filled me, and I felt as languorous as an Egyptian pharaoh ministered to by slaves. If I let my imagination run free, graceful fingers would feed me honeyed figs while other fingers would rub oil into my skin. I knew the fingers weren't corporeal, that if I could actually open my eyes I'd see no man taking advantage where he shouldn't. Instead, I'd see the Mother's magic, and so I capitulated to the feeling. The Mother had requested my presence, after all.

As if waiting for my surrender, the fingers reached under my chiton, toward that softest part of my inner thigh. Other fingers started on my stomach, exploring and tantalizing. Still more fingers ran the length of my neck. Fingers lit across the inside of my thigh, barely touching. I remained still, afraid if I breathed the fingers of delight would desert me.

The ghostly tendrils remained, stroking. Hands lifted my hair and arranged it over my breasts. In my imagination I saw the long dark sheaths of it obscuring my nipples just enough to tantalize—to tantalize Chiron.

No, I wasn't worthy of that thought. I didn't know what kind of mischief the Centaur King was stirring, but his insistence on ruining a perfectly planned alliance made him dangerous. I tried to imagine Lycurgus's hands, his mouth instead, but the Glade's magic stole rational thought.

Fog fingers captured each of my nipples in a light pinch, and liquid heat flooded between my thighs. They pinched both nipples unrelentingly hard; they lifted my breasts and let them fall naturally. Wraithlike palms covered every inch of me—my breasts and nipples, my neck, my stomach.

Fingers looped through my hair and around my breasts. Small caresses stroked my neck, that tender spot behind my ear. Then they traced their way down to my breasts as other fingers parted my thighs.

The exhilarating sensation of those ghostly tendrils left me quivering. The heat between my legs, the silky river, craved relief. Under those fluttering fingers, I lost myself, blossoming, opening.

I wanted more.

I shifted my legs apart. "Please," I murmured. "Please." And I couldn't help it. Chiron's face appeared before me, his sensual lips, the lean lines of his cheekbones. I could almost imagine him—

Then fingers gave that release—sliding completely between my thighs. Fingers glided over my slippery nub, and I writhed in pleasure. Behind my closed eyes, myriad stars burst across a night sky in an extravagant show of beauty. The sensation electrified me to my core, and my body arched with the pleasure of it.

Still pulsing with delight, I drifted in a dreamy haze. Haphazard images flickered through my mind's eye. Lycurgus's heavy-lidded gaze split by a lightning bolt and overlaid by a cold midnight eye, something feline. In my mind, my asp arched in alarm at the cat's eye.

The baying of hounds filtered through my vision, urgent. The scent of danger permeated my languor, and I bolted upright, crushing the bed of ferns beneath me. The foggy day had melted into darkness.

Something feral approached. Without my daggers, without my bow, I fled, seeking the way out of the Sacred Glade.

The white light of the full moon bathed me, lighting the path as I fled. With swift feet I raced, hoping I traveled south. The baying pharaoh hounds sounded closer, leading their master toward me. I needed my weapons. I needed Chiron.

Then I heard an owl's piping hoot. I froze, and the hair on my neck crept—the Mother Goddess. The realization that She'd wakened me filled me with fear.

"Hello?" I called. My voice wavered and that angered me. I was the Mother's priestess. Who was I to fear her? "Chiron?" My voice was stronger.

And then my heart began to pound in earnest, despite my bravado. The dogs' cries were closer, and the robe I'd been clutching had disappeared, as had my clothing—I was in the spiritworld.

The full fat moon on the horizon illuminated the fog rising from the hot ground. I breathed deeply. The sweet scent of the *Albizia* blossoms filled the air. It made me wish for . . . something. A memory of his kiss laced through my veins. Chiron. His hands. His lips. Fear and eager anticipation filled my heart in equal measure.

The light directly in front of me shimmered. Something was coming. Someone.

A beast? Chiron?

No, a man walked toward me—not a centaur. I was sure of this, although only his silhouette was visible in the opalescent moonlight.

The man—whoever he was—was gorgeous: tapered waist, thick arms, broad shoulders. His stomach muscles rippled in the

foggy moonlight. I caught a quick glimpse of his profile, an aristo-
cratic nose and a strong jaw. Could it be possible? Could this
man be as striking as Chiron?

No. Few men could be. Not even Lycurgus.

He walked toward me, hesitant, like he looked for something—or someone. He stopped and turned, giving me a glimpse
of his muscular thighs. He had brawny thighs, completely
human, what Chiron's would have looked like if—

But it didn't matter.

Primed by the foggy tendrils, liquid flame coursed through
my veins. I walked toward him, naked and unafraid.

He didn't say a word. Instead he wrapped his arms around
me and held me like I was the only thing standing between him
and oblivion.

We stood like that for a heartbeat. Maybe two. I knew he
couldn't be real, but questions remained unasked. The darkness
pulsed with magic, and words would've broken the night spell.
Neither of us spoke, not with our voices.

Instead, I tilted my face toward his and saw love, love
adorned with desire. When he bent to kiss me, I didn't question
it. This was a dream—not real. The real Chiron had hooves and
a tail. This Chiron didn't.

The lips of my dream Chiron rested gently, almost chastely,
against mine, and the feeling was so exquisite I could barely
breathe. I wanted him to kiss me. I feared its power, but I
wanted his kiss like I'd never wanted anything.

And then slowly, a time-standing-still sort of slow, he sucked
my bottom lip into his mouth. I remained still as a startled doe.
He ran his tongue over that lip, nibbled it gently. My heart
pounded with the excitement, and that liquid flame licked at
my core.

Stillness was no longer an option for me. Something fiercer
replaced the frightened deer in my heart. My tongue sought his,
not with desperation but with eagerness. I flicked, wanting, and

when my tongue crashed into his, a small moan escaped me. I'd hunted this sensation; in my heart I'd tracked him to this spot. Now that I had him . . .

I wasn't going to let him go.

Our tongues tangled with a beauty belonging to the spirit-world. The stars pulsed in the sky nearly as brightly as camp-fires while the tip of his tongue dancing over mine left me crazy with desire. Even when I closed my eyes I could see the oddly bright stars and the glowing moonlight. And when I closed my eyes, it seemed that only he existed. In my world there was only his mouth and his tongue, his arms—his love.

My arms twined behind his neck, pulling him closer to me. He sucked my lips, first one, then the other. He sucked my tongue, breathing my breath until I had no choice but to yield to him, to give him everything he'd ever wanted—to give him everything *I'd* ever wanted.

His fingertips stroked my sides, my ribs. His touch left me slightly crazy. Insane images filled my mind. I wanted to curl into my bedding with this man. I wanted to be worshipped by him and worship him in turn. I wanted his mouth and hands and cock. I wanted him to explore every bit of my body and my soul.

I wanted to be his.

His lips, filling me with a slick heat, trailed from my mouth down my neck.

My breasts, my nipples ached for him. His hands slid along the base of my shoulder blades, and I arched my breasts toward his hungry mouth, relying on the strength of his hands to support me.

My heart pounded like that of a captured bird as his mouth inexorably slid toward my breast. When his tongue finally flicked over my pebbled nipple, lightning bolts from the Mother's Consort, Earth Shaker himself, couldn't have electrified me any more than he did.

The hot glide of his tongue over my nipple shocked me. He sucked lightly at first, then more insistently. I arched toward his mouth until I could bend no longer and even that wasn't enough. I had an ache between my thighs that I couldn't deny.

He must have sensed it, must have known we were both ready for more. He picked me up as if I weighed nothing, and he carried me in the direction from which he'd come.

As he carried me unerringly down the dark trail, I looked at his face, lit by the unearthly stars. His cheek, the long, straight line of his nose; it seemed I knew the curve of his brow as well as I knew my own.

He carried me into a small round glade carpeted completely with lavender. Tiny owls, like the one that had spoken to me, filled the trees, and they glowed a ghostly bright white. If bone could glow, it would be the color of these owls. And the light was so bright I could see the small purple stars of the lavender, the silvery green of their leaves.

The Mother was giving us her blessing.

Chiron gently set me in the deepest stand of flowers, and the scent from their crushed blossoms filled the night. Lying on the ground, I stared up at him, at the stars in the sky. He was beautiful, the length of his thighs, his throbbing manhood. I couldn't have dreamed a more beautiful moment.

I would have told him so, but words still felt wrong somehow. How did he feel about having human legs, a human cock? That made me think. I sat up with a grin, crushing moss beneath me. I wanted to take advantage of this opportunity, whether the Mother or part of my personal dreamworld sent it. For his pleasure—and mine.

Reaching toward him, I didn't know what I was doing, but I didn't think Chiron would care. Tracing my way down the hard ripples of his stomach, I slid my palm over his shaft. It was hot, amazingly hot, and hard but so smooth.

Taking my time, I ran my hand from the wide base to the very top. Liquid spread over the velvety tip. My fingertips memorized every contour, every change in texture.

Perhaps my touch was too tentative, because he took my hand in his, leaving my fingers curled around his cock. He pushed down, so that his cock strained against my hand. Looking at this face, I could see him contorted in pleasure, and the dripping tip told me how he liked it.

Did I dare take the next step? A piping call from one of the owls filled the night. I dared.

Leaning forward, I licked his shaft, tasted the salty liquid. He groaned, and I wanted to cry out, too. Knowing he wanted me so fanned that fire burning in my core. I'd never felt such an aching between my thighs.

I pulled him to the ground, crushing my breasts against his thighs as I licked him, savoring his musky male scent. He lay back, yielding himself to the touch of my mouth. But my tongue wasn't getting enough of him; my whole mouth wanted him.

Crouching over him, I discovered I could rub my aching nub on his thigh as I pulled his entire cock into my mouth.

It was delicious, this sensation. As my nub slid over his thigh, his cock slid over my tongue. The sliding and gliding, the way he arched into my mouth and pressed his leg against me. Within heartbeats my world shrank to just us, to the points where his skin and mine touched. The heart of the world beat in our mutual throbbing.

And then the pulsing exploded into something that seemed both natural and expected, and surprising. I'd been told, yes, but I hadn't anticipated. I saw exploding stars even though my eyes were closed. I exploded with them, then melted into a puddle of molten lava still pulsing with energy from the earth's core.

For a moment beneath me, his body was as taut and tight as an ancient oak. Then he quivered. Chiron's cock pulsed, and the salty tang of his seed filled my mouth.

Collapsing against his muscular leg, I inhaled his musky scent. I wanted it to fill my nostrils for eternity. "Chiron," I said, almost whispered.

With that word, my world altered. The colors changed in a subtle way—but profound, too. The moon shone with a more natural light and the stars receded to their usual distance. The glowing owls disappeared.

"Chiron," I said, clutching the man beneath me.

But my fingers curled around cool lavender stems rather than hot muscle.

And I might have believed he was just a dream, a figment, but his scent told me otherwise. His masculine musk lingered in my nose and on my tongue as I drifted to sleep.

4

"Princess Akantha," the Lapith King said, waking me with a nudge of his foot on my naked hip.

"King Lycurgus," I said, bolting awake. Standing, I refused to feel embarrassed. He'd only caught me . . . sleeping. "How did—" I tried to mask my confusion. "You've found me."

"I tracked you to this glade."

That thought gave me pause. What kind of prints had I left during the night? Best not to dwell on that. "But I'm glad to see you in good health, Lord Lycurgus. First I'd thought you fallen to a centaur arrow; then I thought you'd fallen prey to earthquake fissures." I crossed my arms around my naked breasts and wished I had my clothing, which had vanished with the vision. "But you seem very much alive."

"Yes," he said succinctly. "You'll take a chill." He wrapped me in his cloak. Seeing Kleio at my throat, he did his best not to flinch. "Did that beast injure you? Where is he?"

The magic from the Mother's Glade still had its tendrils wrapped around my mind. "What beast?" I pulled the cloak around me, grateful for both its warmth and its protection from Lycurgus's gaze.

"The centaur." Revulsion underlay his words.

A beast? "Lord Chiron?" I asked. "He didn't hurt me." But I didn't want to discuss the King of Centaurs, not with Lycurgus. "Thank you for the cloak."

"See?" Lycurgus said, adjusting the collar. "We can find a way toward mutual respect. We mustn't let a clash of our cultures stand in our way of happiness, my lady."

His dark hair tumbled to his thick shoulders, and his eyes were as green as spring grass. Lycurgus would appeal to some women. He'd appealed to me once. "Do our cultures clash?" I replied.

"We mustn't let our cultures stand in the way of love, either," he said, ignoring my question.

"Love."

"It occurs to me," Lycurgus said, "that our differences lie with the centaurs."

"I don't understand."

"If all humans united against the centaurs," Lycurgus explained, "peace would reign on Crete. No force from the mainland could threaten us."

"Are you suggesting a war against centaurfolk?" I rubbed the last of the Glade's enchantment from my face. "But we see so little of them in general."

"We've seen too many today. They've kidnapped you, shot at me. They're constantly inebriated and foul-mouthed."

Shame washed over me, and I couldn't argue the point. Even yesterday, I would've agreed with him. But after the Mother's vision in the Sacred Glade . . . I wondered if I'd been too hasty in my judgment. Today I felt reluctant to call Chiron's mouth foul. His masterful lips gliding over mine were anything but offensive.

"So I've discovered a solution to the problem," Lycurgus

said, stepping back from me and putting his hands on his hips. He whistled three sharp blasts, and then he looked at me expectantly.

"What is it?"

"I'd planned on giving this to you after the Mother Rite, after you were mine. But a day early will make no matter."

"You'd be mine," I corrected. Again.

A crashing sound broke through the forest to our west. Expecting a pygmy elephant or a river hippo, I reached for my ankle dagger, but I had nothing—no weapon, no clothes. Only Lycurgus's robe and my asp.

Seeing my reaction, Lycurgus chuckled. "He won't harm you, Princess."

"What is it?"

But the question answered itself as a large cat—as massive as a centaur—bounded toward us, eyes locked on Lycurgus.

It landed next to the Lapith King with a graceful bound. His sword-scarred hand reached to stroke the beast, which purred and twisted around his hand. Its eyes, staring at me, were mercilessly black, and onyx circles swirled over its amber coat.

"It's a leopard, like the cloak you gave me," I said.

"Yes, from Egypt," he replied, still petting the beast. "A nice pussy to lie in one's lap."

"It looks . . . dangerous." I wished this one were a cloak instead of a living, breathing creature. Something evil glittered in its eyes.

"It is." He flashed me a feral grin of his own. "It's been taught by the pharaoh's own trainers."

"Taught to do what, exactly?"

"Why, to find and kill centaurs, of course."

Lycurgus nodded to a soldier standing in the shadows, and that soldier nodded at another. Finally they dragged in a young centaur woman whose name I didn't know.

Desperation enveloped her. Although her bustier was still in place, her fine-spun robe had been shredded to rags and her hands were bound behind her. Someone had gagged her mouth with a wad of doeskin leather.

"Let me show you," Lycurgus purred, giving a shrill whistle to the cat. "This pussy's quite skilled."

"No!" I shouted, but it was too late. The soldiers holding the girl scrambled away as the cat sprang like some coiled storm. It lunged for the girl, white teeth shining with saliva.

"Watch," Lycurgus commanded, grabbing my arms as I struggled. Horror flashed in the centaur girl's eyes. "Princess Akantha, together you and I shall eradicate this hooved blight from our island."

This girl? A blight? Not with her fine skin and lovely golden coat. "Oh Mother," I said. "No."

I thought my prayer was answered. The girl bucked spectacularly, landing a solid blow on the leopard's chest just before it pounced on her. It fell to the ground, breath slamming from its chest with an audible huff.

But Lycurgus just chuckled, unimpressed by the girl's show of force.

A muffled scream came from behind the gag, and the girl spun on her forelegs, lashing at the circling cat with her back hooves. Her golden tail whipped behind her like a banner.

"Now watch!" Lycurgus demanded, turning his attention to the leopard.

With new respect for the girl's hooves, the big cat paced around the centaur as she fought the bonds tying her arms behind her. For her sake, I was glad her bustier covered her breasts. I couldn't imagine what the leopard's claws or teeth would have done to that sensitive flesh. I didn't want to imagine.

"This leopard has never lost a prey," Lycurgus said. His dark confidence sent a chill through me. "And it won't lose one now."

But the girl had a different idea. She'd quit trying to scream, and she was focused, her eyes tracking the cat. The leopard would not take her unawares.

Then the cat sprang.

She kicked her back hooves but the leopard was quicker. In an amber flash, it landed and sank its claws into her golden equine back. Quick as my asp, the cat latched its powerful jaws around the girl's throat.

"You monster!" I shouted to Lycurgus. "You've made your point, now stop!"

"They're the monsters." The Lapith king didn't take his gaze from the centaur and the leopard.

Using the speed and agility for which centaurs are renowned, she spun and bucked madly. She dropped her head and flung her heels high into the air, twisting at the same time.

Terrible bloody tracks welled on her back as the leopard struggled to remain astride, but the creature kept its inexorable grip on her neck.

I quit struggling in the Lapith's grip. I needed to reason with this man. "Please stop this, Lord Lycurgus. You're above torture and chaos."

"You need to see reason, Princess Akantha, if you're to rule by my side. You there," the Lapith said, pointing to one of the soldiers. "Retrieve the cloak. The cat can scent it when he's finished with this beast."

The soldier retrieved a sack and pulled a long red robe from it. My mouth went dry.

The garment belonged to Chiron.

Lycurgus looked away from the struggle. "I don't know where your centaur princeling has gone, Lady Akantha, but the leopard will find him. And you and I shall follow. It will be a fine hunt, don't you think?"

"No!" I screamed. I slammed my fist directly into Lycurgus's face, then I brought my heel hard into his groin. As he writhed in pain, blood pouring from his nose, I slid his sword from his belt. I kicked him again, and satisfaction filled me as I felt his nose crumple beneath my blow.

The two soldiers stepped toward me, but the girl collapsed in a heap between us, her face blue. The leopard clung to her neck.

Lycurgus's sword was much too large for me. Still I swung it at the cat, awkwardly hitting its head with the flat side of the blade. It landed with a clanging sound. At least the beast released the centaur. Then it yowled, a blood-chilling sound unlike any I'd ever heard. The cry deafened me, and the leaderless soldiers fled.

Cowards.

Then the cat turned its soulless eyes toward me, and I thought the soldiers might have the wisdom of it. It yowled again, and I tried to balance the heavy sword in my grip. My sweating palms didn't help. Neither did the Lapith King. Lycurgus staggered to his feet.

I had no shortage of foes. The cat took a wary step toward me, eyeing the blade. Lycurgus stepped to the other side.

"I don't want to hurt you, Princess Akantha," he crooned. "I want to wed you. Together we'll create a stronger Crete—an undefeatable Minoan empire."

I stepped back cautiously, knowing I couldn't outrun the leopard even if I escaped the man.

But the eyes of the centaur woman, who still lay prone in the dirt, fluttered—no, winked. And her chin jerked in invitation. *Get on*, she told me.

"Lycurgus," I said, hoping to placate him. "I couldn't let your cat kill the woman. I apologize for your bloodied nose." I held the hilt of his sword out to him.

With one hand holding his dripping nose, he made a gesture to the leopard. The beast twitched its tail angrily, but it sat and began to wash its face.

"Beloved," Lycurgus said in a voice made nasal by my blow.

"Please, let us not argue." He took his sword and slid it into its scabbard. Then he held out his hand in invitation.

I held out mine—and then leaped. I landed on the golden back of the centaur girl hard, and I heard her catch her breath.

"What are you—" Lycurgus started to say.

But the centaur girl was already scrambling to her feet. Gripping her sides with my knees, I grabbed her waist and tried to stay off the deep claw wounds on her back.

"I agree," I said. "Let's not argue. Toward that end, I'm leaving."

The centaur needed no second clue; she bounded into the forest.

5

"Thank you for saving my life," I said to the centaur girl. We were still deep in the forest, and I didn't recognize any of the paths.

"You saved mine, too. I owe you equal thanks."

I saw blood still trickling from her back and neck. "Let me dismount."

"Thank you," she said. "My wounds aren't likely to fester, but they ache fiercely."

"I'm Princess Akantha of Palace Knossos," I said. "If you return to the palace with me, we'll get them attended."

"I know who you are." The girl—no, woman—flashed a smile at me as I walked by her side. Her face shone with beauty. "I've seen you in the augury. The Mother Goddess has need of you."

My stomach curled around itself at those familiar words. "Chiron said much the same." And I didn't believe him. But it was difficult to disbelieve this woman. Her golden eyes reflected only honesty. "Perhaps I should've paid closer attention to him."

"I wouldn't have believed it either, if one of your folk brought this news to my village," she said, diminishing my guilt. "I'm called Pholus the Augurer."

"Well, Pholus the Augurer, could you direct me back to Knossos? I have a Mother Rite to oversee, and I've no idea where I am."

"Oh," she said with a disarming laugh. "You cannot return to the palace yet. I'm taking you to the Sacred Glade."

Vision or no, Chiron's scent still clung to me. I'd no wish to return to the magic of that place. "I need to return to the palace."

"My apologies, Princess, but that man," she spat the word, "interrupted the solstice revelation. The Mother still needs you—and the Tears of Eternity."

My face flushed at all the knowledge this young woman seemed to have. "How do you know this?"

"I'm the augurer." She stopped in her tracks. "And I must leave you here."

"Here?" I asked, certain I'd not heard her correctly. "Alone?"

Pholus the Augurer simply nodded, her blond hair waving in the breeze.

"Without a weapon?"

"Blood cannot spill during the solstice in the Glade, not without weakening the Mother."

A great weariness overtook me. When had the world become so complicated? I closed my eyes and sighed. "Very well, Pholus. Leave me."

And she did, the sound of her hooves beating away into the distance.

I looked around, seeking any clue as to my whereabouts. I had no intention on going back into the Sacred Glade, meeting up with hoof-less centaurs. I would go home to my palace. And I would organize my Mother Rite tourney.

As I eyed the surrounding trees, a thought occurred to me. I could rid myself of both Lycurgus and Chiron in one move: I'd forbid Lycurgus a place in the tourney. That way, he'd not take my lands. And if Lycurgus was Earth Shaker's tool—something I highly doubted—he'd be foiled. The final bonus was that I'd not have to permit any centaur in the Mother Rite—Chiron would have no one to battle if I disallowed Lycurgus.

Feeling more in control than I had since I'd laid eyes on Chiron, I looked around in earnest for any sign of a cardinal direction. The sun was too high for shadow. I couldn't hear the gentle murmur of the Aegean Sea.

Instead I spied that eerily familiar wall of gray fog, complete with beckoning fingers.

My maidenhead responded instantly, surging with hot desire. The memory of their caress over my nipples, between my thighs, made me long. Long for what, I wasn't sure. And I wasn't certain I wanted to know, either.

I turned on my heels, grateful for the clue. I knew now where my palace lay—directly opposite of the temptation of the cursed fingers.

Except now the wall of fingers lay directly in front of me.

What? Had I turned too much?

I spun in alarm, but I found my fears confirmed. The wall of fog completely surrounded me, and it was closing in.

Akantha, the fingers called, *Please come.*

But I would not, not willingly. I needed to go home and stop this madness before it went any further.

Then the drumbeat I'd come to recognize filled the air—hoofbeats.

And I knew—I couldn't simplify my life just yet.

"Akantha!" I heard. His rich voice carried easily through the verdant trees. I contemplated running or remaining silent.

But there was no denying him. He'd find me anyway. "Here."

As he grew close, the fog evaporated and an intense rainbow—colors more vibrant than even the frescoes in my chamber—appeared. The rainbow was no taller than a man.

"Thank the Mother, we've not missed the ribbongate," Chiron said, panting from exertion and taking my hand in his callused one. He pulled me toward the rainbow, which strangely resembled a gate.

"Stop!" I said.

He did, but he kept hold of me. The warmth of his hand over mine, his strength—I liked it if I were honest with myself.

But that wasn't the point.

"I've arrived at a decision regarding the Mother Rite," I told him.

He gave me a questioning look. And I wanted to run my fingers over his face, memorize each line until I'd etched each curve of his face in my mind.

"The leopard," I said at a strange loss for words. "And Pholus. Lycurgus has poor manners."

He took a deep breath, eyeing the rainbow, which might have been shrinking. "I don't understand."

"I'm not going to permit him to fight. I'll uninvite him to the Mother Rite."

"Very well." He nodded and started to step toward the shimmering gate, pulling me with him. The opening was definitely smaller than it had been a moment ago.

I dug my heels into the ground. "That means you don't have to take part in the combat," I clarified. "We're free. Go your own way." I pulled my hand from his with a jerk and stepped away.

"Please, Princess Akantha. Come with me."

There was something irresistible in his expression, something in the set of his stormy eyes. Concern and laughter gave him a rugged look that tugged at my heart. I couldn't refuse him.

"Are you certain?" I asked.

"More certain than I've ever been."

I laughed then, because he struck me as a very certain man. Then I bolted toward the rainbow gate and threw myself through with a laugh.

"Our visit here will lend the Mother Goddess strength," he said. Summer grass sprang green and tender to our knees, dampening our legs with early morning dew. "She may actually take on a corporeal form, if we burn brightly enough."

His dark bronze hair, hanging in his wide-set eyes, caught a stray sunbeam and glowed. "What do you mean, 'burn brightly enough'?" I asked.

His expression seemed hungry, and his muscles were so freshly used they rippled across his chest and abdomen when he walked. I'd never in my life seen a man as gorgeous as he.

And when his eyes met mine, I knew exactly what he meant. His words lit a fire deep inside me, and I knew—with absolute certainty—that I'd burn brightly for him.

"Look," he said, pointing to the myrtle trees. "She comes."

In the branches, something fluttered, matching the crazy trembling in my stomach. Dozens of small white owls filled the trees and sang. Like the fabled priestess to the pharaohs, they sang.

They sang the song of my heart.

His eyes turned to mine, heavy with purpose. Slowly, deliberately, his hands circled my waist and he pulled me toward him.

In his arms, time stopped. Peril and strife fell to the wayside. In his embrace, just Chiron and I existed.

My eyelids heavy with languor, I slid my arms around his neck. My breasts crushed against his chest, and my thighs pressed against his.

The speckled silver of his eyes, his intent gaze stirred my heart, and the clear purpose of his expression heated my maidenhead. As his opened palm slid from the small of my back to my bum, that burning heat inside of me did not abate.

I buried my face in his chest, inhaling the delicious scent of him. He smelled like barley and pine intermingled with his own musk. Closing my eyes, I let my fingers drink in his beauty, the play of his muscles under my hand, the breathtaking softness of his human skin. I let my hand, trembling now with desire—and fear—travel past his human skin. He groaned with pleasure as my fingers trailed to his equine coat, which was softer than I'd ever let myself imagine.

He grabbed my hips and pulled me tightly against him. Even as my maidenhead throbbed in pleasure, pressing against the place where human flesh met equine, I felt him change.

The world tilted strangely in my hands, and then the man standing before me was all human; his extremely human cock pulsed, begging for attention as it pressed against me.

"Chiron," I asked. "Are you real?"

"I'm real," he said, gathering me into his arms. Heat from his equine body warmed me against the morning's chill. For the first time since I'd known him, I embraced even that animal part of him. "And now I've let you know the secret of our people."

"Secret?"

"With the Mother's grace, we can alternate between human and centaur form."

"Then last night? You were truly—" I tried to organize my thoughts. "You were human! And you were there!"

"Thank the Mother, I was there," he said with a wicked glint in his eye. "And I anticipate being exactly there again. Come here, Akantha."

"How good are you with those human legs, centaur?" I unhooked Lycurgus's robe. I didn't want anything that had touched him touching me.

Chiron looked down at his legs with a questioning expression, and I took his meaning. His human legs were hewn with muscle. Powerful calves curved into massive thighs so solid they could've been carved of marble.

"True, they look perfectly functional," I admitted.

"Merely functional?"

"Vain creature," I teased. "Let's see how they work." With a wild laugh, I sprinted through the tall grass, pounding the earth. "Catch me!"

He wasn't expecting me to run, but he caught me, and I didn't fight him. I squirmed against him, letting my bum run the length of his cock. I struggled while he spun me toward him, pressing my breasts against the hard muscles of his chest.

But I didn't fight him. I wanted him too much.

"And is this perfectly functional?" I asked, curving my hand around his cock. Like his legs, it looked more than ready to perform.

"Do you wish to find out?"

Laughing at his blatant desire, I took his robe—he'd replaced his red with a roughspun brown—unclasping the bronze hook at his throat, and shook it out. I lay it in the thick grass that surrounded us; it was large enough for both of us.

"Is that a yes?" he asked.

"Come find out."

But Chiron didn't rush, despite my desire—or maybe because of it. With deliberation, he sat next to me, not touching me with his hands, but letting the warmth of his bare shoulder heat mine. His thigh, too, rested against mine, taunting and promising, both.

The early morning sun warmed me, but his naked presence was much hotter. The air between us almost crackled, tight with possibility. It could have been the magic of the solstice, but I supposed it was something more rare than that.

"I should tease you," Chiron said, touching me finally. His index finger curled a path from my shoulder blade to my inner elbow, making me shiver with delight and anticipation. "I should make you laugh until these heavy emotions go back into our hearts where they belong."

"Then why don't you?"

"I find," he said, wrapping his finger around a tendril of hair, "I cannot." He tugged it gently, insistently.

"Why not?" Taking his hand in mine, I looked at him from under my lashes, almost afraid of what I'd see.

"Because of your neck."

I laughed at the absurd comment. "What about it?"

"I find its beauty has rendered me incapable of speech."

"Your words were coherent." I tilted my chin back, inviting him to do something other than talk. "I think you exaggerate."

"Let me show you," he said. His hot lips found that tender spot just below my ear. First he nibbled, then he sucked. My breasts, thrust up and out by my clothing, ached for him, and the wetness between my thighs begged for his touch.

But he didn't stop. His lips and teeth found the back of my ear, and deliciously all of the hairs on my neck prickled.

I rolled my head to the side, inviting more kisses, and as his lips neared my breasts, I groaned.

"That's what I mean," he said. Desire blurred his words, thickened his voice. "How can I jest when you sit like that, tempting me?"

"If you kiss me here again," I said, running my finger just behind my ear. "You might find inspiration."

"It isn't your neck I want to kiss now."

"No?" I traced my finger along the seam of my bustier. "Would you prefer these?" I slowly wrapped my fingers around my breasts and offered them to him, the Mother's gift.

But Chiron's words escaped him for deliciously long moments as we learned the simple pleasure of his hands on my breasts, of his fingertips on my pearled nipples. I arched my back, pressing my tight nipples into his palms.

The feel of his skin on mine felt so pure and good. I knew it gave strength to the Mother. Indeed, the earth beneath us seemed to pulse with power.

His tongue danced over mine, caressing and asking. His teeth tugged my lip as his thumbs caressed my nipples. Heat seared our kiss, pushing nervous fear to the far background. I ran my hand through his hair, savoring its silky weight. And I wrapped my fingers in it, pulling his face closer yet.

He was mine.

The friction of his thumbs over my nipples brought a gasp from me, but also it brought a hunger for something more. As if he knew, he dipped his head and flicked a searing tongue over my nipple.

By the Mother, I'd never imagined this gift.

Then he lifted both breasts and buried his face, licking and teasing and biting. Desire swamped me, flowed over me like a storm surge. I twisted so that he didn't ignore my other breast, enjoying the press of his cock against my maidenhead.

"Don't stop," I said. "Please."

And he knew.

He straddled me. I stretched my hands high above me.

I was his.

But then he found control from someplace. He sat back, softly stroking my thighs, the curve of my waist. He slowed our mad passion, forcing us to savor it.

With a laugh of delight, I tried to sit, to pull his face back toward mine, but he wouldn't let me. Gently pushing me back, he ran his palms over the flat of my stomach. His hands memorized every detail of my waist and hips, the softness just under my belly button.

His hot fingers caressed the curves of my thighs and hips, teasing. His thumbs reached for the apex but then pulled back just as I believed relief was upon me.

"Chiron," I moaned, pushing myself toward him. "Please."

Then he was over me, his chest crushing my breasts, his

thighs asking mine to open. His scent surrounded me, and the heat of his muscled body pressed mine. I sighed and parted my thighs. I wanted this.

His fingers slid and slipped, lighting a fire so hot I quivered on the edge of something unnamable.

With the lightest touch, his tongue teased mine. Then his lips caressed my face, telling me with his every movement that he would not hurt me, that he cherished me.

But I almost couldn't feel his gentle touch. The flame lit by his fingers between my thighs burned too intensely. As he stroked me, I lost any control left to me. His fingers danced and slid around that sensitive nub, and my hips moved in a rhythm dictated by desire, not sense. Enslaved by the delicious ravishment that overwhelmed my senses, I yielded completely.

But he wasn't done with me yet; he wasn't ready for the final stroke.

He leaned down and buried his face between my legs, his finger tracing lazy circles around that nub.

Hi tongue ran the length of me as his fingers worked their magic. But when he sucked I thought the universe might explode. "Don't," I said. "I'm so—"

But his hands reached up to my breasts. His rough fingers caught my nipples and rolled them into hard, tingling tips. He sucked again, sudden and insistent, and it brought me right to the edge. I thrust toward him, begging with my body. I couldn't hold back. He sucked again—and lightning lit behind my eyes, zapping me from toes to fingers.

My core throbbed and pulsed, reaching for something that wasn't there, and I gasped at the intensity, amazed by my body.

"I never knew," I said breathlessly. "That it'd feel so . . ."

Chiron gave me that rakish grin. "I'm not finished with you yet, Princess."

More than the ground pulsed around us. Now the very air we breathed seem to vibrate with power from the spiritworld.

"No waiting," I said. His hard, swollen cock pressed against me, but I didn't flinch. "I'm ready for you, for this."

He slid into me, slowly at first. But when he came upon that membrane, he pushed past in a quick movement. I gasped.

Stilling himself, he covered my forehead with little kisses. "I've not hurt you?"

"No," I said, and it was true. I slid him just slightly deeper with the most tentative glide of my hips. It caused no pain.

Now ravenous for him, I wrapped my legs tightly around his hips and pulled until he sank fully into me, spreading me, filling me deliciously full.

Then I took the lead, inviting him to thrust faster, and harder. I met him there. The magnitude of our desire for each other overwhelmed me. Under him, I could hardly bear the pleasure of his penetration.

I watched his jaw flex in an effort to control himself, but I didn't want control. I wanted wild abandon, his and mine. His shaft sank delectably into me, and I knew I stood on the brink.

"Oh Mother," Chiron groaned.

I thrust myself up and met him in one more gratifying thrust.

"Chiron!" I cried as the orgasm flashed through me in a luscious explosion.

And when he shuddered, his whole body stiffening, I surrendered. Within seconds, I came with him. Deep inside me, the pulsing of his cock and the spilling of his seed satisfied the hunger I'd felt since I'd first kissed him.

This man was a gift from the Mother Goddess herself.

But with my body still shuddering in pleasure, a cold finger of dread curled around my heart. I knew when I opened my eyes I'd see the immortal Mother Goddess herself.

But I was wrong.

6

"Ah, how quaint," Lycurgus said, looming above us. "A charming little love nest." He looked at me, his eyes raking my naked breasts, my exposed thighs—the smear of blood. I felt excruciatingly aware of my swollen lips and my disheveled hair. "And what a pretty little bird you have in it, too."

"Your problem," Chiron said, deliberately wrapping his robe around me, "stems from the fact that you cannot distinguish a woman from a bird."

I watched Lycurgus scowl. "You defy humanity with your hooves," the dark-haired man spat.

I thought this ironic since Chiron was in human form. My champion stood, rested his hands easily on his lean hips, and looked at his foe. "Perhaps envy lies at the heart of your disgruntlement," he suggested. "Though not of hooves."

"To what exactly do you refer, unnatural creature?" Lycurgus said.

Chiron shifted into centaur form as we watched. His perfect thighs and calves took on their animal shapes, powerful haunches, lean stifles, wicked hooves. And for the first time since I'd craved Chiron's touch, his equine parts did not unnerve me. Indeed, the deep muscles rippling across his back and flank made me long to caress him.

"You disgust me," Lycurgus said, his hooded eyes heavy with distaste.

Chiron looked toward Lycurgus's groin. "I'm told that men who aren't particularly well endowed are more inclined to this sort of envy. Do you think that's so?"

With his sword out quicker than I could blink, a feral noise escaped Lycurgus as he lunged toward Chiron. But I knew—not a drop of blood was to be spilled in the Sacred Glade. I could not allow combat.

I stepped between the two men.

"If you continue, Lycurgus," I said, "I'll deny your place in the Mother Rite."

"Your willing submission isn't necessary, Princess," Lycurgus said. The animal-like expression in his eyes scared me, and I stopped myself from stepping back. How could this creature honor the Mother Goddess?

"Yes, it is."

"Perhaps I even prefer you in an unyielding frame of mind."

He sounded like Earth Shaker's minion. Then I realized—I could determine Lycurgus's alliance for certain. If I had the courage.

Lycurgus strode toward me, but I stood my ground. He bent, and my stomach squirmed but I kept my feet in place, my back straight. My expression remained haughty even as he brushed his wet tongue over my bared nipple.

Then Lycurgus encountered Kleio's bared fangs. The Lapith king jumped back, colliding into Chiron—and I knew. His fear of snakes was more than normal caution. Lycurgus hated serpents.

Lycurgus belonged to Earth Shaker.

Fury overtook me. This man would have won the Mother

Rite tourney. I would have handed my palace and all her alliances to him.

In a heartbeat Lycurgus regained his composure and brandished his sword—but he threatened *me* this time, not Chiron. I grabbed Kleio, mentally apologizing to my scaly friend for what I was about to do.

"Lycurgus," I said. As his eyes met mine, I threw my asp toward his face. He shrieked like a maiden as Kleio coiled around his neck.

Chiron grabbed Lycurgus's arm and twisted it hard behind him. Lycurgus tried to spin away from the cruel grip, but Chiron was stronger, even in human form.

We had him.

Suddenly, the dark hues of the forest shifted, some coming into focus while others disappeared altogether. I stood, and a small white owl stood on the ground before me.

Then I realized: it wasn't an owl—it was a woman.

But she was no ordinary woman. The Mother Goddess, taller than I, held a black serpent in each hand, and they writhed angrily.

Lycurgus ceased his attack on Chiron. "You whore!" he said to the Goddess. "Earth Shaker should be here, not you! What have you done to him?"

"Nothing he didn't enjoy," she said with a sweet smile and unexpectedly tossed a snake.

Instinctively, Lycurgus tried to catch it, but he missed. The snake hit his wrist and slithered across his forearm. Before he knew it, his wrist was bound to a small tree, which had sprung up behind him. "What the—"

But the Mother Goddess was tossing the second snake at Lycurgus, even as a third appeared in her hand. The second snake bound his other wrist to the tree. She tossed the third snake and a fourth, which jerked his ankles apart, then tied them to the tree trunk.

"Look at me, Lycurgus," she demanded, her voice as creamy as fresh milk. "What do you see now? A whore? Truly?"

Her flounced skirt fell gracefully to the ground, covering her feet and ankles, and an apron made of fish scales covered her sex. A tight belt snaked around her tiny waist, making her bared breasts seem incredibly large.

"What do you see?" she insisted.

Lycurgus looked at her face. The power of her gaze hurt him somehow. The black pools held death in their depths, even I could see.

"Power," he said. Finally.

The owl perched on her head nodded slowly in approval, but the snakes holding Lycurgus's wrists and ankles began to writhe and hiss, opening their mouths so that their venom dripped on his skin. Their fangs glittered.

Lycurgus began to shriek, high-pitched and unmanly. "Earth Shaker! I need your aid!"

The noise filled the forest, but the Mother Goddess shrugged and turned. Suddenly no sound came from the Lapith King, although his mouth gaped and he appeared to be shouting.

"What will you do with him?" I asked, unafraid of her now.

"That remains to be seen. Mostly it depends on you." Then she threw a snake toward me.

I caught him perfectly. "Kleio!" I exclaimed as he slithered around my arm and to my breast where he belonged. "Thank you!" I said to her.

"Your asp friend would like me to tell you he enjoyed his task," she said, winking one of her kohl-lined eyes. "Apparently, Kleio enjoys a good jest."

"Naughty snake," I said with admiration, caressing his smooth scales.

"My lady," Chiron said, bowing to her. She lent him the glow of an immortal. "What is your desire, Mother Goddess?"

"The Tears of Eternity."

"The Tears," I said, trying not to scoff. "Their existence has no factual basis."

The owl on the Mother's head laughed, a light tinkling sound. "They exist, a result of past mischief by Earth Shaker," the Mother Goddess said.

"And I suppose they grant your heart's desire." Sarcasm probably wasn't the best attitude to use with the Mother Goddess, but I couldn't help myself.

"The Tears deliver fate," she said. "Deliver them, and I'll rid Crete of Earth Shaker's trouble."

Something hardened in Chiron's expression. He doubted. "What if we use the Tears on Earth Shaker ourselves?" he asked.

"The Tears are not for mortals," the Mother Goddess said. "It's true they'll deliver your heart's desire, but they'll wrench something precious from you, too."

I had no intention of using them, but if retrieving them would free our land from Earth Shaker—his quakes and patriarchical ways—I would find them. "Where do we get the supposed Tears?" I asked.

"Hunt the leopard."

Chiron shook his head, and the sunlight lit the coppery glints in his hair. "There are no leopards on Crete."

"Lycurgus brought one with a particular taste for centaur flesh," I said.

"Let us hunt, then," he said.

"No." Both the Mother and the Centaur King looked at me. I thought of the way the leopard had sniffed Chiron's robe, the ecstasy that had crossed its feline face. "I'll do this on my own. This is my quest, my responsibility."

The owl on the Mother's head laughed, filling the verdant Glade with the sound of tinkling bells. Our bows and daggers appeared at the Mother's feet, quivers full.

I turned toward Chiron and said, "Meet me back at the palace."

"You ask too much of me, Princess." The gray in his eyes was clouded. "I cannot leave you alone."

His desire to protect me—to adjoin his strength to mine rather than to replace it—grabbed my heart and twisted it. "Track me while I track the beast, if it pleases you then."

I'd defeat the leopard before it scented Chiron.

Not a twig crackled beneath my careful feet. No dried leaves gave me away. The Mother Goddess had set us on the leopard's trail, and I could still feel the pulsing of her power through the earth, though we'd left Her glade a while back.

My progress was unusually steady, and I was proud of it. Although I ached deep within my core from my early morning's activities with Chiron, it was a good ache, and I felt strong. Traversing a particularly deep drift of leaves, I didn't made a sound.

As if rewarding my care and self-assurance, the Mother gave me a gift. Among the thick debris of forest, a surprising bare patch of mud lay before me. And that was the gift: the mud had captured the leopard's print.

Without making a noise, I indicated the track to Chiron, who remained several steps behind me. He didn't step toward it or inspect it, to my chagrin; I would've liked to smell him, to feel the heat of his skin near mine. I would've liked to run my—

But I stopped that thought as he nodded at my find. I needed to remain focused. Kleio flicked his dry tongue on my shoulder in agreement.

Ignoring the almost physical sensation of Chiron's eyes on me, I turned my gaze back toward the leopard track. Pointing north, the print was fresh. The delicate edges hadn't yet begun to crust, and no pollen or detritus had accumulated within the small valleys made by the animal's pads.

Even if I'd never seen the deadly beast, I would have known from the size of the foot that the cat was huge, masculine. In my mind's eye, I could envision the play of muscle and sinew covering him; I could see the raw power emanating from him—the beast was like Chiron that way.

Kleio slithered from one breast to another, reminding me to keep my mind on the task. I looked at the track again.

Making no sound, I stood, listening. Where had the beast gone? I heard nothing from the cat. No panting; no purring. No cracking of bones as it ate.

The passage of this hunter through the forest even silenced the birds. Now, I heard only the gentle noise of the Aegean Sea to the north, lapping the shore of my beloved Crete.

I took a silent step toward the forest's interior but still saw nothing. Breathing quietly I scanned the surrounding foliage. I tried to fight a growing panic; I saw no clues.

Then leaves rustled almost imperceptibly to the east, making my heart pound. The leopard was close.

Walking up the path, I slid an arrow from my quiver and nocked it to my bowstring. Keeping three fingers on the sinew, I started my silent walk again.

After several steps I stopped. The path I'd been following had opened up. Where had the creature gone? The topography didn't suggest a direction.

I knew what I had to do.

Closing my eyes, I opened myself to the Mother, beseeching Her to guide my senses. My asp, curled around my breast, relaxed his muscles. Kleio's trust calmed me, and I felt no sense of pressure, no urgency. The need to impress Chiron, to snag his attention, had subsided as well. Now, only a quiet confidence in my ability to track this cat imbued me.

I could do this, with the Mother's help.

Finally the Mother Goddess spoke, in her own strange language. Heat from the ground beneath my bared feet pulsed up my legs, leaving me dizzy. Kleio's tongue flicked over my nipple, a sure sign the Mother was close. Her touch spiraled around my knees and up my inner thighs. When the power swirled through my stomach and across my hardened nipples I knew the Mother Goddess would guide me.

Then I opened my eyes. My gaze fell immediately on a silky strand. The hair, caught on a long, red raspberry cane, was fat and shining in the gold sun. I could see the change in the color: black at the root, to a red-gold, and then back to black.

It belonged to the leopard.

The raspberry cane was adjacent to the eastern path. Drawing back the bowstring just a bit more, I headed east. I could smell the big cat's musky scent. He was so close.

I didn't want to sacrifice stealth for speed, but a new urgency was upon me. The Mother was directing me, I was sure of it. She wanted me to hurry.

Placing my feet on sandy spots, avoiding twigs and dried leaf litter, I stepped more quickly. My heart was pounding now. My fingers clutched at the sinew string and pulled it back a little tighter.

Then the huge beast dropped on me from the tree over my head. Saliva-coated fangs and outstretched claws flashed before my eyes. The stink of cat filled my nose.

But the Mother had my hand, and my flint-tipped arrow, strong with the power of my ancestors, flew unerringly to the beast's throat. It hit with a solid thud, and a shower of hot blood splattered me, filling my mouth with that copper taste.

"Yes!" I cried in pleasure at my success. The huge body of the animal somersaulted over me and hit the ground. It was dead. Surely it was dead.

With bunched muscles, Kleio slithered from my breast to my neck, tasting the cat's blood from my cheeks, testing it.

"Yes!" I cried again into the quiet forest. I wanted Chiron to know I'd succeeded. I'd found and conquered the leopard!

But my celebration was too soon.

A cloud passed over the sun and I looked down at the cat.

The leopard at my feet blinked at me a moment, and I blinked back, sliding my hand toward my bronze dagger.

Wasn't it dying? Locked on mine, its dark eyes flashed with hatred. The life and intelligence I saw in the animal's gaze frightened me. I thought I'd killed it.

Then I saw something else. My carefully fletched arrow was buried at least a handspan into the animal's throat. Shallow arcs of blood were landing in the sandy dirt and pooling. The leopard should be dead; it must be dying.

My hand relaxed its grip on the hilt of the knife and the cloud moved away from the sun. A golden sunbeam caught the cat's dappled fur, illuminated the dense black spots, the swirls of amber and onyx.

But then the sun flashed over the cat, and its fur turned white. Or so I thought as I blinked again. The giant cat leaped to its feet and disappeared into the wood.

The trail of blood it left in its wake was real, clearly red. When I touched it, it was hot and sticky.

Something in me hardened. White-furred or spotted, I wanted the animal dead.

I stood to track the beast again.

I wasn't quiet as I sprinted along the blood trail. Seeing wet, crimson spots splattered over fig leaves, I crashed through bushes, heading into a section of forest I'd never explored.

"Akantha," Chiron called from behind me. How had he gotten so far behind me? The sound of his fading voice was shocking—but not shocking enough to stop me. "Wait!" he called again.

I didn't wait. This was my quest—I had to kill the leopard. Ignoring the lure of Chiron's deep voice, I burst past another clump of foliage. Blood pumped in my ears and I struggled for breath—but then, I found the leopard.

My eyes hadn't deceived me. His black-on-amber spots had truly disappeared. The animal before me, coolly lapping from a sky-blue pond I'd never seen before, had turned as white as the clouds above me. He stood in a field of flowers, the white carnations used to celebrate a queen's choosing.

The leopard stopped drinking and stared at me. My arrow was gone from his throat, and I saw no blood on his bone-white fur.

"Akantha," the leopard said. His voice came out somewhere between a growl and a purr. It made my blood run cold. "You like animals—why don't we fuck?"

I spun around looking for Chiron, wishing I hadn't left him so far behind. I suddenly felt naked.

And Kleio was gone from my breast, too, which meant only one thing—I was no longer in the physical world.

"Oh, Mother," I breathed.

The cat grinned at me, feral and wicked. "It's just you and me, Akantha. No Chiron, no asp." He yawned a huge yawn, showing me his razor-sharp teeth. "And no Mother, either, that bitch."

With clenched teeth, I nocked another arrow, wishing I had my flint arrowhead, wishing I could throw the weight of my ancestors at this unnatural creature.

The white leopard casually licked his shoulder, cleaned his fur, while I took aim. His eyes were as coldly blue as the pond at his feet. I loosed the arrow, and it flew true, right into its chest. A surge of satisfaction coursed through me.

But then I saw the strike brought no blood. The arrow was buried deep in his chest, but it caused no wound. Instead his powerful haunch muscles tightened, and the cat launched toward me quicker than an arrow.

The animal's paws flung me flat on the ground as the leopard landed on my chest. Its weight immobilized me. Teeth bared, it knocked my breath from me and took it for its own.

7

Shades of gray danced before my eyes as the leopard cut off my breath. As its dank breath wafted around my nose, I knew. It was my time to die.

But then something exploded above me, crashing through the shrubs with all the power of a tidal wave. I saw a flash of bright sorrel, and I saw the underside of hooves.

Chiron. He'd found me in the spiritworld. He'd risked his life and the Mother's to save me.

His massive body careened into the leopard at my throat, and the beast flew off me, ripping the tender flesh of my neck.

Still, I lived. I gasped for breath, and my hand scrambled for my dagger even as I registered my bow beneath me, crushed. Finally my world quit spinning, and I stood.

What I saw horrified me.

Centaur and leopard rolled over each other in a blur. The leopard's claws were fully extended, digging into Chiron's stomach. The dagger-sharp things had sliced through his skin until pink muscle shone through.

But Chiron's powerful hands gripped the cat's neck, strangling the animal that strangled its prey. The leopard's breath rasped through its throat. Chiron would soon put an end to it—if the beast didn't eviscerate him first.

I stood one leg behind the other. Putting my weight on my back leg, I drew my dagger hand behind my ear. Then I waited.

I did not want to hit Chiron with this blade. In practice, my aim was good and I hit hard. But I wanted to hit leopard flesh, not centaur.

I wanted to throw my dagger but couldn't. Chiron rolled to the top, throttling the leopard beneath him, but then the leopard flipped him over. It didn't help that blood stained the white cat fur so that it nearly matched Chiron's chestnut color. I couldn't tell one from the other.

Finally I had my chance: a patch of cloud-white along the line of a rib. I threw the blade with all of my might, and it flew true. It hit the beast with a reverberating thud.

But the leopard didn't die.

Chiron flipped the cat onto its back, and it dug its claws further into my beloved's stomach. He didn't have much time, but the beast was not dying.

It hadn't died before. Why did I think it would collapse now?

And then I saw the pond. Really saw it. The color wasn't true—it was too blue. It was the color of polished gems or the summer sky extending across the horizon into the forever.

It was the Tears of Eternity.

I jumped into the water, shocked at its chill, which was colder than anything I'd ever felt, but I didn't care. Cupping my hands, I splashed water at the beast. "Begone Earth Shaker!"

And the Tears killed the leopard like arrows and blades did not. The white fur regained its amber-and-onyx coloration, and the beast collapsed into a heap beneath Chiron. Not an eyelid flickered.

And for a heartbeat I thought the Tears had killed Chiron, too.

He lay unmoving, blood pouring from the wounds along his equine stomach. I looked closer and saw intestine. He would not survive this.

"Chiron," I called from the pond. "Don't go! Don't die!" With my cupped hand full of water, I walked over to him, careful not to spill a drop. "The Tears of Eternity can heal!"

"No," he croaked when saw what I was about to do. "You've already incurred one curse. Let me," he gasped, "do this one."

He took my hand in his and dumped the water along the wounds. "Heal me," he commanded of them, and the wounds mended themselves, closing as if time flowed backward.

I looked at him, at the wounds, wondering if my eyes could be believed. "Are you . . . ?"

"By the Mother Goddess, that hurt," he said, standing to his feet. The blood on his coat and skin dried and blew away. His copper hair and coat shined, as if a smith had polished him to a high gleam. "But Earth Shaker is . . ."

"He's gone," I said. "For now."

Chiron shifted from centaur form to human, running his broad hand over his abdomen. "I feel wholly myself."

"Are you sure about that?" I asked, raising my brow at his throbbing cock. "All of you?" I let my fingertips trail over his chest. "Shall we make certain you're correct?" With that I flicked the tip of my tongue to his lip, and he was mine. He leaned into my kiss as the scent of crushed flowers surrounded us.

His lips drank in the soft skin along the top of my breasts. My nipples reached for him. "You saved my life, Chiron." My tongue savored the salt of the sweat on his chest.

"And you saved mine."

His intention lit that flame of desire in me. "We need to get these Tears to the Mother, and what about Lycurgus?" I asked.

"He can wait." Chiron scooped me into his thick arms and ran his tongue between my breasts. "But I cannot."

Then he laid me back, our mouths blending, tongues flowing in concert to music only we could hear.

We embraced on the crushed carnations. Like the flowing sea, our movement swelled into a promise of orgasm. Our bodies joined, sex to mouth, mouth to sex. Then sex to sex.

Finally, exhausted, my lips and tongue strained, my nipples and core aching, I opened my eyes. Chiron was worshipping me with his eyes.

"I could envy you mortals, when I see love like this," the Mother Goddess said.

Where she'd come from and how long she'd been watching, I didn't know. I cared not, either. Still, we both stood in her presence.

"The Lapith King failed to satisfy you?" Chiron asked.

I thought it a bold question but the Mother just laughed, stroking one of the black serpents that twisted around her forearm. "I fear I wore him out."

But then the owl on her head screeched, "Truth!"

The Mother added, "But he's escaped, and he's gone to your palace, Princess Akantha."

"To Palace Knossos?" I asked stupidly. "Couldn't you stop him?"

She didn't take umbrage at my tone, though I regretted the impetuous words as they fell from my mouth. Still it was my palace on which Lycurgus and Earth Shaker would wreak havoc. I didn't want my villagers homeless and destitute as were those of Palace Phaistos.

"Without the Tears I lacked the strength. Earth Shaker still lends Lycurgus power—I couldn't exorcise him."

"Hope," the owl said, preening its wing with its hooked beak.

"My pretty one," The Mother crooned, stroking the owl as

it hopped to her arm. "Thank you for the reminder." She looked up from the bird and said to me, "Yes, hope exists thanks to you two for finding the Tears of Eternity. I still lack the ability to free the Lapith man of Earth Shaker's hold—the mortal likes it too much—but he'll no longer have the ability to shake the earth on his whim."

"So we can defeat him," I said.

"Bring him down, and I deliver the Lapith to his fate—I'll remove him to . . ." The Mother Goddess seemed to sift through options in her mind before she decided. "Thessaly. Defeat Lycurgus at arms, and all Lapiths shall find themselves in Thessaly, which should keep them from causing mischief here."

"And Earth Shaker?" I asked.

"The sands of time will find him in Thera," she said, "if you succeed. Which brings me to your fate. I told both of you that the Tears weren't meant for mortals, and you both used them."

Feeling the warmth of Chiron's arm next to mine, I knew that whatever the cost, I wouldn't regret it. But that bravado didn't quiet my nerves.

"What's the cost, Witch?" Even in the presence of an immortal, Chiron radiated command.

"Do you know how the Tears of Eternity came to be?" she asked.

"No."

"An immortal loved a mortal, and such a love cannot be. Their tears made the pond."

The owl turned to Chiron and said, "Fate."

"Yes," the Mother agreed. "Fate. If you vanquish Lycurgus, Lord Centaur, fate will grant you both eternity; you'll live forever."

"Forever." Chiron said the word flatly.

"You will live long enough to see people forget the names Earth Shaker and Mother Goddess, only to learn new ones, forget those and learn anew—you will see cities erupt from the ground and blow away with the dust. You will gain such wisdom that the immortals will send their children to you." The owl looked at him and blinked. "Yes, Lord Centaur. You will both live forever."

Then the Mother Goddess gave Chiron a sassy grin. "You have your chance, Lord Centaur."

"Chance?"

"She's seen your skill with one sword; show her your skill with the other."

8

Even as we galloped over the fissure-ridden ground toward my palace, I could see something was wrong.

Folk were gathered around the arena, and royal pennants from the surrounding palaces flew from the dais—from my dais. The octopus of Palace Kato Zakro flew next to the dolphin from Palace Gournia, and I'd invited no one, not yet.

Worse, hundreds of soldiers filled the area, and each wore the emerald green of the Lapiths. The Lapith King was hosting the Mother Rite—the choosing ceremony for the champion who'd rule beside me for the next seven years.

"This is preposterous," I told Chiron. "The Mother Rite cannot be held without me."

"Well, you're here now, Princess, but don't go running up the dais quite yet." He slowed to a trot and then a walk behind the bull barn.

"Why not?" The clanging of swordplay filled the air. Someone was trying to choose my champion for me. I could not permit this under any terms.

"You're naked, love, save your snake." With a wicked gleam in his eye, he pulled me into his massive arms and kissed me. Hard.

"I could say the same to you."

"Now wish me sweet fortune before I enter that arena and flatten every man, every creature, who tries to come between me and you."

Dressed in my formal flounced skirt and my fitted bodice, I pushed my way to my throne. The Queen of Kato Zakros narrowed her eyes at me as I walked past her—Lycurgus had influenced her, I saw.

The combat had paused the moment my constituents heard of my arrival. The situation was not beyond repair.

"People," I called, once I'd gained my throne. Letting my voice carry over the gathered throng, I held up my arms to command their attention, and my sea-green robe hung theatrically, perfectly complementing the forest-scene fresco behind me. But it wasn't pygmy elephants and river hippos painted on walls that interested me today.

"I'm glad you've had the opportunity to prepare yourselves for this event!" I nodded to the combatants standing at ease in the arena. "Today I will choose my first champion," I said in a booming voice. "As is the right of every woman in our land!"

The crowd hooted and cheered, but I could feel Earth Shaker's dark presence. Lycurgus's soldiers glowered on the sidelines, and evil pulsed in the air.

"People!" I said again. Keeping my arms above my head, I let the strange afternoon sun glint off my bronze battle vambraces. I wanted to remind the gathering of my power, the power held by the Minoan Queen.

I could override generations of tradition, and I planned to do it. Waiting until the noise fell back, I paused before I said,

"Unlike any Mother Rite of the past, this one will be open to humans—and centaurfolk."

Dissatisfaction simmered among the villagers, and I heard a noblewoman hiss in her breath beside me. "What?" someone cried from below me. "They're hung like ho—"

I knew objections would come, and I wasn't mistaken.

"You've a death wish, Princess!" someone called.

"But what a way to go!" This came from a woman standing behind me.

I held my temper. My people didn't know the worth of our hooved neighbors, but they'd learn—assuming Chiron and I succeeded in subduing Earth Shaker.

A black cloud had gathered on the horizon, and the wind blew cold in unpredictable gusts, whipping arena dust into our eyes. The same volatile mood fermented in the folk below.

"If a worthy centaur exists today," I declared, "he will rule beside me until the next choosing!"

I'd hoped for sporadic cheers, but chill silence met my proclamation. Led by the Lapith soldiers, people shifted discontentedly. Then angry murmurs filtered from the sidelines up the dais. "This cannot be, Princess Akantha," a riled voice called from the crowd, breaking the silence.

Lycurgus's work. Or Earth Shaker's.

"I challenge you!" he said. Ezio, a man of minor nobility from Palace Malia, walked across the arena toward me. He had the lanky grace of a bull leaper. "I challenge your right to allow centaurs!"

My heart thudded as the clouds continued to coalesce on the horizon. If I had to best Ezio to allow centaurs in the tourney, so be it. The lanky man's skill lay in graceful leaps over running bulls, not in swordplay or archery. Women of my line had been leading men into war against the mainlanders for generations.

"Ezio," I said. "I'll slaughter you like a goat for a sacrifice."

"Prove it, Princess."

Shrugging from my robe, I vaulted over the short wall into arena. I landed with my dagger extended, a handspan from his chest. "Daggers," I said, naming the weapon. "Arm yourself."

"A woman's choice," he spat.

"Then it should be natural for you, Ezio." Who did he think he was?

"You won't win this, Princess," he said. "No one wants Knossos to be ruled by a centaur."

"Make no mistake, Ezio. I and only I rule this land—regardless of today's outcome."

Then I turned toward the throng. "Move back," I shouted. I didn't know who had already battled for the right to take part in the tourney, but I needed to invalidate it. "The match between Ezio and me," I declared, "shall initiate the Mother Rite!"

Still Ezio stood before me empty-handed, his dark bull-leaper's braids dangling to his shoulders.

"What?" I said to him. "Are you missing something critical?" I let my gaze fall suggestively to his crotch.

"I have what I need," he said, slowly pulling his blade from his belt.

"Are you certain?" I asked. "That's a remarkably . . . short blade." I taunted him with a grin. I knew exactly how anger could interfere with good sense.

And it worked. Ezio lunged at me with none of the grace for which he was famous. Hoping my full skirt of flounces didn't hinder me, I stepped to the side—and stuck out my toe.

Ezio tumbled to the ground at my feet, ire reddening his face.

"Do you really seek to rule by my side?" I said as he stood.

He wiped dust from his loincloth. There was something about his stance . . . Ezio feinted toward me, but I was ready.

His blade glanced harmlessly off my left vambrace. I let it slide the length of my forearm as I spun around. My skirt swooshed around his shins, and I hoped it distracted him. Years of vaulting bulls had made him strong, and resisting his blade was difficult.

Still, I did resist, and this pushed him off balance. As his blade hit the lip of my vambrace near my elbow, I jumped toward him, quick as a snake. Ezio leaped back—but not quickly enough.

My blade found his throat and pressed against it.

"Do you give?" I asked as the crowd shouted around us.

"She wins!" he shouted. "I do not denounce her right to invite centaurfolk to the tourney."

But ill grace lurked hard behind his eyes. I'd not won a friend here. "Let men and centaur decide the Mother Rite by the sword!" I said, and the crowd cheered their approval as I walked back to my throne.

As I sat, the gate screeched open, and the tattoo of galloping hooves filled the air. In a mad flurry of sword and tail, Chiron cantered toward the dais. He slid to a stop before me and flashed his sword in a show of agility.

"Who will take me on?" he challenged. And my heart pulsed with pride, for when the villagers saw the brawny centaur, the leaf-shape blade of his sword glinting in the sun, men retreated. The ease with which he held his sword, the grace of his blood-red cloak billowing behind him—these made him look mighty.

Chiron was magnificent.

"I'll take you on, centaur," a mischievous voice proclaimed, and the crowd turned to look. With his bay coat shining, Demoleon trotted into the arena carrying a bronze sword of his own. His black tail flowed sensuously behind him.

"My sweet Mother," I heard a woman in the crowd say. "This'll be a fight to remember."

For a brief moment, fear lashed through me, as hot and bright as lightning across a night sky. What if Chiron lost? What if Demoleon hurt Chiron just enough so that he couldn't defeat Lycurgus?

Together, Demoleon and Chiron bowed to me, and I had no choice but to return the acknowledgment. I'd hoped Chiron would confront Lycurgus fresh, but it was not to be.

"Let it begin!" I said, and the two men met in the middle.

"I've come to see how well you've learned all I've had to teach you," Demoleon taunted Chiron loudly enough for all to hear. He swung his sword in arcs, sending hard glints of sunlight into the rapt crowd.

"And now the teacher can be the student," Chiron called. Demoleon's inky tail flowed behind him as he loped in easy circles around the arena.

And then I understood—Demoleon was the centaur swordmaster.

"So be it," Demoleon called.

The two centaurs spent no time on niceties. Sword song filled the air, almost joyously. Sitting at the edge of my throne, I couldn't tell where one man's sword ended and the other's began. Silver sparked from the bronze, and the noise became deafening.

Flashing hooves danced as the bronze blades arced above them. One man spun, trying to land a blow on the other's shoulder—it was Chiron, I saw, trying to hit Demoleon. But Demoleon stepped neatly out of reach and spun on his own hindquarters.

Demoleon followed that spin through, blade flashing, and I gasped as his sword landed on Chiron's forearm, his sword arm. Blood dripped to the dust at his hooves, and my knuckles whitened as I grabbed the throne's arms.

Despite my fear, the blow didn't stop Chiron.

With all of his weight behind it, Chiron swung the sword. It looked like the swoop of a bird's wing, graceful and elegant in its efficiency of movement. The sword hit Demoleon's exactly at the hilt, and his sword went flying free, landing blade first in the dust. The metallic ring of the vacillations filled the awed silence.

Chiron had bested his master.

Gracefully Demoleon bowed to his competitor. "Thank you, Chiron. You've indeed learned all I've had to teach and then some more." Then Demoleon turned to me and said, "Enjoy him, your majesty."

"I plan—" I started, but the gate squealed opened again.

"King Lycurgus," I announced as he strode in, hands on his hip, sword heavy on his hip. "You're not welcome here." The clouds on the horizon had moved toward us, and a few drops of cold gray rain began to pelt.

"You'll welcome me to your bed tonight, Princess."

"Not if I have anything to say about it," Chiron said.

"My sword longs to drink your blood, centaur."

He held his blade aloft and allowed the crowd to admire it. Lycurgus's blade also was leaf-shaped and bronze. Red jewels glittered in the hilt, which was thicker than any I'd seen before. His sword also bore straight crossbars running perpendicular to the blade. I'd never seen such a thing.

"Then your sword will die of thirst, as will you when blood pours from your veins," Chiron said. He wiped his bleeding arm across his forehead, leaving a red smear.

I stood. "King Chiron," I called.

"My lady." He turned to me and bowed, his muscles rippling.

With a neat flick, I tossed him my battle vambraces. The last remaining sunbeam caught them as they flew across the arena. "May these bring you good fortune, sir, as you protect the way of our land."

And with those words, with that action, I declared war on the Lapiths.

Chiron clamped the armor on his forearms, and I watched supreme confidence cross the face of King Lycurgus as he tightened his own vambraces. He might not be able to cause earthquakes, but he was no simple mortal man.

Thus it began. Lycurgus lunged at Chiron with a grin and a roar.

Where the dance between Chiron and Demoleon had been beautiful, filed with an efficiency of movement and predictable pauses between the sound of metallic tangles, Lycurgus attacked Chiron with a ferocity bordering on rage.

He threw himself madly at Chiron, but his anger didn't hamper his skill. His wrist and forearm flicked with perfect precision. And more than that, Lycurgus fought with a supernatural strength, with Earth Shaker's strength.

Still, Chiron kept pace, nicking again and again at Lycurgus's swordhand.

Then I saw the function of Lycurgus's strange crossbars. They protected his hand against Chiron's sword. The crossbars made Chiron's subtle strike useless. Time and time again, the clanging sound of Chiron's sword tip hitting Lycurgus's heavy crossbars filled the air.

Bronze squealed and clanged. Hooves and booted feet slid and pummeled the ground until dust obscured the men from their knees down.

And then a huge peal of thunder made the audience gasp. Rain began to fall in earnest, dampening the powdery soil. For a moment, it appeared to refresh Chiron, washing away his sweat and the nicks of blood. But Lycurgus's ill-gained strength was telling, draining away Chiron's ability.

I could see the moment real exhaustion took hold. As Lycurgus harried him, pushing him farther and farther down the long end of the arena, I could see the tip of Chiron's sword sinking lower and lower. His hooves weren't so quick; he didn't lift his knees so high.

The rain began to turn the dust to mud, and Chiron was scrambling to his feet; Lycurgus had knocked him to his knees. A new wheal on his chest oozed bright blood. As Chiron regained his footing, Lycurgus struck again, mercilessly raising another wheal just under the first.

"Oh, Mother," I gasped, but it was Earth Shaker who had hold of me. A sudden vision of Lycurgus's hand squeezing my breast with cruel detachment assaulted me. I could smell his breath as his mouth latched onto my neck, his actions claiming my body even as my mind resisted. "No," I groaned. I couldn't sit here and watch.

That thought rang through my mind again: I couldn't sit here and watch. But why was this required of me? I'd broken tradition to include centaurs in the Mother Rite. I'd break tradition again—I'd make this Mother Rite a true choosing.

Ripping the flounces of my skirt to my knees, I pulled my daggers from my ankle straps and leaped into the arena.

Another clap of thunder ripped through the sky as I ran toward Lycurgus, overwhelming any sound from the crowd.

As I slipped in the mud toward the combatants, I watched in horror as Lycurgus sliced another wheal into Chiron's chest, and with dread I realized that Lycurgus merely toyed with the Centaur King.

Rain fell cold on my face, dripping into my eyes, but I still had surprise on my side. Ten paces behind Lycurgus I stopped and aimed for the spot between his shoulder blade and spine. I pulled back my dagger hand then let my blade fly.

But the wind whipped my blade, or maybe the rain made my aim untrue. The dagger merely pierced the fleshy muscle of the Lapith's bicep.

With a bull-like bellow, Lycurgus turned toward me. What I saw in his eye wasn't human, wasn't sane.

As Lycurgus stalked me, Chiron found an opportunity and swung his sword at Lycurgus's neck with all of his strength.

It should have decapitated him, but the blow didn't stop the Lapith. Lycurgus remained standing in the pelting rain.

Undeterred, Chiron moved in and swung again, catching the crossbar of Lycurgus's sword with the tip of his own. Rain poured down on us so hard, I could barely see, but I saw Lycurgus's blade fall to the ground, useless.

With a deft step, Chiron hooked his hoof behind Lycurgus's heel and shoved hard with his elbow.

My hair was matted across my face, but I didn't wipe it away. Instead I sent a prayer to the Mother Goddess and let my second—and last—dagger fly.

Disarmed and off balance, Lycurgus fell as a third clap of thunder reverberated across the sky.

Chiron slammed a knee on his opponent's chest, his bronze sword at the other man's throat. But my dagger had already buried itself there, and Lycurgus was dead.

9

I didn't need to inspect the corpse to verify the demise of Lycurgus and Earth Shaker—all of the Lapith soldiers had vanished. Along the arena fence, on the dais, my folk looked around in wonder for the missing men. I wished Thessaly much enjoyment of them.

The pelting rain was gone, too. The sky was achingly blue, and only large puddles around the arena confirmed the storm's existence.

"Akantha," Chiron said, letting his voice roll over the syllables like he had when we first met. It grabbed my heart, my core. We looked at each other, blood and mud smeared over our faces—and we grinned.

As if we'd lost our minds.

And the crowd started cheering: "Kiss her! Kiss her! Kiss her!"

Chiron gave a jaunty bow to the crowd and closed the two strides between us. A dangerous gleam lit his eye, and I knew it lit mine, too. He looked the way I felt . . . feral.

"Akantha," he said, stopping before me. "The crowd expects a kiss."

"And you, my lord?" I asked. "Do you?"

"It seems you've left me little choice."

"Don't let it be too much of a hardship, King Centaur."

"You know nothing of hardship," he said.

"Then show me," I taunted. "I've a great wish to experience something . . . hard."

"As you wish, your Highness." He bowed.

His words were innocuous, but his gaze . . . Chiron looked at me, and my heart nearly stopped. A searing intensity filled his gaze.

If that wasn't desire, I was a squirming octopus yanked fresh from the Aegean.

"You want me," I said. "You love me."

"Yes," he said, but he walked close to me, so close his body heat poured over me. He pulled me toward him. "I've come to make you queen, Akantha, and to do that I must kiss you."

A ragged breath escaped him as he claimed me with a demanding kiss. His lips covered mine with a deliberate slowness, and he crushed me to him as if could pull me into his own body.

His hand slid behind my neck, and he pulled my face even closer to his. It hurt, oh Mother, it did. But the pain was exquisite as he worked his free hand into my hair. He forced me to yield completely.

But I'd yielded already, in the fields and glades as we uncovered the Mother's secrets hidden in birdsong and the whisper of the breeze in the leaves. I'd yielded when I leaped from the dais to help spare his life.

And I yielded now.

His salty lips parted mine, moved over mine with a searing hunger I'd only dreamed in the Mother's visions. My shallow, quick breaths mingled with his.

"That should please them," he said pulling away. I staggered on my weakened legs; my hands and lips and tongue ached for him. Chiron turned to the hooting crowd, whom I'd forgotten completely, and waved. "I present to you, Queen Akantha," he shouted. "Ruler of Palace Knossos and all of Crete!"

The crowd cheered wildly, but I looked at them blindly.

"Wave," he said at me. "Or blow them a kiss."

He'd earned his right to rule beside me for the next seven years, but he hadn't earned the right to order me around like a kitchen maid.

"No," I said.

I erased his incredulous expression, kissing him as possessively as he'd kissed me. Just as Chiron's sword had tangled with Lycurgus's, my tongue twisted over his. I bit his lips, almost too hard, and I sucked.

I heard the crowd calling around me, but I didn't care. I took his face between my hands and took his lips in mine. "You are mine, Centaur King," I breathed into his mouth. "At least for the next seven years."

Then, and only then, did I blow my kiss to the waiting throng.

"And after that?" His lips spread into a wide smile, flashing his white teeth. "For eternity." Then he flashed me that wicked grin that made my heart pound. "Let's not waste a moment of it."

THE DREAM WELL

Dawn Thompson

1

Was he the only one aboard who heard the siren's song before the galley struck the Land's End shoals? Something nudged him hard, buoying him toward shore, and Gar Trivelyan, Knight of the Realm, hauled himself up out of the creaming surf and collapsed on the strand, coughing up what seemed like gallons of seawater. Drifting mist caressed him, like hundreds of probing fingers, groping, stroking—covering him like a blanket. He struggled to his feet and staggered like a blind man into the wraithlike whiteness that all but hid the full Samhain moon from view.

He was aroused. Had he come that close to death? He'd heard such things occurred when a man was dying. Raising his codpiece, he soothed his burgeoning cock as he blundered into the mist. It seemed to be leading him inland. Until that moment, the urgency in his loins had canceled the pain in his arm. He noticed it now, for it bled profusely, running in rivulets over the hammered gold bracelet coiled like a snake just below his elbow.

Tearing a piece of homespun from the hem of his tunic, he

cinched it tightly above the wound with the aid of his teeth, and staggered on, his good arm carving circles in the air ahead of him. The mist had become a thick, meandering wall impenetrable by the eye. It was as though he'd stepped off the planet. Where had the storm gone that ran the ship aground? Why was it warm here, not bitter cold as it had been when the cruel November sea had spat him out upon these shores? Could he have crossed over into the Celtic Otherworld? He'd heard of seafarers doing just that after shipwreck in Cornish waters.

He didn't see the well until he'd run right into it, a low round affair. A gurgling spring edged with stacked stones, rising from a whitethorn grove, the trees' branches aflutter with bits of colored cloth. *A Celtic dream well?*

According to myth, if one in need of a dream fulfilled dipped a bit of cloth into the water of such a well and tied it to one of the trees that guarded it with proper tribute and incantation, the dream or wish or petition requested would be granted. He had never believed in such nonsense before, but his arm was nearly severed, and it couldn't hurt to try. There seemed no other help in the offing, and he tore another strip from his tunic, dunked it in the satiny black water, and tied it to a whitethorn branch among the other bits of cloth hanging there. Then, slipping the hammered-gold bracelet from his wounded arm, he groaned and prayed, and tossed it into the well.

No sooner had he done, when the water began to roil and bubble up, spitting over the edge as the perfect form of a naked woman broke the surface, his hammered-gold snake bracelet coiled about her upper arm. She was without blemish, her skin like alabaster, her hair teasing her buttocks with a long cascade of silken waves the color of copper burnished by the sun. It was surprisingly dry for having come from the depths of the well, and none covered her pubic mound. It was hairless, her entrance beneath resembling not the sexual organ of a woman, but the column of a rare and costly orchid whose flushed lips and purple bud beckoned irresistibly in the eerie half-light. His wound forgotten, Gar could not take his eyes from it as she stepped from the well and floated toward him, rubbing her nipples to tall hardness between her thumbs and forefingers.

What sorcery was this? And what sort of fool would he be if he didn't take advantage of it? Ripping off his codpiece, he exposed his thick, hard cock to her gaze, and groaned as she took it in her hands. Sucking in his breath, he made a strangled sound as she ran her cool fingers along the blue-veined surface in a spiraling motion from its bulky root to the ridge of its mushroom tip. His mind was speaking to her then, screaming what he dared not speak aloud—not even to ask her name—for fear she'd evaporate before his very eyes: *the tip . . . touch the tip! Run those cool, soft fingers over the head of my cock and make it live, my beauty. . . .*

As if she'd heard, the woman did just that, sliding the tip of her finger over the rim of his sex, moistening the sensitive head with the drops of pearly pre-come leaking from it, her forefinger lingering on the puckered opening, inviting more pearls to form.

"Your wish is granted," she murmured. "Your wound is healed."

So it was! Gar hadn't even noticed until now. That cool hand riding his hot, hard shaft had canceled all thought except plunging into the petals of that exquisite orchid between her thighs until he'd filled her.

Lifting the globe of one breast, she offered her nipple. "You may have me for a little if you wish," she said. "Every year when the moon waxes full at the Samhain feast, I am allowed to rise from the well and take a lover . . . if the tribute is well to pass." She nodded toward the bracelet on her arm. "'Tis a fine trinket, this."

It had to be a dream. He had died in the wreck, and this was his torment. He slipped his arm around her waist and drew her closer. No, this was no dream; this was real flesh he was feeling, as smooth as satin and as fragrant as the night lilies blooming in the water.

"Have I died, then?" he finally said. "Which are you, angel or demon?" Not that it mattered. He was enthralled.

The woman smiled. There was a provocative little beauty spot above the right corner of her lip. "I am neither, Gar Trivelyan," she said. "I am called Analee, handmaiden of Annis, Goddess of the Wells. This well is mine."

"How do you know my name?"

"I know much, knight of the realm," she returned. "Will you drink . . . or not?"

Gar cupped the offered breast and took the nipple in his mouth. It was hot and hard, the areola puckering taut as he laved the tawny bud with his tongue until she purred like a contented cat.

Overhead, the Samhain moon peeked down through drifting clouds like a voyeur as he nipped and sucked and drank her essence. She tasted golden, of the sun, of honey and bee pollen. Could this be happening? His mind said no, but his cock said yes as she let it go and stripped him of his tunic and breeches. He'd lost his cloak, sword, and sandals in the sea.

"Come," she said, leading him into the mist.

She led him through lush fields burgeoning with all manner of wildflowers, across streams and brooks swathed in the ghostly mist that seemed alive the way it followed them, weaving in and out among the trunks of ancient hawthorns and young saplings that seemed to sigh and sway and carry on hushed conversations with each other.

All at once, a red-and-white-striped canopy came into view; a tournament tent of the kind used by revelers at routs and feasts and festivals was nestled deep in a little clearing in the whitethorn grove, where it gave way to oak and ash. The flap was turned back, and a bed made with petal-strewn quilts of satin and down beckoned. Once inside, the goddess of the well drew Gar to her, her hands flitting over his moist skin as they explored his naked body until, unable to help himself, he drove her down beneath him in the bed.

Nothing seemed real, and yet it was. Otherworldly visits were hazardous at best. Dangers lurked in wait at every turn for mortals sojourning in the parallel dimension—dangers that could trap a man forever, or devour him body and soul. Had he fallen into a trap? Was he about to lose his immortal soul? These were natural concerns. But then, in the arms of the captivating Analee, while her deft fingers were exploring his body, touching him in places no woman had ever touched him before, while her sweet essence nourished him as he suckled at those perfect breasts, nothing mattered but the moment, and the beautiful Goddess of the Well.

Straddling him, she knelt there, her hands flitting over his body, exploring the rock-hard muscles that had tensed in his biceps, in his broad chest and roped torso. Inching lower, she gripped his cock in both her tiny hands, for one hand could not do it justice, and began pumping it in a spiraling motion like she had done before. Slow, deep revolutions along his shaft made him harder still, as she teased the mushroom tip just enough to drive him mad. Meanwhile, his fingers found her nipples, pinching, tweaking, until she writhed against him, grinding the parted lips of her slit into his bulging testicles, into the base of his cock as she played with it.

Gar groaned. He felt her release as she rubbed up against him, felt her juices flow, moistening his genitals, and the throbbing, shuddering palpitations of her climax. Her pleasure moans were throaty and deep, as she threw her head back until her long coppery hair rippled over her buttocks and grazed his thighs beneath her. It was more than he could bear. His cock was bursting. Profoundly grateful that she had come, he rolled her over on her back and in one motion thrust into her, parting her orchid-like nether lips, gliding on her wetness until he'd filled her.

"You said that I could have you for . . . a little," he panted, undulating gently, for to drive himself into her now would bring him to climax in a heartbeat. As it was, he'd begun to pray to forestall the inevitable; a tactic that had always given him more staying power in the past. But that was before Analee, Goddess of the Dream Well. She had bewitched him.

"For a little, yes," she purred. How beautiful she was, with her hooded eyes dilated with desire, her full lips parted to receive his kiss, her fair skin rouged with the fiery blush of sex. She was like a rare orchid, indeed, and Gar longed to open her petals one by one.

"How little is . . . 'a little'?" he asked, for that would depend upon what happened next. If she were to evaporate like the mist at any moment, he would make the most of it, but if there was time, he could address his immediate need and then love her properly. How strange that the word *love* had formed in his mind. He was a seasoned warrior, and he had bedded many, but love had nothing to do with it. He was of the firm belief that a warrior should have no truck with love. Thus far, he'd managed to dodge Cupid's darts, but that, too, was before the magical goddess of the well. Though it was plain that her advances toward him were pure lust, she had reminded him that there was such a thing as love, and that it was missing from his mundane existence.

"Until the dawn," she murmured.

Wrapping her legs around his waist, Analee wound her arms about his neck and threaded her fingers through his dark, wavy hair. He wore it long, below his ears. Her touch was like a lightning strike, the grip of those skilled fingers sending shock waves through his loins. Gritting his teeth, he shut his eyes and groaned, and she fisted her fingers tightly in the locks at the back of his neck, and arched her back, drawing him closer.

"Pleasure yourself, Gar Trivelyan," she said, her voice throaty and soft, "even as I have done. I am yours till the sun chases the moon . . ."

Gar could feel her womb. There was barely room for his cock in the tight confines of her sexual seat. She felt like hot silk, her juices laving him as he pistoned into her again and again until he cried out as the petal soft lips of her vagina gripped his shaft, milking him dry of every drop

The orgasm was like no other. He filled her to overflowing, as his heartbeat matched the pumping, throbbing, shuddering rhythm that drove his cock relentlessly inside her. The pulse beat in his sexual stream was so acute he feared it would drive his heart right through his heaving ribcage.

He collapsed into her kiss, his brow running with sweat, his cock slow to go flaccid inside her, for the petals of that exquisite orchid between her thighs gripped him still. How could he part with such ecstasy at dawn? How could he bear never to feel again what he'd felt in the arms of this goddess? There was no question that she had bewitched him. Angel or demon, he was beguiled.

Time stood still, then. Gar had no idea how much had passed before he withdrew himself and lay beside her, content but not sated. He could still feel the rhythmic contractions of her vagina, involuntary or deliberate, he couldn't tell. It didn't matter. He wanted to live inside her again and again.

"I think you have bewitched me," he said through a heavy sigh. "One moment I was struggling to stay afloat in a freezing maelstrom of high-curling seas and flesh-tearing winds, the next I am here, with you in this warm misty place. Have I died? Have I crossed over? Or have I somehow breeched the span and entered the Celtic Otherworld?"

"Shhh," she murmured, grazing his moist brow with her lips. "Our time has just begun. We must not waste it."

Gracefully, she rose from the bed and padded to a trunk in

the corner. How lithe she was, as if she floated on air. Raising himself on one elbow, he feasted on the sight of her slender curves. He salivated over the roundness of her buttocks, over the perfect globes of her milk-white breasts, their tawny nipples standing out in bold relief against the opalescence of her skin. How the breathtaking sight of that body teased him, half veiled in the silken fall of coppery hair, like a sun-kissed halo about her.

The shock of her hairless pubic mound drew his eyes when she turned, and his cock responded to the sight, swelling to life where it rested against his corded thigh. He was hard again, and he swung his feet over the side of the bed, rose up, and approached her. But she held him at bay with an armful of what looked like cloth made of spider silk, spangled with stardust. For its sparkle was blinding.

"Put this on," she said, handing him a sheer garment, so fine he feared to force it over the contours of his muscular body. Nonetheless, he did as she bade him and found it to be quite sturdy. It fit him like a second skin, as if it had been made for him, a sheer garment the color of winter spangled with snow. ". . . And this," she added, handing him a headdress with antlers and a half-mask attached. Nodding her approval as he slipped it over his head, she swirled a billowing cape about her made of the same spangled cloth that hid none of her charms, and raised the hood.

Gar looked on enraptured as she donned a shimmering winged mask; her eyes, the color of dark water, glazed with desire burning toward him. What passion smoldered in that sultry gaze, passion he had not yet tasted. He could but stare, consumed by lust and longing, his quick hot breath puffing back against his face from inside the mask. Her mystical allure was infectious.

She held out her hand. "Come," she said, "we must join the others."

2

Gar followed the goddess into the mist to an open clearing where others gathered around bonfires. They were drinking honey mead and wine, dancing and feasting upon nuts and apples and roasted meat. Here, the mist parted to permit the moon to beam down upon the revelers. Faery lights flickered, and Wills-o'-the-Wisp danced on the distant marshes. Gar had celebrated the Samhain feast many times, but never in the Celtic Otherworld, and never in a warm climate, for it was the harvest feast.

As if she'd heard, Analee said, "It is never autumn or winter here, so we make it so with costumes when we feast."

They were the only two dressed as frosty winter, all the rest wore earth colors, their costumes fashioned of leaves and moss, their headdresses wreaths of vines, studded with acorns, nuts, and succulent berries.

"I rule here," she said. "I wear the winter white at Samhain to tell the masses all will be well at the Winter Solstice. It is a sign of hope. You are garbed as the winter stag, because you are my consort . . . for a little."

Gar wished she wouldn't keep reminding him it was only *for a little*. All around him revelers had paired off, dancing around the bonfires to the music of flute and lyre. Scantily clad wood nymphs danced around him trailing yards of spider silk spangled with some anonymous iridescence. It reminded him of the ethereal phosphorescence in the sea he'd just come from. Would he ever see the mortal world again? Or was he trapped in the Otherworld for the rest of his days? Gazing at Analee in her near nakedness, that did not seem like an unpleasant prospect.

The nymphs came nearer, almost touching him as they crowded close in their dance. How exquisite they were, one more beautiful than the next, their long hair whipping him as they passed him by. They smelled of incense—patchouli and sandalwood, angelica and yew. It was like a drug, besotting him until his head reeled, and his body swayed to the plaintive music. All the while, the goddess looked on, her sparkling eyes riveted to him through the eyeholes in the winged half-mask she wore, her dewy lips parted.

Many men in stag antlers appeared from among the trees wearing precious little else, save leaves for loincloths, and surrounded Analee. How long had they been standing there camouflaged by the tertiary bark and branches that blended with their antlers? She spread her cape wide, inviting them to touch every angle and plane, every orifice and recess of her body as they danced around her. As they did, the nymphs began to fondle him in the same intimate manner.

"They make you ready for me," the goddess said, "just as these make me ready for you."

Scarcely able to believe his eyes, Gar watched the masked and costumed men fondle Analee's breasts. He watched them follow the curves of her body with light strokes, their hands flitting over her pubic mound, their skilled fingers riding the length of her slit, and she spread her legs apart, leaning into their caresses, writhing against the pressure of their strokes, as one by one they fondled her. They were aroused, even as he was, as the nymphs opened the crotch of his garment and exposed his cock to their caresses.

Cool, skilled hands rode his shaft and kneaded his testicles, as each in her turn rubbed up against his swollen cock, while the others groped his hard muscled chest and buttocks, and played with his taut nipples. But he could not tear his eyes from what was happening across the way, as the aroused males laved and stroked and petted Analee until she uttered throaty moans that resonated wildly in his loins.

Gar had never experienced such an arousal. Watching the revelers bring her to the brink of ecstasy, watching her alabaster skin turn pink with the sultry blush of sex attacked his loins like fiery pincers, without the nymphs' caresses.

These Otherworldly creatures lived to pleasure themselves and each other. Their carnal cravings were like the lightning, untamable, and unpredictable, like the sea that had spat him out amongst them. He had heard it was thus in their world. He was seeing it firsthand, something granted only to the chosen few. Would he remember it after? Was there even an *after*? Was death or to be lost among the fay the price for this excruciating ecstasy he had been granted *for a little*?

Someone passed him a wineskin and he drank until rivulets ran down his chin, throat, and broad chest. Where had the garment Analee had given him gone? Had they torn it from his body? He was naked and the nymphs were licking the wine from his skin; so many hungry mouths, so many groping hands. Every cell in his body, every pore was on fire, his cock bursting, aching, begging, demanding release, and yet it would not come. What sorcery was this? What torment!

One by one, the revelers began to leave Analee and pair off with the nymphs that were fondling him. Wine still glistened on his golden, battle-tanned skin as the goddess approached him. All at once, she gripped her cape, raised her arms above her head, and whirled around him closer and closer. It was plain that she meant to cocoon him in the gossamer folds and drive him down in the cool, dewy grass at the edge of the thicket. But Gar resisted, not even knowing why. Something in her strange gyrations suggested entrapment, as if he wasn't already caught in her web.

"Why do you hesitate?" she murmured. "'Tis all part of the ritual."

"I would rather stand back and feast my eyes upon you, my lady," he returned. She shrugged and continued her strange dance, until she'd spiraled to the ground, her mantle spread out wide.

Gar dropped down beside her. The tall grass was cool around them, and fragrant with scents he had never smelled before, some otherworldly species of wildflower. It reminded him of the heather that grew on the Cornish moors, ruggedly sweet, with the barest trace of the salty mist that drifted overland from the sea. He couldn't see the flowers. All his eyes showed him was the sight of the Goddess of the Dream Well, naked in his arms, divested of her spider silk cloak. All else around them had vanished.

Where had the bonfires gone? Where were the wood nymphs and male revelers? Where were the faery lights? All that remained were the Wills-o'-the-Wisp bobbing about in the distance, and the moon beaming down upon their trysting place. It had not yet reached its pinnacle. Soon it would sit high in the indigo vault above, and all too soon thereafter it would begin its descent to keep its rendezvous with the dawn. What would happen then, when his time in Analee's arms was up? He would know soon enough, but now, oh, now! Her soft flesh was underneath him, grinding against him, her slender back arched to welcome his cock. That was all that mattered.

Gar crushed her against him in a smothering embrace. Ghostly mist drifted close, reminding him that when the full moon shone down upon the feast of Samhain, the veil between the living and the dead was at its thinnest. Which was he? That thought kept trickling back to haunt him, along with Analee's warning that he could only have her for a little while—till dawn. Time was short, and he beat those thoughts back in the rapture of her embrace, for they were both aroused beyond the point of no return.

Lying on the cool ground wet with dew, Gar could almost feel the pulse beat of the land beneath him, for indeed it had a heart, thumping to the rhythm of his own heart. Under the Samhain moon, the Otherworld had a sensual pulse. He'd felt it in the real world, too, but never as strong as now, among these creatures. Even the trees had a pulse; he could feel their roots stirring beneath him, moving in the soil beneath the tall, swaying grass. They were all celebrants in the harvest ritual—living and dead, fay and mortal conjoined under the full round November moon that seemed to shine upon both worlds.

Analee's arms were clasped about his neck as she straddled him. Raising her up with hands that spanned her narrow waist, he lowered her upon his shaft, watching it enter her inch by inch until he'd filled her, gliding on her juices. She felt like liquid silk inside, warm and welcoming. She, too, had a pulse. Right now, it beat for him. But it would not always be so. Once this little interlude was over she would lie thus with another, for that was the nature of the creature she was, this Otherworldly goddess, this sorceress of the well that had granted him ecstasy, but only until dawn. How glorious it would be if such a passion could be had among his own kind. To live in the arms of voluptuous flesh to the end of his days would be rapture, indeed. Such was the stuff of dreams, he knew, but it was a pleasant thought as he raised her up and down along the thick, veined bulk of his cock from root to rimmed tip, gazing at the glisten of her dew upon his skin, upon his shaft as he pumped in and out of her. Engorged, his penis was flushed blue, aching for release, throbbing to the beat of the astral plane palpitating in the very ground beneath him.

He could finally bear no more. Rolling her on her back, he raised her legs and thrust into her in mindless oblivion. She matched him thrust for thrust. The flower of her vulva from clitoris to vagina opening to him petal by petal until she'd captured him totally, rotating beneath him, gripping him with such sucking force his hips jerked forward as he came deep inside her, filling her with the hot rush of his seed.

All was still around them. Not even the wind sighed, though it fluttered the grass bed beneath them. It was a moment before Gar collapsed alongside her, his breast heaving as he gulped air into his lungs. They were alone, but movement among the nearby trees caught in a moonbeam called his eyes there. Someone or something had been watching them, and he strained his lust-glazed eyes, dilated in the darkness, trying to make the image come clear. A horse . . . no, a man . . . no, a *centaur!*

The pulse in the ground beneath them took on a new meter. The thudding of the creature's heavy hooves reverberated through the grassy bed they lay upon. It had an angry beat, though the beast didn't move from its position among the ash and oak trees in that quarter.

Gar raised himself upon one elbow, taking stock of the watcher in the moonlight. It was a magnificent creature, its body the dark four-legged form of a feather-footed destrier, its torso that of a muscular man, whose dark hair worn long was caught at the nape of his neck with a ribbon of vines. Their eyes met, and the creature pawed the ground. The gesture had a ring of warning to it.

"Who . . . *what* is that?" he said, nodding toward the centaur. For he truly thought the strange wine he'd drunk had had its way with him.

Analee shrugged. "'Tis only Yan," she said. "Pay him no mind. He's out of sorts."

"He looks a bit more than simply 'out of sorts,' " Gar observed. The creature looked about to charge, and they were in the open. He got to his feet and took her hand, raising her up alongside. "I think we'd best find suitable shelter elsewhere," he said. "I have no wish to be trampled. Those hooves of his look mean enough to do the job, and I have no sword to defend you."

"There is no need," Analee insisted. "I rule here, Gar Trivelyan. Yan is jealous. Eons ago, he angered the gods, and ever since on all eight sacred feast days throughout the year, he becomes the centaur. That is his punishment. When all the rest are coupling, he is denied me. He is my consort otherwise, you see, but cohabitation while he is in the body of the beast is strictly forbidden him, and so he sulks, and routs, and strikes the ground with his heavy hooves, but 'tis all bluster. He will not harm you. But he is why you can only have me till the dawn, for then his curse is eased. When he is a man again I cannot speak for your safety."

Gar eyed the centaur dubiously. "Yes, well, I still would put some distance between us, if it's all the same to you," he said, leading her away.

"No, not that way," she said, turning him toward a little lake beyond the clearing. "We shall have a sail if you fear him. Yan cannot follow there. The lake is too deep for the centaur."

"I fear no man or beast!" Gar defended. "But I have no weapon to defend you, and unless my eyes deceive me, that thing is armed!"

"I have no need of defending," Analee said. "Yan would never harm me, or you, either. He knows the rules well, though he doesn't like them much, I'll own. But that is his fault, isn't it? Come . . ."

Her words were scarcely out when the twang of an arrow whizzed through the air. It struck the ground inches from Gar's foot. Spinning around, Gar clenched both fists and started back toward the ash grove, but the goddess's quick hand arrested him.

"Pay him no mind," she said. Her voice was soothing and slow. "He will tire of the vigil. It has been thus for many ages. Believe me, he will not harm you, for then he would have to contend with me."

"No harm, eh?" Gar growled. "I just nearly lost a toe."

"No, you did not," Analee said, leading him again. "If he wanted your toe, he would have hit it. Yan is an expert marksman. He always hits his quarry. You are a seasoned sailor, Knight of the Realm, have you not ever had a warning shot fired across your bow upon the sea?"

Gar considered it, a close eye upon the centaur. The irate creature had reloaded his longbow and taken aim again. Analee saw also. Stamping her foot, she spun into a whirling cyclone, parting the tall grass and lifting dead leaves and mulch off the forest floor where the centaur stood among the trees. Puffing out her cheeks she blew a mighty wind that bent the whitethorn, furze, and bracken that hemmed the thicket. Bolting, the creature reared back on his hind legs, pawing the air amid the stinging blizzard of swirling leaves and twigs, acorns and pine needles her ire had raised, and galloped off deep into the forest.

They had reached the edge of the lake. Overhead, the moon had risen to the pinnacle. It would begin its descent now, each moment bringing it closer to the dawn. There wasn't much time left in the arms of the goddess who had granted him her favors for what reason he had yet to discover.

Yes. These were sexual creatures. It all seemed quite natural to them to pair off and enjoy the pleasures of the flesh. But then, he was a seasoned warrior and he had known his carnal moments also. Still, this was different. She had dazzled him with her magic and her beauty, and though he knew it couldn't last beyond the dawn, he had to believe there was a reason for her favors aside from the obvious. She was up to something. He would probe that issue, but not now. Not when the moon was sliding low and the beautiful Goddess of the Dream Well was standing before him naked and willing and ready to pleasure him as he had never been pleasured before.

They had reached the water's edge. It was warm, lapping at their feet and ankles—comfortable, just as everything was in the mysterious Celtic Otherworld, everything except jealous centaurs with longbows. It was bizarre moments like that when Gar was sure it was all a dream, but then he could still feel the wind the arrow made as it struck the ground so close to his foot he felt the shudder of its vibration. One did not feel such things in dreams, but they did feel such in enchantments.

Everyone knew the power of the fay. Didn't the Irish leave their front and back doors open a crack at night to give access to the wee folk that they might pass through unhindered in their night revelries? And didn't the Cornish pay tribute to the knockers in the tin mines to ensure that those little folk would lead them to the richest veins of ore? What had he bought with the tribute he'd tossed into the dream well, the coiled snake bracelet catching glints of moonlight on Analee's arm? Why was he the chosen one? What did it all mean? He longed to know, but feared to ask and break the magical spell she had cast over him.

Analee had taken his hand. A little boat resting in the lapping surf appeared at the edge of the lake. She was leading him toward it. Long and slender, in the shape of a swan, the boat bobbed gently as the calm ripples nudged it. Inside, it was made like a bed, with satin sheets and feather-down quilts. Silver bowls heaped high with grapes and plums and pomegranates set about the bow and stern made his mouth water.

"Come," she said as he handed her into it. "There is much I would show you before the dawn parts us, Gar Trivelyan, but first a moonlight sail."

3

They drifted with the current along the narrow ribbon of moon shimmer on the water as if it were an avenue. Balmy breezes fanned their naked skin, moist with the sweat of sex. There was no need of oars, or rudder. The little swan boat seemed to know the way. Cradled in the arms of the goddess, Gar had eyes for nothing else but the copper-haired, wide-eyed beauty in his arms, until another creature appeared.

Breaking the water's surface, a seal cow appeared; its limpid, human-like eyes seemed strangely familiar. It let loose a mournful wail, melancholy and sad, and lumbered alongside the boat, resting its front flippers on the side rail. Poised there, it peeked in at them, its gaze intense.

Analee vaulted upright. "What do you do here?" she scolded the creature. "Your time is not yet. Get you back to your revelry and leave me to mine, little sister."

The seal wailed again, and to Gar's great surprise, it reached to pet him with its silky flipper, its adoring eyes taking him in with much interest. The creature's touch was scintillating, its body aura charged with iridescence in the moonlight like a halo. An evocative scent of ambergris and salt drifted toward him from its pelt. It blinked and purred and shuddered in the water, making little ripples on the breast of the lake that spread out wide, like a stone makes skipping over the surface, just as her touch sent ripples of sweet sensation radiating through his loins. Instinctively, Gar reached to stroke the creature's sleek, wet head, and it closed its eyes and purred again, leaning into his caress.

Analee vaulted to her feet, nearly upsetting the little boat. "Away, I said!" she commanded the seal. "This will not be borne! Get you gone!"

The seal pushed off then, spiraled down into the water with another heart-wrenching moan, and a spectacular show of tail before it disappeared beneath the trail of moon shimmer that was growing steadily wider as the moon descended.

"Why did you chase her?" Gar asked. "She was doing no harm."

Analee sank back down in the boat and reached for him. "She knows her place," she said. "Right now that is in your world. She has no business here now."

"You called her your sister," said Gar, perplexed.

"I call the wood nymphs my sisters, too," the goddess replied. "Otherworldly deities each have their place. They must remain in it. But we all have our alter egos . . ." she added, as if to herself. "And on feasts anything is possible."

The last made no sense, except that it smacked of jealousy. He ignored it. "She is an astral deity, then, that seal?" he asked.

"She is a *selkie*. When the full Samhain moon unites the autumnal currents and the streams collide, the selkies shed their skins in your world. Some mortal men will steal those skins and if they do, the seals that shed them must remain with their captors. There are many wonders in our world, Gar Trivelyan. We of the astral choose with care those mortals favored to know our secrets."

"Why have you chosen me?" Gar blurted out. He had been dancing around asking that question since he met the Goddess of the Dream Well.

"Mortal men are too full of logic," she responded through a sigh that moved her naked breasts seductively. "Is it not enough that you have been chosen, knight of the realm? Must you have a reason?"

He shrugged, sinking into her arms. "There must be one," he persisted. He'd brought up the issue. There was no turning back now.

"There is," she said, playing with a lock of his hair, "but it is not for you, a mere mortal, to question the will of the gods." Her finger traced the scowl lines on his face. "Is it so important, really? Are you not pleased with the wonders you have seen here . . . with me?"

"Will I remember them when I return to my own world?" She hesitated, and his heart nearly stopped. It was the bravest question yet, for he had no idea if he would be returning.

"That depends," she said at last.

"Upon . . . ?"

"The gods," she said. "They have granted us this time, but it grows short, and we must not waste it . . ."

Fisting her hands in his hair, she pulled his head down until his lips met hers, but Gar had one last question, and he held back, focusing upon the provocative beauty spot above her lip, for he dared not look her in the eyes for this one.

"For all the passion here, there is no love, only lust," he said. "How is that possible?"

Again she hesitated. "The astral is a sensual plane of existence," she said. "What you mortals call love does not exist here. We of the astral view what you call by the name of *lust* as being as normal as breathing. It is a natural function that brings pleasure. We put no moral connotations upon it. This is what divides our worlds, why one will never understand the other, and why it is best that they be kept apart. Do not look too closely at the giver, Gar Trivelyan. Simply take the gift."

"And yet there is jealousy," Gar continued, trying to ignore her caresses. "That centaur . . ."

Analee laughed. "Yes, there is jealousy," she said, "and possessiveness, but not because of love. You are an intruder here, and the enemy! Have you forgotten who it was that caused the fall that separated our worlds when time began? Man's memory is weak, but not that of we of the astral. Our recollections go back to when mankind and the fay coexisted side by side in one world—before the fall—before the Great War that rent our worlds in two."

Gar gave it thought, but there was still one more thing troubling him. "That seal before," he said. "There was love in her, I sensed it—I felt it . . ."

"The selkies are a breed apart," said Analee. "That is because once shed of their skins they take on human traits, and sometimes actually become human—*too* human."

Gar uttered a guttural chuckle. "I sense a little jealousy here, too," he observed, pulling her closer.

"Rivalry is a more accurate term," she snapped back. "Enough! Do you see that moon up there?" She waved her arm toward it then swept it down toward the shimmer it painted on the breast of the water. "The lower it sinks, the wider the swath," she said, "the wider the swath, the closer the dawn, when we must part. Take the gift, Gar Trivelyan."

Bypassing her mouth, the goddess pulled his head down, feeding him her nipple; it was hard and cool to the touch as he laved it with his tongue, making it harder still. It would not do to anger her in this melancholy mood that had come over her since the seal appeared. He was in her world now. He must play by her rules, but he couldn't free himself of the selkie's touch. His skin still tingled from the caress of that satiny flipper, and her dark eyes with lashes that made them seem so human haunted him still.

Perhaps it was her wide-eyed innocence that had so captivated him, or the love he felt in her caress that was so conspicuous in its absence among the rest. Whatever the cause, he longed to see the little seal again if only to dispel what she had ignited in him. Meanwhile, the Goddess of the Dream Well had twined her legs around him in the plush bedding that lined the little boat. How smooth and silky soft it felt against the fever in his skin.

Analee trailed her hand in the water, then moistened his lips with it, slipping her index finger inside his mouth. Gar laved it, licking the salt from it, sucking it as her fingertip jousted with his tongue. His hand glided over her belly and thighs and slipped between, parting the petals of her sex, spreading her juices as he probed her layer upon layer until he'd slipped two fingers inside her. How warm and welcoming her body was, thrumming to the rhythm of his caress as her vulva gripped his fingers just as they had gripped his cock.

Straddling her was precarious in the narrow swan boat. Gar's tall, hard-muscled body barely fit in it with her as it was, without managing coupling positions. It would have been safer were she to straddle him, but she made no overtures in that direction, reclining on her back upon the feather-down quilts, her long coppery hair fanned out about her on the bolster beneath her head. She looked her Otherworldly incarnation, as if she wasn't real at all, but an illustration in a fine old tome of collected myths.

Lifting her legs, he raised her hips and entered her, watching his hot, hard shaft slide inside her, gliding on the wetness of her arousal. Again and again he thrust into her as she clung to him, fisting her hands in his hair, arching her back to take him deeper still. Writhing against him, she slid her hands over her breasts, working her tawny nipples into tall, hard buds between her thumbs and forefingers just as he had done. Looking on through hooded eyes dilated with desire, Gar watched the wide areola of those perfect nipples pucker taut, watched the globes of her breasts flush and harden. His shaft plunged deeper. The sight of her thus sent waves of drenching fire through his loins, each shuddering thrust bringing him closer and closer to climax until at last he could bear no more.

Bending, coupled as they were, was difficult in the close confines of the boat, but he longed to take those nipples in his mouth, longed to lave them with his tongue until she begged for more, until he could feel the contractions of her release as he brought her to climax. Shifting position, he cupped one breast in his massive hand, lowered his eager mouth, and suckled.

Analee let loose a guttural groan, primeval and deep. Her hips jerked forward and she lurched in his arms as he filled her, matching him thrust for thrust, gripping his cock with her vagina until, on the verge of orgasm, he shifted position and took her deeper still.

The boat began to rock to their rhythm. Faster and faster it heaved from side to side, taking in water, for it was shallow. Swamped, it keeled over when Gar scrambled to his feet attempting to steady it, pitching them both into the lake. As it spiraled down beneath the surface of the water, the swan's neck–shaped prow struck Gar a blow on the head as it sank.

Down, down, Gar plunged dazed into the still, dark water. He'd lost sight of Analee, though he groped for her as he plummeted. He had always been a strong swimmer—even injured— which is what had saved him during the shipwreck, but the glancing blow he'd taken to the head had rendered him nearly senseless, and he fought to stay conscious.

All at once a stream of phosphorescence glided toward him. He felt a sharp nudge that propelled him upward. Something silky soft leaned against him, something vaguely familiar. It raised him up until his head burst through the water and he filled his lungs with great gulps of air as it nudged him upon the lakeshore, coughing and sputtering helplessly.

Rolling on his back, he opened eyes smarting with salt to the sight of the little seal cow bending over him, her head cocked to the side, her enormous eyes sparkling down at him dazzling in the moonlight. There was a large lump on his brow, where the boat's prow grazed him as it sank. Glancing up, he could see the angry bruise surrounding it. The little seal saw it, too. Before he could raise his hand to soothe it, she laid her flipper over the lump. How soothing and cool it felt against the fire in the smarting bruise.

Stroking it, she purred like a cat and sidled closer, flopping down alongside him. How warm her body was, considering that she'd just come from the water, and how comforting as she nuzzled against his heaving chest with her sleek wet nose. Her whiskers tickled. When he brushed them away, she nuzzled his hand, and patted him with her flipper the way she had done in the boat earlier.

Gar couldn't help but smile. "You're a friendly little thing, aren't you?" he said. "I suppose I should thank you. I might have drowned if you hadn't rescued me, little friend. Well done!"

Iridescence glowed around her like a halo in the moonlight at his words just as it had before, but her purring vibrating against his skin alarmed him. It had erotic overtones about it that flagged danger, and he vaulted erect, all but toppling her over. He was aroused. Was it because he'd had another close brush with death, or had this strange selkie creature made him hard with her gentle petting?

He had to keep reminding himself that he was in the astral realm, where all creatures exuded sex as a matter of course and a natural function no more profound than drawing breath.

There were no moral strictures here. Creatures went about naked, and mated in public whenever and with whomever they pleased. Having come among them, he'd been caught up in the magic—obliged to behave in like manner, for he'd been chosen by the fay, and one did not refuse that privilege or treat it lightly or without respect, else he fall to disfavor with the astral realm. No one dared risk curses of the Celtic Otherworld, least of all a seasoned warrior who depended upon all the supernatural favors he could glean on his campaigns.

Gar raised his hand to his brow to find that the lump was gone. Had she healed him? She must have. Now, she flopped around him in the manner of a seal, and seemed to be taking his measure. There was a childlike innocence about her that made her all the more irresistible. One could not help but be endeared to such a creature. It was his natural instinct to embrace her, to stroke her head like he had done in the boat. Something made him resist the urge. Instead, he sat spellbound as she waddled around him, her silky flipper petting first his arm, then his hip, then his leg. There was discovery and awe in her touch, as if she had never seen a naked man before. The tactile sensations spread by that gentle touch set his loins on fire. Every cell, every pore in his skin responded to her touch. There was no question as to the cause of his arousal now, and when her raised flipper approached his erect cock, he vaulted to his feet.

"That will do, my curious little friend," he said through a nervous laugh. He stooped and finally succumbed to stroking her head. She looked so forlorn at his rejection of her caress, he couldn't help himself. He couldn't bear the hurt in those huge limpid eyes. She seemed all eyes then, gazing up at him longingly. She was half human after all. "Hadn't you better go back as your sister said?" he urged her. "You wouldn't want to anger her, would you?"

"It is far too late for that!" said the goddess, plowing out of the lake. She approached them, arms akimbo, her long hair curiously dry for having risen from the water. "Get you back where you belong!" She charged the seal, chasing her toward the water's edge.

The seal barked a protest, her reluctance to leave evident in the way she flopped and waddled around him until Analee finally drove her back into the water with the aid of a stick that had washed up on shore. Again the creature wailed. The mournful sound pierced Gar to the core. Their eyes met for the briefest instant before the seal splashed into the water and dove beneath the surface, dodging the stick Analee hurled after her. Seconds later as if waving farewell, the creature rose up and plunged again, her broad tail rising into the air, dripping luminous pearls of water back into the lake, then disappeared.

"So!" the goddess said. "The minute my back is turned, this is what I find. Is this how you would repay my generosity, Gar Trivelyan?"

Gar shrugged. "That creature saved my life, my lady," he defended. "But for her—"

"*I* saved your life, knight of the realm," Analee reminded him, "and gave you my favors. It would do you well to remember that."

"How could I forget?" he returned, the words spoken on the cutting edge of sarcasm.

"Ummm," the goddess grumbled. "However needs must, you would do well to remember your benefactress. Our time is not yet up, Gar Trivelyan."

Gar glanced up at the moon, then toward the still breast of the water and the silvery shimmer that had swallowed the little seal. He recalled the gentle thump of her body that had guided him toward shore. It was not unlike something similar he'd felt after the shipwreck. He'd heard the siren's song then felt something nudging him toward the strand before he stumbled out of the surf. Could the strange little creature have been with him all along? Had she guided him to the Otherworld in the first place when the galley struck the Land's End shoals? So much was unclear, and yet one thing was very clear, indeed. The little seal had touched his heart, and he wondered if he would ever see her again.

4

Gar was leery of the forest, for it was dense and dark, the moon scarcely showing through the canopy of diverse branches intermingled overhead. Here, oak and ash, elm and yew coexisted with pine, the ground grizzled with hawthorn, bracken, and woodbine. They had left the willows behind beside the lake, for willow trees so loved the water and lived beside it in both worlds, it seemed. All manner of magical tree and plant life lived here, and the trees seemed alive, as curious as the little seal as he passed among them following the Goddess of the Dream Well deeply in.

Leaves, vines, branches, and tendrils groped him as he followed a narrow footpath, acutely aware that he was being watched. The centaur, he had no doubt, though Analee didn't seem to notice, or if she did she made no mention of it. Gar was beginning to part the veil she'd cast before his eyes to mystify and confuse. He was beginning to see her intent for what it really was. He was not her guest, as she would have him believe, he was her *captive*, until the dawn. What happened then evidently depended upon what he did while under her spell.

Gar had heard of people disappearing after an encounter with the fay, never to be seen or heard from again. The Celtic Other-world was populated with creatures, one cleverer than the next, who delighted in playing pranks upon mortals. It had been thus since the fall that separated the races and split the worlds in two. Yes, they were, indeed, a clever lot, but so was mortal man, and Gar was beginning to regret he'd ever stumbled upon the dream well and its enigmatic goddess guardian. But it was too late for those thoughts now. He would have to play her game until dawn, and hope he could outwit her and escape. He had no desire to spend eternity in the Celtic Otherworld. The trick would be to manage it without invoking her wrath. Judging from the look of her now, from the staccato spring in her step, the stiff set of her lips, and her silence as she led him deeper and deeper into the wood, it did not bode well.

"Have you dominion over these?" he asked her, gesturing toward the trees, meanwhile removing one branch that had gripped his torso familiarly as he passed it by.

"I am the Goddess of the Dream Well. There is where my dominion lies. Only the greater gods have dominion here among the ancient ones."

"But they heed you," Gar said. "I see them genuflect as you pass by."

"They show respect, yes," she said. "It is unwise to disrespect any deity. Why do you ask?"

The path they followed narrowed suddenly, or was it that he'd just begun to notice the trees on either side crowding close? He opened his mouth to speak, but too late. The goddess waved her hand, and a sturdy oak reached out its branches and tethered him by the arms to its vine-covered trunk.

". . . And they do my bidding!" she concluded. Strolling back and forth before him, she pointed to the obvious. "You are aroused," she said. "The little seal's doing, while I was left beneath the lake!"

Gar popped a bitter laugh. "You cannot fault her for this," he said. "I've been aroused since I arrived here. You have seen to that. And as to leaving you, the sinking boat struck me in the head. But for that little seal, I would have drowned. She saved my life."

"*I* saved your life," she reminded him.

"Yes, you did," he returned, "and you gave me your favors until dawn. There is still some time left before that, and I can hardly do you justice tied to this tree. Turn me loose! Believe me, I perform much better as a guest than a captive."

She continued to stroll around him. "In due time," she purred.

He shrugged. "You are the one continually telling me time is short," he said. "Suit yourself."

Her eyes flashed, and she seized his cock, wrenching a groan that smacked of an odd mix of lust and surprise that startled even him. "Do you mean to say that little seal didn't cause this to harden?" she demanded. "I saw you two just now!"

"Then you saw naught but the sort of affection a man might have for his faithful dog." That wasn't entirely true, for he saw something in the little seal that struck an affectionate chord and touched his heart. Inside that sealskin, there lived an entity that could take the form of a woman, a woman who could be his for the taking if he possessed her pelt. A woman with childlike innocence possessed of a tenderness that he had never known. There was something magnetic about such a tender nature. Something once tasted no man could resist, least of all Gar Trivelyan, who had never known the like.

Secretly, he longed for the little seal's tender touch, longed for her adoring eyes and benevolent nature, for that truly was a nurturing facet of the little creature's makeup, an attribute conspicuously absent in the goddess. But it wasn't the animal. It was the creature within shining through that so enthralled him to the point that he was becoming obsessed with seeing that creature in its human form. He was haunted by the longing to see if the attributes he so admired in the seal carried over in her human incarnation.

These secrets of the heart he could not share with the goddess. It would not do to anger her. His future was still suspect. For all he knew he would never return to his own world. It was more than likely that he would remain a captive in this plane of existence ruled by libidinous lust for the rest of his life, if in fact he still had a life. It did not bode well.

Her hand tightened around his cock and he sucked in a hasty breath. There was no question that she had the touch, no argument that she possessed the power to arouse and fulfill like no other he'd ever known. Her deft fingers were picking out the distended veins in his shaft as she sidled closer, flaunting her nakedness. She'd come so close he could feel her body heat radiating toward him. She was on fire, so steamy hot he feared his cock would burst into flame under the friction of her touch. He could feel the blood thrumming through the pulsating veins she stroked so skillfully. She was about to finish what had started deep within his loins when the little seal nearly touched his genitals on the lakeshore. The difference was the enigmatic little selkie did not have to touch him to set his pulse racing and riddle his loins with drenching fire. If he were to come now, it would be the selkie's doing, not the hand of the goddess that stroked him so relentlessly. For it was a different hand entirely that stroked him now, playing his body like a fine musical instrument. As skilled as that hand was, there was no love in it. No. This, he would not let on to the Goddess of the Dream Well.

"I do not like tethers," he said. "Have this ancient one unhand me else I break its branches. I am well able, you know. That I remain thus is out of deference to you, but I grow tired of this game. It would be wise to let me go now."

"You change the subject easily enough," she observed. "You have not answered my question."

"I give no credence to it," he said succinctly. "What you accuse is too impossible to deserve an answer, and a moot point. What you are doing there is about to make me come. Would that not be more enjoyable if I had the use of my arms, my lady?"

"Oh, I don't know," she purred, sauntering closer still, so close her hardened nipples touched his chest and his cock leaned heavily against her slit. "There is something very provocative about bringing a bound man to climax." She began rubbing herself against his shaft, slow undulations that threatened to drive him mad. "See how it lives for me?" she murmured.

She ground the petal-like folds of her vulva harder against him, and he strained against his tether. To his dismay, he found that he could not break his bonds as he had boasted. The tree branches were possessed of superhuman strength. They were enchanted, as were the vines that roped him now, climbing his body, binding him to the trunk of the ancient tree, while she had her way with him.

"It must be nearly dawn," he said. "Can we not find a more comfortable way to couple?"

The goddess laughed. "Time means nothing here, knight of the realm," she said. "Dawn here and dawn in your world are two entirely different things."

From somewhere deep in the fuzzy labyrinth of his memory, Gar recalled hearing that time as mortals knew it did not exist in the Celtic Otherworld. A pity he hadn't remembered earlier. But he would not dwell upon that then. It was clear that Analee wasn't going to release him until she'd satisfied the lust that was inherent in her, the libidinous drive that powered all the fay. There was much he needed to know, much he needed to ask her, but not while her skilled fingers were setting fire to his moist skin, and her body was charging his loins with unstoppable lust. While she was his guest, his slave, his *captive*, he was under her spell. She had made him what she was for the duration of his stay. How long would that be? How long before the dawn? He was almost afraid to ask these questions, though what flimsy shred of humanity he still possessed in this enchanted place demanded he do so, just not yet . . .

"Umm," she hummed. "I see your point about your tethers. Something is lost this way, but I know a way to get it back, maybe even stronger."

With no more said, she began pumping his cock in slow, deep, spiraling revolutions that wrenched a troop of throaty moans from him. A beam of moonlight spilled over them through the trees' leafy branches. Glancing down, he saw that his shaft was blue with engorged veins, the head a desperate shade of red, slick with pre-come. It wouldn't take many of those motions to bring the climax, and though he fought against it with his mind, his body jerked, and his loins jutted forward as if his body were possessed of a mind of its own.

A captive of the passion, his whole body throbbed like a pulse beat. It echoed in his ears like the beat of a galley drum, thumping—hammering—begging for the release her cool hands promised. He began to drive himself against those fingers relentlessly.

Gar shut his eyes. He was on the brink of ecstasy, but they wouldn't stay closed. Was there any part of his anatomy that didn't have a mind of its own? Instead, his hooded gaze fell upon what she was doing to him, and to herself, for she had begun to stroke her slit with her free hand.

Exposing her clitoris, she began to rub it in the same slow, shuddering rhythm as she stroked his cock. He could see the hard bud slick with the wetness of her arousal, and the swollen nether lips beneath as she parted them, inching deeper inside the petal-like folds of her vagina.

Gar's breath was coming short as she quickened the rhythm of her strokes upon his shaft to match that of her deft fingers caressing her genitalia. She pressed up against him, grinding her hard nipples into his chest as she stroked herself, and Gar could bear no more. He groaned as his hips jerked forward, and he thrust himself into her hand faster and faster as she undulated against him, his heart hammering against her, his whole body convulsed in wave upon wave of heart-wrenching contractions.

There was no stopping, no holding back now. He could no longer watch what she was doing to him, to herself. It didn't matter. He could feel, oh how he could feel! Pistoning into her hand as she stroked him again and again, he matched her thrust for stroke until the thick lava flow of his seed erupted from him. It rushed out of him in long shivering spurts that spilled over the leaf mulch on the forest floor like rain. The riveting sound it made combined with the goddess's orgasmic murmurings quickened his heartbeat, wrenching another groan from him.

A wave of Analee's hand released him from the tree, whose branches once more reached toward the sky as if they had not ever tethered him. The old oak seemed to sigh, the sound whispering through its uppermost branches. It was almost a human sound that called Gar's eyes to the treetops, where the silvered moon was visible in fleeting glimpses.

Analee ran her finger along the side of his cheek. When it reached the corner of his lips, she slipped it into his mouth. It tasted of herbs and bee pollen, and of her musky juices, dark and sultry. Why did he think of ambergris then? How strange that in the fragrant forest, rich with the scents of lush foliage, herbs and the peppery tang of pine, he could smell the mysterious sea, in all its evocative splendor.

"Come," she said, leading him deeper into the wood. "A place has been prepared for us to wait for the dawn."

Gar breathed a sigh of relief. Those words held a glimmer of hope. This was all very well, but he had begun to fear that the dawn would never come for him in the goddess's realm. She was a skilled seductress, and a more formidable adversary than any foe on the field of battle that he had ever come up against. She used her sexuality like a seasoned warrior used his sword, and with it, she possessed the power to maim or kill or to enslave. Which fate had she planned for him? There was no question that she had a plan; he could see it in the little smiles that did not reach her eyes, and in the way she avoided answering him directly. Like a poisonous serpent paralyzes its victim, so had she paralyzed him with her wiles, with the secret powers of the astral that had been known to drive men mad. That he was still aware of that was a good sign, and he called upon what few threads of his humanity still knitted him together to burnish it into his fogged memory.

They walked a while in silence. There were so many questions banging around in Gar's brain demanding answers, questions that he was almost afraid to ask. He was hoping they were heading toward some body of water where he might see the little seal again, but this was not the time to broach that subject. The Goddess of the Dream Well was possessed of a temper, and this wasn't the moment to test it.

"What happens when dawn breaks?" he said at last.

She cast him a sidelong glance. "That depends," she said.

"Upon you, I know," he returned. "But surely you know by now what you mean to do with me at sunrise."

"That depends," she repeated, "but not upon me, upon *you*."

Now he was intrigued, though he decided to leave that for a bit. "You say time does not exist here," he said. "How much mortal time has passed since I washed up on your shore?"

"I do not know time, mortal or otherwise," she replied. "It has neither meaning nor purpose here in the Otherworld." She shrugged. "Some who have visited here return to find their loved ones long gone to their reward, while their stay here seemed no longer than what you mortals call 'hours.' And others . . . never return." Her voice deepened with the last, and her hesitation troubled him, but he went on nonetheless. He'd come this far. He needed to know what to expect.

"Because they chose to stay here, or was it something else?" he asked her.

She stopped in her tracks and faced him. She was wearing her long flowing mantle again. When had she put that on? She was as naked as he was when she emerged from the lake. It didn't matter. The garment was as transparent as a morning cobweb spangled with dew, catching glints from the low-sliding moon. The trees were thinning and the moonbeams picked out the firm, round shape of her buttocks and the perfect globes of her breasts. Her tawny nipples straining against the gossamer fabric held his gaze relentlessly.

"Some choose, and some are chosen," she said.

It was clear that she wasn't going to give him a straight answer, and the more important his questions seemed, the less she was going to divulge. He attempted a casual attitude, as casual as he could manage possessed by Otherworldly lust madness in the company of a nearly naked sex goddess who was flaunting her charms.

"I see," he said. "And where do I fit in that number?"

She smiled. "Are you so anxious to leave?"

Gar laughed. Did it sound as blatantly nervous to her as it did to him? "It is only natural that I would be concerned for my fellow shipmates," he said. "That galley was bringing us home from a long campaign in the north. It was the last lap of a harrowing journey over land and sea. The knights were battle weary, longing for home, and here I am safe in the arms of a beautiful goddess. Is it any wonder that I would be anxious?"

"You were not so anxious a moment ago, when I held this cock in my hand, Gar Trivelyan," she purred, fondling his shaft, which had begun to rise again. "But your member here is anxious, isn't it? I fear we may not make it to the perfect place to wait upon the dawn."

"Because you have enchanted me," Gar said.

"I have granted your wish," she murmured, "and awarded you my favors, but only for a little . . . until the dawn. I have said so from the start. I promised no more, or no less. Is your arm healed?"

"Yes, but—"

"Have I not given you my favors?" she interrupted him.

"You have, my lady, yes," he responded.

"Then I have kept my word, knight of the realm, and I owe you nothing more."

"But the dawn has not yet broken," Gar persisted, "and as you have so often said, time grows short. I would know how short, my lady. It is a reasonable request." There! It was out. She would have to answer him now. It was a direct question.

The goddess smiled a smile that chilled him to the bone. "Like I've said," she purred, "and I do not like repeating myself: That, my impetuous knight, does not depend upon me. It depends upon *you*. Come now, the best is yet to come."

5

Gar said no more. He was at the mercy of the Goddess of the Dream Well. It was that simple. Everything he'd heard about the Otherworld was coming back to haunt him as they walked through the forest among the thinning trees toward a little clearing beyond the thicket, where a blanket had been laid among the sleeping wildflowers. It was no ordinary blanket, but a thin veil of transparent stuff spangled with the morning dew. Bowls and platters set upon it were heaped high with fruits of the harvest, nuts, apples, plums, grapes, and succulent pomegranates, along with fragrant breads and cakes made of tender unborn grains glazed with honey. There were slabs of soft cheese, flagons of sweet wine, and crocks of mead, a veritable feast for the gods. She waved her hand and a ground-creeping mist rose like a cottony fog surrounding them.

Gar was suddenly very hungry. His mouth was watering over the array of food spread out before him. Above, the moon was slowly sinking toward the horizon. Soon the sky would lighten and he would finally have the answer to the question he so longed and dreaded to hear all at once: What would become of him when dawn broke?

Analee knelt upon the shimmering cloth and beckoned to him to join her. Gar dropped to his knees and reclined on a pillow, watching her examine the food. As good as it all looked and smelled something nagging at the back of his brain brought a constricting lump to his throat. It was common knowledge that one must never accept food from the fay. To do so meant captivity in the Otherworld for all eternity. Was this what the goddess meant when she said it was up to him? If that were so, he knew what would happen to him if he did eat the offered food. The question was what would happen to him if he didn't?

"None for me," he said, as she offered him a succulent grape from the bunch in her hand. "I am sated on your love alone." Why did the word *love* addressing her taste so bitter on his tongue? There was no love in her, only lust. There was more love in the soft flipper of the strange little selkie seal than there was in the goddess's whole voluptuous body. And why did the word evoke the little seal's image?

The goddess bit into the grape she'd offered him. A little rivulet of the juice trickled over her lower lip, glistening in the moonlight. The moon seemed to have frozen in the sky. Its position hadn't changed since they sat down on the gossamer cloth.

Gar nodded toward the heavens. "We seem to be frozen in time," he said, as casually as he could manage.

"You mortals are always so obsessed with time," she returned. She caught a drop of the juice on the tip of her finger and sucked it clean. "If you only knew how much better you would fare in your world without it."

Gar couldn't imagine a world without time. Nonetheless, he was held captive in one now, and if he wasn't very careful, very clever, he would find himself a prisoner in the Otherworld forever.

He laughed. "And you, I fear could never become accustomed to the restrictions of time were you in my world, my lady," he said.

"Perhaps not," she admitted. "But then, I will never have to."

Of course she wouldn't. There was no entity powerful enough in the mortal realm to bind her there against her will as she was going to attempt to do to him in her world.

"And yet, time must exist here for you to have stopped it," he served.

"All here is illusion, knight of the realm."

"Even you, my lady?"

"Ask that there between your legs if I am 'illusion.' "

Gar was about to reply, when the whiz and twang of an arrow finding its mark struck the cloth beneath him dangerously close to his left thigh, where his erect cock rested. He felt the breeze it made and vaulted to his feet, searching the drifting mist for some sign of the bowman who had launched it. But all was still, and he seized the arrow, broke it over his knee, and tossed the pieces aside. No sooner had he done so and begun to resume his seat, when another arrow whizzed past him, coming to ground exactly where he would have reclined.

Analee laughed as Gar disposed of the second arrow as he had done the first one. "Yan is anxious for the dawn as well, I think," she tittered, rocking back on her heels where she knelt on the cloth.

A third arrow sailed through the air. This time it struck close to Analee, and her demeanor darkened. All trace of her levity had disappeared as she surged to her feet, tossing the grapes down with force enough to squash them.

"Perhaps he is the one in need of tethers," Gar said, as the centaur pranced out of the mist, his dark glower menacing them both.

"I will deal with this," the goddess said. Swirling her transparent cloak about her, she strode toward the creature, who had reloaded his bow.

"Put that down!" she commanded the centaur.

"You mean to keep him!" the creature said, waving his arm toward the sky. "This is not like the other times. I saw you in the woods." He thumped his chest with a scathing fist. "*I* am your consort. Him, never! He will taste my arrow if you detain him here."

"You overstep your bounds," she warned him, stroking his sleek destrier body. "In due time, things will be as they were between us. You must be patient, Yan."

"And meanwhile I am trapped thus!" the centaur said, rearing out of her reach. "I am denied you in the body of this beast, while you lie with that . . . that *human!*"

She *had* tampered with time—his time, at any rate. Gar had his answer now. His worst fears were realized. She did not mean to let him go, she never did. She had tricked him—bewitched him—beguiled him with her fay glamour, and he was at her mercy. Cold chills riveted him to the spot where he stood. That was the other thing he should have remembered: The fay could never be trusted. They were tricksters and pranksters, and no matter how sweetly they seduced a man, he was doomed if he were to succumb to their wiles.

"You do not rule here, Yan!" the goddess shrilled. "Remember yourself, else you learn to love your present incarnation."

"Keep him, and I will *kill* him, Analee. You were right when you told him my aim was true, that if I wanted to hit him I would have done."

"You heard that, then?"

The centaur nodded. "You forget that I hear everything! You go too far. Keep in mind that I can redeem myself with the gods exposing you. Mother Annis would not take kindly to the way you have abused your office were she to learn of it. She has dominion over all the wells—and you, my sweet!"

"You wouldn't dare!" she shrilled

"Oh, wouldn't I? Do not think to put me to the test! And as to your human, I do not want to kill him. He is just as much your victim as I am, but take no comfort in it, for I will if needs must. I will not be made the laughingstock—no longer!"

Unconsciously, Gar reached for the sword missing from his hip and cursed under his breath. He felt doubly naked without the two-edged weapon of Toledo steel he'd sacrificed to the sea during the shipwreck, for it weighted him down in the water. How he wished he had it now, safe in its leather scabbard at his side.

"You make too much of this," the goddess murmured, attempting to stroke the irate centaur again, and again the creature pranced and reared and sidled out of her reach. "It is *Samhain*!" she went on. "Let me have my bit of fun. All will be as it was between us come the dawn. You have done as I bade you, haven't you?"

The centaur nodded. "And that's another thing! I do not hold with cages, I—"

"Silence!" she snapped. "Come away. He will hear!"

"Promise me no harm will come to—"

"Be still, I said!" the goddess demanded, leading him away.

Though they spoke still, they were out of earshot, and Gar sank back down against the pillow. Supporting himself upon one elbow, he strained his ears and searched the mist that had swallowed them, but he could neither see nor hear them now except for the buzz of incoherent mumblings. Analee was definitely up to something. The quirk of fate that had pitched him into the Otherworld had left him ill prepared to deal with whatever that might be. He would have to rely upon his wits to outwit the goddess, and what faery myths he'd been fed at his mother's knee. So far, the latter had served him well enough. He knew enough not to trust any entity, or accept food in the Otherworld. The trouble was most of his Otherworldly edification came in the form of prevention, rather than cure. He knew what to do to avoid captivity, but not how to escape from it, if there even was a way to escape. It did not bode well.

Presently, Analee parted the mist, returning. Gar knew she would not leave him long unattended. He watched her approach, raking her with eyes hooded with desire. He could not help himself. She had bewitched him. Torn between a passion she commanded and the last shreds of his humanity, he gritted his teeth and held his breath, waiting for her to speak.

"He will bother us no more," she said, kneeling down beside him.

"I cannot say as I blame him much," Gar said, reclining full length, his hands beneath his head in as casual a pose as he could muster. "If the situation was reversed and you were my permanent consort, I would be feeling jealousy myself."

"He will get over it."

"Does he really mean to kill me if you keep me here?" It was a risk, but he needed her to know he'd overheard at least that much of her conversation with the centaur.

"You do not understand him as I do," she said. "He will not harm you. Once the dawn has come and gone—"

Gar waved his hand toward the sky. "The moon has not yet moved, my lady. That tends to make his assessment of the situation somewhat trustworthy."

"Forget him," Analee warbled, reaching to stroke his cock. "He means nothing to us. This is the place I spoke of, where we wait for the dawn, where I award you the last of my favors. Put Yan and his jealous nonsense out of your mind, and submit to me this one last time before we part."

Her cool hand riding up and down his shaft had made him harder than before. She knew just where to touch, just how to stroke to bring him to the brink of ecstasy, coming near, but only teasing those erogenous points that set him afire from the inside out. Right now, it was his testicles she teased, her skilled fingers flitting over them with the lightest touch, like that of a butterfly's wing. He shut his eyes and groaned. There was no help for it.

"You have a very persuasive touch, my lady of the well," he murmured.

"You have a very willing member, knight of the realm. But you must keep up your strength. Did you have something to eat while I was gone?"

"My hunger is only for you," Gar said, his voice a seduction. Two could play at her dubious game.

"But it is such a pity to waste all this," she said, pouting. She plucked a grape from the bunch she'd discarded earlier and slid it between her teeth. Bending over him, she lowered the fruit to his lips. "Take it from me," she murmured. "Quench your thirst in the sweet juice of this fruit of the vine, and I will give you pleasures you cannot possibly imagine."

Gar turned his head aside. "I am not fond of grapes, my lady," he hedged. He dared not let a single drop of the grape juice into his mouth, for to taste it would damn him.

The goddess sucked the grape between her teeth and bit down, releasing its juice while she swallowed the rest, then lowered her dripping mouth to his. "Kiss me," she whispered only inches from his lips.

"I told you," he replied. "I do not like the taste of grapes."

"A nut, then?" she coerced him, slipping one between her teeth.

"Thank you, no," he said. "As I said, I have an appetite only for you."

The goddess frowned, and her hand tightened upon his cock. "Do you know how rude it is to refuse my hospitality, a goddess of the Celtic Otherworld?"

"I did not ask for such a feast, and you did not promise it," Gar said steadily. "It is more than enough that I feast upon you for what little time I have left."

"Then I must insist that you take the tiniest morsel out of respect for the many hands that have prepared it especially for you. We fay are easily insulted. You would not wish to be the cause of any such insult, would you?"

There was no way out now. He looked her long in the eyes, and had the good sense to take back his cock from her before speaking. "My lady, any fool knows not to take food from the fay," he said. "And there is no use to try to trick me, for such tricks have no power. As tempting as the prospect is of lying in your arms for the rest of my days, I wouldn't last long with your Yan stalking me. His arrow came a little too close to my cock just now for me to put any trust in him if we were to consort on a permanent basis." He gestured toward the heavens. "So you may as well unbind the moon, and let dawn break."

The goddess shrieked like a banshee, crushing two bunches of grapes in her white-knuckled fists to pulp and rivulets of sticky juice. Surging to her feet, she kicked the bowls and trenchers, scattering the rest of the food in all directions. Nuts sailing through the air quickly became the prize of scurrying squirrels and chipmunks. Larger woodland creatures made off with the fruit, and field mice gobbled up the crumbs of cheese, while birds flew down from the trees at the edge of the wood to fight over the bread.

A burst of deep masculine laughter erupted from the mist. Yan, no doubt, Gar surmised. The triumphant sound only angered the goddess more, and she dropped to her knees, smearing the crushed grape pulp none too gently over Gar's face and chest, over his engorged penis and swollen testicles.

Gar vaulted upright and seized her upper arms, shaking her. His hand grazed the coiled gold serpent bracelet he'd given her as tribute what seemed an eternity ago, and very well could have been, considering her command of time.

"Have you forgotten this so soon?" he said, flicking the bracelet with his thumb.

The goddess laughed. "You have received favors that far surpass the value of that trinket, knight of the realm," she chided.

"Whose fault is that, then?" he retorted. "You made the rules, gave your favors, enchanted me with libidinous lust to have your way with me. I have been your slave, woman! How is such as that my fault, eh?"

Analee relaxed in his grip. "Very well," she said. "Perhaps I have been hasty. I do not often get so skilled a lover. You are a lion, Gar Trivelyan, a rampant lion, like the device upon the crest of your people. Can you blame me for wanting to tame you to my will? Look at what you have made of *me*."

Gar clamped his teeth over his tongue for fear of saying, *you, my lady, are like a puff adder, and I had naught to do with your making.*

"But let us part friends," she went on, her voice dripping honey. "Let me love you just once more before the dawn."

The whole erotic episode had hardened him like steel. The tactile feel of crushed fruit ground into his skin, into his cock and the taut skin of his testicles filled him with an insatiable longing that she lick him clean of it.

But the moon hadn't moved overhead, and again he nodded toward it. "Once I see that you are in earnest," he said, waiting.

Analee waved her hand, and the aura around the full Samhain moon flared. "Done," she said. "Watch, and you will see it move among the stars if you do not believe me."

The centaur's laughter had ceased echoing from beyond the mist. Acutely aware of the danger of arrows, Gar could only hope that the creature would also see the moon's descent and leave his longbow unloaded.

His eyes hooded with desire, Gar watched the goddess kneel beside him, and groaned as she began to lave the grape pulp from his chest. He shut his eyes altogether as she licked the sweet, sticky juice from his face. She was very thorough, and seemed to be rubbing her genitals at the same time. Her soft, warm tongue was fulfilling his fantasy as if she'd read his mind, but then, who was it that had put the thought in his mind to begin with? It had to be her doing, just as everything she had done to him since he tossed the bracelet into the well had been her doing. A captive of her seduction, he did not open his eyes again until she'd begun to concentrate upon his middle.

The first thing he looked toward was the moon. Yes, she had kept her word. It had begun its descent, and he began to relax as she straddled him and inched lower along his torso, laving his cock from root to tip. How he longed for her to suck him hard until he came, but she did not. Moving lower still, she laved the pulp and juice from his testicles, until she'd cleaned away every trace, before returning to his cock.

Gar threaded his fingers though her hair as she took his penis in her mouth and began to suck in long, spiraling plunges, meanwhile flicking the tender skin of his shaft with her tongue. Again and again, she traced the distended veins as she took him deeper into her throat, avoiding the sensitive head of his cock until he begged for her to lave it, his hips raised for her to take him deeper still.

As her plunges grew more rapid, her hardened nipples scraped against his corded thighs until he could bear no more. As if they possessed a will of their own, his hips jerked forward as what felt like white-hot tongues of liquid fire rushed through his loins. The pumping, pulsating climax drained him of every drop.

His lungs gave up his breath in one long shuddering exhalation. It was a moment before he opened the eyes he'd screwed shut, and her image came clear. Something triumphant in her gaze trained upon him flagged caution and his eyes flashed toward the indigo vault above. He breathed another sigh, this time in relief. All was as it should be. The moon was still descending. Could he have misjudged her? Had she finally met her match and yielded to his will?

Rolling her over, he straddled her, intending to plunge into her while his cock was still hard, and pleasure her in kind, but she stopped him with a gentle hand.

"No," she purred. "Do to me as I have done to you, knight of the realm. I want to feel your tongue inside me . . . deep inside me. We have not done it thus as yet."

Gar did not speak. It seemed a reasonable enough request, since it was their last time together, and he spread her legs and moved between them, running his tongue first over her belly and pubic mound. Inching lower, he spread her petal-like nether lips and found the hard bud of her clitoris with his tongue. Erect, the distended nub looked purple in the moonlight. He laved it slowly at first, his tongue sketching little whorls around it, making it harder still. He could feel the pulse in it through the sensitive tip of his tongue, as laving became sucking and sucking became nipping.

She fisted her hands in his damp hair. "Enough," she panted, ". . . before I come without *my* fantasy fulfilled. Take me with your tongue, knight of the realm. Take me deeply!"

Gar spread her open wide and thrust his tongue inside the musky mysterious darkness of her nether lips gliding on her sweet juices, her sweet *familiar* juices. What was he tasting? His whole body stiffened as she held his head firmly against her slit, against the first layer of the petals of her sex he longed to peel away. But he could penetrate her no deeper. Beyond that point, she was closed to him. Something round and hard blocking her entrance pressed up against his unsuspecting tongue.

"Take it!" she cried, as her pelvic muscles forced the grape she had inserted there against his mouth. "Swallow, and be mine forever!"

Gar scrambled back from her and spat out the fruit, wiping his mouth with the back of his hand. "*Bitch*!" he seethed. "You would attempt to trick me anyway?" He surged to his feet, both hands fisted at his sides. The mist had begun to thin. He saw the centaur before he heard its laughter, where he stood close by at the edge of the thicket. He had obviously been watching them.

"Well done, my fellow consort!" the creature trumpeted between rousing spurts of guttural chuckles that boomed through the quiet. "Well done, indeed!"

Gar glanced toward the sky. The moon was still descending, but the Goddess of the Dream Well, on her feet now, let lose an earsplitting shriek as she spun in a cyclonic whirl, raising severed wildflower heads into the air like a scythe had decapitated them. The dew-drenched blooms rained down over them as she slowly spun to a stop. Then waving her hand, she pointed, parting the mist to reveal a sight that all but stopped Gar's heart. A wailing sound so mournful and forlorn pierced the predawn darkness, and Gar swayed as if he'd been struck. Before him stood a cage fitted with a large, heart-shaped padlock. Trapped inside was the little seal, her flipper reaching toward him through the bars.

Blinding pinpoints of white-hot light starred Gar's vision. The poor creature was begging him for her freedom. Her cries pierced his heart, and he ran to the cage, but to his horror, he ran right through it. It wasn't real, but a ghostly illusion, and the little selkie had no corporeal substance. The image vanished into the mist as he spun and whirled about in the decapitated wildflowers trying in vain to make the vision reappear, but all that remained was the melancholy echo of the little seal's mournful wail.

Gar faced the goddess, whose laughter rose above the rest. "Where is she? What have you done with her?" he demanded.

"That is for you to find out, knight of the realm," Analee triumphed. "Did you actually believe you could outwit me—*me*? You dream. Now then, surrender to me and I will set my sister free. Deny me, and she will rot in that cage, for though she can live quite long out of water, she needs to return to it to hunt for food, and caged she will surely die. That will happen even sooner if she sheds her skin and takes on human form."

"She cannot die. Selkies are immortal!" Gar thrust at her.

"She will be dead to you, knight of the realm," she purred, "for she will spend her eternity caged and hungry. Submit to me, I say! You cannot win. Surely you see that now."

Gar glanced toward the sky again. The moon was sinking low. "Make it stop!" he thundered. "You, who have no truck with time, hold back the dawn, like you did before, and release the selkie. Do this and I will submit to you."

"I think not," the goddess drawled, sauntering nearer.

Gar clenched his hands in and out of white-knuckled fists at his sides. How he longed to clamp them around her neck and squeeze until her head burst like the grapes she'd crushed had done.

"I rather like the end to this that you have designed," the goddess went on, undulating around him. "We shall let the dawn come. You will have until first light to find my selkie sister and free her from her cage yourself. Either way, I win, you see. You are mine already, you always were. I would have rather had you stay willingly. That is why I offered you my favors—few can resist me—but since that is not to be, I will settle for this game instead. Save the selkie if you can. You have until the dawn."

"Wait!" Gar trumpeted, for he sensed that she was about to leave him. "I beg you, stop the moon's descent as you did before and give me a fair chance to find her!"

The goddess shrugged. "I have kept my part of the bargain," she said. "I promised you naught past the dawn, if you recall. It comes quickly now, knight of the realm. You were the one who begged me to make the moon descend a few of your precious mortal minutes ago, as I recall. This should teach you to be careful what you beg for in the Celtic Otherworld, Gar Trivelyan. You might just get your wish . . ."

Gar opened his mouth to speak, but the goddess had vanished before his very eyes. The centaur was gone, also. He stood naked and alone in the mist that had suddenly thickened around him.

6

Gar stood riveted to the spot. Gooseflesh attacked the cold sweat that had washed over his naked skin. He would go to his grave with the sight of the little selkie's pleading eyes begging him to set her free. He would hear her mournful wail for the rest of his eternity in astral captivity. It had ripped a tear in his soul. He had to find her.

The conversation he'd overheard between Analee and the centaur came trickling back across his memory. She had asked the centaur if he had done as she asked, and he'd said he had, but that he didn't hold with cages. So this was the cage they were speaking about. That meant the centaur knew where the selkie was. He was the one who had imprisoned her. If only he had his sword. If only he hadn't sacrificed it to the angry sea!

There might be another way. The goddess would never tell him where the little seal was, but the centaur might if Gar could find him. The creature didn't want him there any more than Gar wanted to be there. Could the centaur be a kindred spirit? It was worth a try to find out, but he wasn't going to be able to do that standing in an empty field of beheaded wildflowers that had been severed from their stems before they'd even had a chance to open with the dawn.

Without a second thought, he stalked off in the direction he'd last seen the centaur. That course took him into another darker part of the forest, where ancient oaks and pines coexisted. Their long, sweeping branches groped him as he passed among them, for there was no path in this quarter. It seemed as if a thousand eyes were watching him. He had no doubt in his mind that Analee and the centaur's eyes were among them. Of course they would monitor his progress, and hinder him if he came too close to finding the little selkie, at least the goddess would; he was certain of it. That didn't matter then, nothing did but that he find the cage and set the little seal free.

Gar crashed through the undergrowth, a close eye upon the moon's progress as he glimpsed it through the treetops. It was no longer a matter of saving himself. He considered his freedom lost. He would never escape from the Otherworld now, but there was hope for the little selkie, who had showed him naught but kindness and admiration in her innocence. All that remained was to find her and get her out of that cage.

Even when he closed his eyes he could see that adoring face, those huge limpid eyes, so human-like, with their long, dreamy lashes. He remembered how her whiskers tickled when she nuzzled him, and how she tilted her head when she explored his body with her gentle flipper. Something pinged in his loins as he recalled that gentle caress.

The scent of ambergris ghosted past his nostrils. Was the little seal near, or had his longing to see her again conjured the fragrance? It didn't matter. It was his link to her, and it was somehow rooted in *his* world, not this dark and deceptive astral plane he trudged through now. True, she was a selkie, but it was her human side that bled through and struck a chord still thrumming in his heartstrings. If anything were to happen to her, he would never be able to bear it. The trouble was, the Goddess of the Dream Well had honed in on that deep recess of his private self, and she was using it against him.

Gar had taken Analee at her word. He had judged and trusted her by human standards; that was his mistake. One could not do that with the fay. He knew that now; he'd really always known it, but until the shipwreck, he'd had no encounters with Otherworldly creatures. He'd always thought such things were fantasy, nursery tales contrived for children. It had never occurred to him, a seasoned warrior in the very real world, that such things could be true.

When he tossed the bracelet into the well, he never imagined conjuring a goddess. It was a pleasant fiction, and his last hope, since his wound was deep and he had lost much blood. It was simply something to try. And then, the goddess appeared, and he believed her—trusted her. He should have remembered then that no fay could be trusted. The minute he accepted her favors, he was caught in her snare. The sad thing was, she hadn't lied—she'd told him the truth, just not the whole truth. She had bewitched him, and he racked his brain, probing the cobwebs of his nursery days for the means to undo the spell she'd cast over him, but no answer came. He either hadn't ever heard of a means to outwit the fay, or there wasn't one.

Gar couldn't dwell upon that then. He bitterly wished he hadn't been so gullible, so easily beguiled, but there was no use lamenting that now. The little seal that had showed him naught but kindness, the gentle little creature that had saved his life, was in grave danger. It all came back to the same thing; he had to find her.

The trees were thinning, and the wood finally ended abruptly. Beyond, the mist thickened to a bleak gray fog that barely let the feeble moonlight through. Hesitating on the edge of it, Gar's eyes snapped in all directions. Which way? How vast was the region the goddess ruled? Was she watching from some-where hidden in the mist? A trickle of cold laughter replied to that thought as if she'd read his mind.

"Where are you?" he called. "Show yourself! I have served you well in our short time together. Show yourself, I say!"

"*Too* well, knight of the realm," the goddess tittered, step-ping out of the mist. "But for that, you would be safely home by now." She sauntered close, circling him, and seized his penis, snuggling up to him while she stroked it. "If you were not such a skilled lover, the dawn would have come long ago. As it is now, I have possessed this fine cock of yours. See how it grows hard for me at the slightest touch?" She ran the tip of her finger over the sensitive head of his erect member and he shuddered. "See?" she said, sliding his cock between her legs. "See how it lives for me?"

Thrusting her hips, Analee moved back and forth, rubbing her slit against his shaft until it hardened like granite between her thighs, until it had grown so long he could feel the pucker of her anus. Gripping his taut buttocks, she trapped him with her nether lips as he rode her slit deeper, until he could feel the hard bud of her clitoris, and the warm wet juices of her arousal laved him to the brink of climax without penetrating the hot, musky depths of her.

"Forget the little selkie," she murmured in his ear. Her warm, moist breath riveted his body with cold chills. She had almost made him forget that he was on a desperate quest to find the little seal and free her. That was the hellish danger in her en-chantment. The fay possessed the power to cloud men's minds until they forgot all that linked them to their humanity.

Gar shook himself like a dog and shoved her away. Seizing his cock, he tried to soothe the aching, burning, throbbing need she'd ignited deep inside him. It was as if she'd set fire to his loins. It was no use. She had taken him beyond the point of no return, but he wouldn't pleasure her with the engorged sex she'd hardened like steel. Instead, he gripped his shaft. Three rapid spiraling thrusts and he shut his eyes and groaned as his seed spurted over the pine needles, mulch, and ground-creeping vines that carpeted the forest floor.

The goddess beat her thighs with white-knuckled fists and stamped her foot, then lowered the flat of her open palm hard across Gar's face. She'd caught him off guard, with his eyes closed, and he staggered back from the stinging blow.

All at once she began to spin in a circle, her motion lifting the loose matter beneath her feet in cyclonic whirls that rose around her like a great funnel. "You will regret this!" her voice boomed from the cyclone. He was almost glad he couldn't see her face then. Her rage was palpable. "You had best resign yourself," she raged on. "You will never leave the astral, knight of the realm. Give over searching for the selkie. You will never find her. You have just *killed* her, Gar Trivelyan!"

She was gone in a blink, her high-pitched shriek living after her, and Gar slumped against the trunk of a young ash tree. He cast his gaze toward the heavens. The moon had nearly run its course. Soon dawn would break, but that didn't matter anymore. He was lost, a prisoner of the Otherworld. He had fought his last campaign. He would never see his beloved Cornwall again. He may as well have died in the shipwreck off the Land's End shoals. All was lost to him the minute he accepted the goddess's favors. He was convinced that it was what he deserved, but he could not conscience that the goddess would revenge herself upon the blameless little selkie. Why? There had to be a reason for her to treat the little seal so shamefully. Analee was jealous, yes, but it had to be something more that jealousy to prompt her to do murder.

Gar pushed himself off from the tree trunk. He didn't matter anymore. He couldn't let her harm the selkie. Nothing had changed. Somehow he had to find the little seal and free her despite the odds against it. Then he would resign himself to his fate, but not until, and he scanned the misty landscape ahead for some sense of direction, some clue—anything that would give him hope of helping the innocent little creature who had saved his life. With that obsession to drive him, he bolted toward what looked like open moors scarcely visible through the mist, only to be jerked back against the trunk of the young ash tree again.

One supple branch snaked its way around his waist, giving a sharp tug, while the other pointed its outermost twig on the opposing branch in another direction. Gar stared as a labyrinth took shape before his eyes. A wall of high hedges marking a narrow maze led into swarthy darkness. Was it showing him the way, or leading him on a fool's errand?

"What?" he murmured. "Are you showing me the way?"

The tree made no verbal or mental reply. Instead, it seemed to hug him for a moment, then the branch that tethered him slithered away from his torso and shoved him toward the labyrinth. Gar turned and studied the tree; its branches were swaying in the wind, but there was no wind. It seemed to bow, its leaves rustling against each other. Of all the creatures he'd seen in the astral realm, the trees impressed him most. There was a silent majesty about them that commanded respect. He'd never given trees more than a passing thought in appreciation of the shelter they provided. He had never thought of them as entities in their own right, possessed of the power of thought and comprehension. Now, as he watched this tree's performance, he understood why men erected shrines in the forests for passersby to leave a token for the ancient spirits who lived in tall silent columns of bark and moss and vine-laced branches. He had never practiced such devotions, but he made a secret vow to do so if he ever found his way back home. The strange exhibition continued. Captivated, Gar could do naught but stare. He had never seen a tree perform such a ritual. The ground beneath his feet began to vibrate as the tree's roots beneath the ground began to shift and jig about as if it were dancing. Still Gar stared, and the branch nudged him toward the labyrinth again, harder this time.

He heard the cosmic crackle and hiss of the lightning bolt before he saw its blinding snake-like energy spear down and strike the young ash tree, severing the branch that had just nudged him. The severed limb struck the ground, trailing smoke. He heard the shriek of a female voice in pain. Did the tree scream? The sound turned his blood cold, but another sound turned it colder—a burst of the goddess's laughter assailed his ears.

"Go!" she tittered. "Run! But it will serve you not, knight of the realm. It is already too late. Look to the east. See? That is first light breaking over the horizon. Your 'little while' is up!"

Gar needed no more proof of the ash tree's intent. She, for the tree was female, swayed in pain, soothing her severed limb, and without a backward glance, he streaked off over the open field between and entered the dusky labyrinth.

Dawn may have broken elsewhere, but it was still as dark as night between the high hedge walls of the maze as Gar groped his way along like a blind man. The heady scent of rich fertile soil ghosted past his nostrils; it was earthy and evocative, bringing visions of home. He ran on, stirring the mist that his feet displaced, but all that met his eyes was deeper darkness, until the goddess's voice stopped him in his tracks.

"It is not too late to surrender to me willingly," she said, her voice coming at him as if through an echo chamber. "You were mine from the start. You have only to accept it to have me for all eternity. If you had only eaten the food, there would have been no need of this. You would have submitted willingly. But you did not, and that has forced me to this. Remember how it was between us? It could be that way forever, as my consort, you—"

"You already have a consort, and a jealous one," Gar interrupted. "What of Yan? How long do you suppose it would be before I took his arrow?"

"Yan controls nothing. I am goddess here!"

"I have no powers to protect me in your world, but Yan does," he returned, praying that the centaur was within hearing distance. If ever he needed an ally it was now.

"You need no powers. You have me, knight of the realm. Yan has no dominion here."

"I do not think he is aware of that," Gar said through a guttural chuckle. "What? Do you mean to kill him as you plan to kill the selkie?"

"I am the Goddess of the Dream Well!" she shrilled. "*I* will decide who is to be my consort. Do you foolishly imagine that I haven't the power to grant my own wishes?"

Gar felt a tremor in the darkness, a four-legged, heavy-hoofed tremor. He smelled the musk of horseflesh, and he went on speaking quickly with a rush of euphoria in his voice that he prayed the goddess was too enraged to detect.

"So you would kill him, then? How would you do it, with a lightning bolt, the way you tortured that poor defenseless tree just now?" She was still somewhere ahead in the darkness, by the sound of her voice, and though he searched the maze with narrowed eyes, he saw no sign of her.

"That is not your concern," she replied. "Do not delude yourself that Yan was my first lover, nor will he be my last, nor will *you* be for that matter. But for now, you will do quite well, quite well, indeed, Gar Trivelyan."

"Still, I'm curious," Gar persisted. "How do you mean to kill the centaur?"

There was silence. When she finally broke it, an audible breath preceded her words. "I sense your disapproval," she said at last.

"You sense correctly," Gar returned.

"Why? What has it to do with you how I dispose of a consort that I have grown tired of? Why should it concern you?"

Gar laughed in spite of himself. "That should be fairly obvious, my lady," he said. "It concerns me because one day you will do the same to me!"

The mist began to drift away as the sky began to lighten, and the goddess stepped out of the darkness into the light. Gar's heart sank. To his great disappointment, the centaur was at her side.

If he didn't know it before, he knew he was on the right track now. The little seal was close by. The goddess hadn't disposed of her yet. If she had, there would be no need for this confrontation. He was approaching a large break in the maze that offered a choice. He had passed by many such breaks, both narrow and wide, that led to other avenues along the way, but not this time. The goddess strolled closer and, almost without thinking, Gar sidestepped her advance and darted through the gap in the hedge, running on long, sinewy legs over the gravel path.

He hadn't gone far when something shook the ground beneath his bare feet. Glancing over his shoulder, he saw the centaur approaching at a gallop. The creature hadn't loaded his longbow, but Gar took no comfort in that; the centaur was bearing down upon him with nostrils flared like a rampant bull.

The creature was gaining on him, though his legs were pumping as fast as he could make them. When the centaur reached out and seized his arm, Gar resisted. "Let go of me!" he demanded. "Let go I say!"

"Up!" the centaur charged him. "Hurry, there isn't much time."

For one long suspended moment, running alongside the creature, Gar hesitated, before fisting his hands in the centaur's shaggy coat and swinging himself up on the creature's back. Of course the centaur would know where the selkie's cage was. He had locked her in it, after all, hadn't he?

"Good!" Yan said, streaking on at a gallop. "Now hold tight. She thinks I am running you to ground for her. She will not be far behind."

"Aren't you?" Gar blurted.

"No," Yan returned. "You do not love her, I know that, but I *do*. You do not understand our Otherworldly ways. You are learning, elsewise I would have made an end of you to keep Analee for myself. You must trust me now. You seek the selkie. I will take you to her, but dawn is breaking, and once the sun has cleared the horizon, I am a two-legged creature once more and of precious little help to you."

"She said she would kill the selkie!" Gar said, gripping the centaur tighter.

"Analee cannot kill her," Yan said. "The gods would never allow it. It would be like killing herself. But she can ruin her. Analee can cause her great suffering and bodily harm."

"I do not understand."

"I know. I told you, you do not understand our ways. The selkie is Analee's alter ego, her better half, if you will—the innocent part of her that she relinquished to become the goddess. The personification of her lost innocence transferred to the body of the selkie was a sacrifice the higher gods imposed upon her. They demand much for privilege; this was the price of Analee's becoming the Goddess of the Dream Well."

It was almost beyond Gar's comprehension. "So, they are one entity?" he said, trying to imagine it.

"No," Yan returned. "They *were* one entity when what you know as time began. They are two entirely separate beings now. They are like what you mortals perceive as sisters."

"But why a selkie?" Gar said, thinking out loud.

"Because that is what Analee was in the beginning," the centaur said. "A selkie can exist in the mortal world as a mortal.

The only way Anya, that is the selkie's name, will ever be safe is to leave the Otherworld and live among the mortals, where Analee cannot touch her; Analee has no dominion there anymore. That privilege ended when she made the sacrifice and became the goddess."

"Analee told Anya to go to my world. I heard her myself, and Anya did as Analee bade her. What I do not understand is if she would have been safe there, why did she return?"

"Because of you," Yan told him. "She is enamored of you, foolish mortal! If you can cross Anya over and take her sealskin, she will never return. She will be safe and content with you in your world, and I will be safe and content with Analee in mine. *That* is why I help you, Gar Trivelyan, but it still remains to be accomplished and the rest of this maze is difficult for me to travel in my current incarnation. Now hold fast!

7

The centaur was right. Gar did not understand the ways of the Otherworld, but he could hardly contain his euphoria. For the first time since he'd dragged himself out of the sea and collapsed upon the shore of the Celtic Otherworld, he had hope of returning home, and of taking the little selkie with him.

The centaur sped through the maze at a pace Gar would have thought impossible for such a hulking creature. Yan was a ruggedly handsome entity, his long hair bound in vines, his face a brooding mask all angles and planes. He wore his centaur guise well, as Gar imagined he would his human-like incarnation. Somehow, he trusted the creature. The centaur had much to gain from Gar's happy outcome. That, and that alone, filled the young knight with hope where all else smacked of doom, and he prayed to whatever deity would listen that he hadn't put his trust in yet another fay deceiver.

The centaur slowed his pace when an almost invisible break in the hedge loomed before them. The openings had grown progressively narrower the deeper they traveled into the maze. It was a tight squeeze for the hulking beast, but Yan forced his way through the virtual wall of privet into a long unkempt lane steeped in shadow. It was darker there, the walls of the hedge so close together they scraped Gar's legs as the centaur carried him toward an alcove, where the selkie's cage came into view. This time, it wasn't an illusion, and Gar jumped down from the creature's back and ran to the cage, examining the lock. Inside, the little seal was making the saddest sound Gar had ever heard, a trembling wail, like hiccups, as though she had cried her heart dry. At sight of him, she flopped close to the latch, reaching her flipper toward him through the bars.

"Gods on their thrones! How do I get this open?" Gar thundered, rattling the heart-shaped lock. How inappropriate was *that*? The Goddess of the Dream Well didn't have a heart. She couldn't have to have penned the poor little harmless creature up like a wild beast.

"Stand aside!" the centaur commanded from behind, his voice booming like thunder.

Gar spun around. Yan had loaded his longbow and taken dead aim on the cage. Even from where he stood, Gar could see the centaur's jaw muscles ticcing. The creature's eyes had receded beneath the ledge of his brow as he squinted down the arrow shaft. For one terrible moment, Gar thought that arrow was aimed at him, or the little seal. She evidently thought so, too, for she shrieked and cowered and began to tremble, trying to shrink back against the bars in the corner, as far from the centaur's line of fire as she could. The poor thing was terrified, and Gar's eyes snapped between her terror and the centaur's steely dead aim as he tried to comfort her.

"Shh!" he murmured. "I will not let you come to harm!" Sliding his arm between the bars, he thrust it in front of her. It was an empty promise, but she snuggled against him, hiding her eyes. She was trembling so violently it was all he could do to ease her quaking enough to hold her out of range of what seemed to be Yan's dead-center aim.

"Keep her *still!*" the centaur shouted. "And keep the cage from shaking! There is time for only one shot! Analee will be here any second. You must trust me, for all our sakes!"

Gar could not read the centaur's expression. Did he dare trust the creature who only a short time ago had aimed that bow at his manhood with deadly intent? There was no time to consider it. Praying that the centaur was in earnest, he froze spellbound as the twang of the bowstring and the whirr of the arrow in flight whizzing past so close he felt the wind it created all but stopped his heart. The missile struck the keyhole in the lock dead center, springing it, and the lock spiraled off as the cage door fell open and hit the ground with a rasping clang that echoed through the unnatural quiet that had fallen over the labyrinth like a pall.

In the blink of an eye, the little selkie flopped out of the cage and waddled off into the maze at a speed Gar would have thought impossible for a seal, her terror-struck wails echoing after her.

"You are on your own, fellow consort!" the centaur shouted. Spinning on his hooves in the close confines of the narrow lane, he staved in the hedge and scattered privet in all directions. "I will keep Analee occupied as best I can, but that will not be for long. Do not lose sight of the seal. You will never find your way out of the maze if you do. She knows the way."

"Hail and farewell!" Gar called after the creature, for the centaur was already in motion, galloping back the way he had come.

Gar regretted not having trusted the creature at the last, but that couldn't be helped. If he'd learned nothing else from his experience in the Otherworld it was that the fay could not be trusted. That knowledge was all he did trust any more.

It didn't matter now. The little seal was free, and he never would have found her if it weren't for Yan. He turned back just in time to see her enter another break in the maze. Darting after her, he called her name, but her fright was such that she kept on waddling into the labyrinth, her frantic snorts and wails siphoned off on the dawn breeze.

"Anya, wait!" he called. "It is I, little friend. I mean you no harm."

But the little seal lumbered on, then made a turn and disappeared altogether into one of the multiple breaks in the hedge that presented themselves in that sector. Her vocal fright was so acute Gar was certain she hadn't even heard him. What torments had she suffered in that wretched cage to cause such a fright? He could only imagine.

Gar spun in circles, poking his head first through one break in the hedge and then another, calling the little seal's name until his voice broke, but no answer came. All was quiet behind. Evidently Yan was keeping his word and occupying Analee. But that couldn't last, and Gar plunged headlong into the alternate avenues in the maze one by one.

He'd barely begun the search when a cyclone formed in his path, a tall whirling funnel from which Analee emerged, her gossamer mantle billowed wide. For all its yardage, it did not hide her nakedness. It was as transparent as the spiderwebs clinging stubbornly to the hedges and ground-creeping vines spangled with the morning dew. He had never seen anything so beautiful, or so deadly. Her eyes were burning toward him like live coals, and her hair was fanned out about her on a wind that didn't exist anywhere else. It was a fearsome sight, but her body was as tempting as ever, and she flaunted it, spreading her mantle open, thrusting her perfect breasts and hairless slit as she sauntered closer.

"You may as well give it over," she said. "You will never escape me. You don't really want to. I can see the lust in your eyes, knight of the realm. You are my creature, and you will remain so until I tire of your company."

The pull of her lure was great, but the pull of another was

greater now. The little selkie needed him, and every second counted. He had to find her before it was too late, before she disappeared in her fright and he'd lost her forever.

"I took you at your word," he said, "and I expected you to keep your part of the bargain—you imposed it, after all. You cannot keep me here against my will. It will serve you not!"

Analee burst into riotous laughter. "I can do whatever I will," she assured him. "This is *my* world. I make the conditions here."

"You can make all the conditions you like, but you cannot make me abide by them. Our time is over. Let me go!"

"Never!" she purred, running her hands over his hard-muscled chest and torso as she crowded closer. "I can make you forget . . . everything . . ."

Her hands were cool as they played his body the way a musician plays a fine instrument, her warm breath intoxicating, puffing against the sweat glistening on his hot skin. Gar had no doubt she could make a man forget everything; hadn't she done just that to him until now? But as he steeled himself against her advances, against those skilled hands roaming over his buttocks and his hardening cock, he sensed that she had something in her arsenal of seductions that he hadn't seen before, and time—the time that did not exist in the Otherworld—did exist in his mind. It was running out for him, and for the little selkie.

The goddess stepped back and spread her gossamer mantle wide. "You have only to come into my arms, Gar Trivelyan," she said. "Embrace me. Let me fold you in the gauze of forgetfulness, and your eternity with me will be a paradise beyond your wildest imagining."

The mantle! What was she saying, that to let her cloak him in it with her would wipe his memory clean? His mind reeled back to when she'd first donned that garment. It was in the tournament tent, when he'd first arrived. Why hadn't she used it then? Could it be because she'd thought she could seduce him to her will without resorting to that tactic? And there was something else . . . for a time she wore no mantle, but then, she suddenly appeared wearing it again. He remembered questioning when she'd put it on. He remembered now, that was when she led him to the banquet she'd prepared to trick him into eating while they awaited the dawn. Of course! No doubt she would have used it then if the centaur hadn't interrupted them. What had he heard of such mantles . . . that the victim must succumb willingly?

Gar backed away from her. "You will not entrap me with that!" he said. "I will never come to you of my own free will. I command you to set me free!"

The words were scarcely out, when a shaft of blinding white light speared down alongside them, a column of snake lightning that rent a tear in the labyrinth floor and shook the hedges all around.

Gar staggered back from it, though it was not aimed at him but, to his surprise, at Analee, who cowered from it, as another lightning strike streaked down, and with it the ethereal shadow shape of a woman robed in silver gauze. Could it be Annis herself? Had Analee finally brought the wrath of the goddess of all wells down upon her own head? The way Analee cowered in this strange deity's presence, Gar was certain of it.

The specter, for that is how the entity appeared, spoke not a word. Instead, she spread her arm wide, swirling the lightning over Analee, and in a blink they both were gone, vanished before Gar's very eyes.

"Go!" said a disembodied voice. "I have done what needs must to see you and the selkie to safety. It is in the hands of Mother Annis now. She will mete out Analee's chastisement. It is not the first time. But you two must be gone before her justice is accomplished, for none of us is safe from Annis's wrath here now. She is most displeased. The balance has been disturbed, and so has she, from her repose. You have been spared for the moment, my fellow consort. Such things are rare. Take the gift and go!"

Gar spun in all directions, but there was no sign of Yan, though it was indeed the centaur's voice he'd heard. It didn't matter. Spinning on his heels, he streaked down the lane with only one thought to drive him. He had to find the little selkie, and take her home.

Three passages came to dead ends, but the fourth led into a mist that somehow seemed familiar. Yes, wherever this was, he'd been here before. He remembered the willows. *The well!* Had he come full circle? There, at the edge of the grove, alongside a whitethorn tree bedecked with many strips of colored cloth, stood the low stacked-stone well with its satiny black spring rippling gently inside. The little seal was perched on the edge, poised to dive into the water.

Her eyes wide with fright, she loosed a bloodcurdling moan and dove, but so did Gar, grabbing fast to her tail as she plunged headlong into the well. "There! I've got you!" he cried triumphant, only to freeze in horror, for he didn't have her. All he clutched in his hands was her soft, sleek sealskin. The rest of her had disappeared beneath the dark, misty water in the well.

8

Gar tied the sealskin tightly around his waist, stepped up upon the rim of the well, and dove in after Anya. Down, down he plummeted through blackness that rivaled the fabled *outer darkness*. A sane man would have been terrified, but Gar considered that he'd run mad or died long since. Convinced that he could not die twice, he swam on, expecting to meet the gods head on at any moment.

He was a skilled swimmer, but his breath was coming short, and he had no idea where he was going. It was an enchanted well, after all, and Analee did preside over it. The legendary goddess of the well, or *Annis* herself, who ruled all the wells and had let him go, could change her mind and block his path at any moment. Anything was possible with the fickle fay, but all he could think of then was finding Anya, the gentle little selkie who had given him back his life. He had to believe, no matter what else he believed, that the gods weren't so cruel as to take that life away from him again now, after all he'd been through.

All at once, the water brightened overhead, but only slightly. His lungs felt as if they were going to burst as he broke through the surface of choppy water that was roiling and swelling and crashing toward shore beneath leaden skies and lightning snaking down. Flotsam and jetsam floated all around him. Crates and spars, lines and sheets and timbers struck him glancing blows as the waves carried them where they would. Even bits of bedding and clothing washed over him. *The shipwreck!* He had come back to the midst of the shipwreck?

All at once soft, slender arms slipped around his neck, and a rippling cloud of coppery hair fanned out about his shoulders. It smelled of ambergris. Supple female curves, petal-soft and smooth as satin, leaned against his naked skin, arousing him, and he blinked the salty water from his narrowed eyes and stared. The last thing he saw before consciousness evaporated was the largest pair of dreamy limpid eyes he'd ever seen, gazing into his with something akin to worship.

Gar awoke to the gentle touch of a woman's hand flitting over his body much as the little seal had done. At first, he thought he was dreaming, but then, he glanced down into the same extraordinary eyes he had seen before he'd lost consciousness. She was lying beside him, her head resting upon his shoulder, her exquisite body pressed so close against him it was as if their skins had become one.

For a moment, he thought it was the goddess; she was so like her, even to the little mole above her perfectly bowed lips. But there was something different in the eyes, something soft and serene, a wide-eyed, child-like innocence that had so melted his heart when he looked into the limpid gaze of the curious little seal.

"Anya?" he murmured.

She nodded against his shoulder as she nuzzled it. She was making a contented purring sound that thrilled him. Throaty and primeval, it was a mystery of her species, something feral, deeply rooted in nature, as erotic and ancient as the pulse beat of the earth itself. He could feel it through his skin, humming in every pore, the sensual vibration echoing in his very soul. Moving her naked body contentedly against his side, she had aroused him, and his cock began to rise through the gap in the sealskin still tied about his waist. She could have taken it back while he lay unconscious. Why hadn't she?

"Why did you run from me?" he said, slipping his arm around her. Her skin was warm, and as soft as silk against his raw male roughness. "Surely you knew I wouldn't harm you?"

She gave a start. "I was not running from you—never from you," she said. "I was running from the centaur. He is Analee's consort, you know. He is the one who put me in that cage. He is well skilled with bow and arrow, a deadly shot. When he raised his longbow and took aim, I feared he would kill me! That is what she wanted. It would have been sacrilege for her to do it herself. I feared she'd convinced the centaur to do it for her."

"The centaur helped me find you," Gar said. "I questioned his motives, too, at first, but he only wanted to free you and be rid of me so he could have Analee all to himself again."

"I did not know that," she said. "I was running for my *life*! He is limited in the places he can go while he is the centaur; his bulk prevents him. I knew he couldn't fit through some of the breaks in the hedge in that sector, but I could. All I could think of was escaping those deadly arrows of his."

"And you have escaped," he murmured, soothing her with gentle hands. "You need never return to the Otherworld again."

"I cannot return without my skin," she said.

"Why didn't you take it back while I was unconscious?" Gar said, fingering the sleek, soft pelt tied around his middle. "You could have done, you know, at any time."

"I did not want to take it back," she mewed. "I want to stay here in your world, with you."

Gar crushed her close in his arms. "And so you shall," he whispered against her brow. "But only if you are certain."

"I knew I wanted to the moment I first set eyes upon you," she confessed.

"In the swan boat," he recalled. "I remember your touch. I've never forgotten it. It has haunted me ever since, little selkie."

"Oh, no," she said. "We met long before the swan boat. I am the cause of all your woes. It was I who crossed you over into the Otherworld. I love the storms, and I was swimming in the sea when your galley broke apart upon the rocks. Did you not feel me nudge you? Did you not feel me keeping you afloat?"

Gar stared into her beautiful eyes, so brimful of admiration. "I did feel . . . something," he said.

"You are so beautiful," she purred, stroking his corded biceps. "I could not let you die in the water with the rest, so I took you home with me, but I hadn't the power to heal you, so I left you near the dream well for my sister to mend. I didn't want to, but if I hadn't you would have died. But then, she would not give you back to me. She wanted to keep you for herself."

"Well, you have me now," Gar said, grazing her hair with his lips. "So, you saved my life not once, but thrice, counting this now and it is yours, my little savior, for we mortals have a code that says when someone saves a life it belongs to them." He glanced about. They were in some sort of shelter as far as he could tell. It was unfamiliar to him, lit only by fractured beams of diffused light filtering in from above. "Where is this place?" he asked her.

"It is a cave," Anya told him. "There are many along the Land's End shore, and farther on along this coast, natural hollows of rock and sand carved out over time by the sea. We selkies love to play about in them and sun ourselves upon the rocks on golden days. Here, we collect the gifts of the sea. Some are very beautiful, and some are very sad. The saddest would have been your poor broken body dashed against these rocks. I could not allow it. So, here we are, alive instead! The caves flood at high tide, but we will be well away by then, my lord."

"You say the goddess is your sister. There is a remarkable resemblance, but how can that be so?"

"It will be hard for you to understand, being mortal," she responded. "We selkie are eons old. Analee was once a selkie just as I am. She seduced the gods to favor her with divinity. The price was sacrificing all in her that was innocent. She had to be divested of all feeling inherent in us in order to rise above the others and dwell in the company of the gods. All the love and gentleness, all the virtue, conscience, and soul in her was left behind in me, when she stepped out of our skin and became the Goddess of the Dream Well. We were one and the same—one entity. I am her alter ego, her other self, if you will, that she left behind when she became divine. It is why she hates me so. In me, she sees her loss. She has passion, but only the passion of lust. She is incapable of love. All such emotions are beneath her now. That was the greatest sacrifice. The price she paid to walk among the gods. It is sad, but it is a mystery of the divine that we must not question. There are many such mysteries in the Otherworld, my lord, but that is mine, and you needn't let it trouble you. You will see the goddess no more."

"And you cannot return to the Otherworld," Gar realized.

"I do not wish to return," Anya said with passion. "I only wish to stay with you, if you will have me . . ."

Gar stared down at the exquisite creature in his arms. "You are real, aren't you?" he murmured. "You shan't vanish before my eyes?" Any Otherworldly entity was suspect to him now, and would be evermore.

Anya smiled. Taking his hand, she cupped it around her breast. His thumb grazed her nipple and she cooed in delight, writhing against him. "Does this not seem real to you?" she said. Her gaze was intoxicating. A man could get lost in the liquid depths of those beautiful eyes, in the invitation of those petal-soft lips. He was beguiled by the wide-eyed innocence in her, by the worship in those haunting selkie eyes, so sad, and yet so filled with ardor. Each gaze, each languid blink was a rhapsody, unlike anything in his wildest imaginings. Not in all his days of knightly lust and torrid passion had he ever known such pure ecstasy as he felt in this creature's arms.

Gar untied the sealskin about his waist and set it aside. His cock was bursting. Sliding his hand the length of her torso he reverenced every inch of her. She was without blemish; the only hair on her body crowned her head in rippling waves of coppery gold that fell over her shoulder and down her back like a gossamer cloud. She smelled of ambergris and the sea, and she opened to him like the petals of a rare flower, inviting him to peel the fragrant layers away one by one.

"You say that you and Analee are eons old," he murmured against her hair as he drew her closer still. "Are you saying that in all the ages that have passed you have never taken a mate?" It was hard to believe that anyone as exquisite as she had lived a solitary life.

"All creatures mate with their bodies, especially the fay, my lord," she said. "It is in their nature, like coming into season, like drawing breath or sleeping. It means nothing. It is the mating of the souls that matters, in this world and in the Otherworld as well, and I have never found a soul mate that could tempt me to leave my heritage and my home until you. You see, I have no powers to dazzle and tempt a mate the way Analee does. You must admit that she is hard to resist, and most men I have met have followed the path of least resistance . . . until you, my lord. That you denied her at the last gave me hope that I had found my soul mate and could be free of her at last."

Her hands flitted over his body as she spoke. There was magic in those skilled fingers that touched and stroked, gentled and fondled. His eyes had become accustomed to his surroundings. They were lying upon a bed of seaweed, a salty cloud of the sea's dried leavings, as light as air, a marriage bed that somehow seemed sacred. Her touch was not unlike the little seal's had been, full of awe and sweet innocence, yet charged with the power to arouse as he had never been aroused before.

His cock was malleable in her hands, ready to burst as she ran her fingertips ever so lightly over the distended veins along its smooth surface. Pearls of pre-come glistened upon the mushroom tip as she straddled him, taking him deep. She was like layer upon layer of hot moist silk inside, as the walls of her vagina closed in upon him, threatening to suck him dry as she moved to the rhythm of his thrusts, matching his passion throb for shuddering throb. The sound of her buttocks slapping against his rock-hard thighs, mingled with the music her juices made laving him as he raised and lowered her on his shaft, played havoc with his senses. He seemed to rise above himself and enter another plane of existence. Never had he felt the searing heat of such desire. Never had his loins responded so totally, so helplessly, so primitively to the body of another. Was it lusts of the flesh? Yes. But this flesh that possessed him now was afire with brighter flames, a firestorm of ecstasy, of passion, and of love. She worshipped him. He'd glimpsed it in the wide-eyed little seal, and saw it now in full bloom in the soul of Anya, the woman. How Mother Annis of the wells deemed him worthy, he would never know, but he vowed as his cock came to life inside this winsome, adoring creature, that he would spend the rest of his days earning the gift he'd been given.

Cupping both breasts, he palpated her nipples erect, and a deep throaty groan escaped her as she ground her slit into his pubic hair, riding him to the rhythm of his ragged heartbeat beneath the hands she's splayed out on his hard muscled chest. He could scarcely bear it. Fisting his hands in her hair, he brought her head down and took her lips in a fiery kiss. Her gentle purr became a throaty groan as he deepened it, caressing the little darting tongue that put him in mind of a hummingbird seeking nectar, as she explored the sensitive depths of his mouth.

Circling her waist with his massive hands, Gar raised and lowered her on his shaft again, watching it ride in and out of her, slick with her juices. When she cupped his face with both her hands, his hips jerked forward. No one had ever done this to him before. It was magical. Turning his head to the side, he captured her thumb with his lips and sucked it into his mouth, laving it with his tongue as he took her deeper still.

Anya's climax was riveting, wave upon wave of involuntary contractions that gripped his cock relentlessly. He massaged her hard distended clitoris with his thumb as she came, and the breath left her lungs in a steady stream, a guttural rush, a living rapture as she rode him in mindless oblivion. She surrendered to it, her head thrust back until her long hair dusted his thighs, triggering a release in Gar like no other. He had felt such before in the arms of the goddess, but never like this. Anya had the same sexual skills as her sister, but the emotional charge that went with them was like nothing he had ever experienced before. It was as if his bones were melting from the inside out as she milked him dry of every drop of his seed.

At first, Gar thought the little cave had begun to darken around them because of the starry pinpoints of white light exploding behind his heavy eyelids. The orgasm had nearly drained his consciousness. But no, the light was fading. He could have sworn it was just past dawn when he woke in her arms there earlier.

"It grows late," he said. Withdrawing himself, he took her in his arms. "We should be mindful of the tide."

Anya smiled. Rising, she took his hand and pulled him up alongside her. Raising her head, she sniffed the air. "Do you smell it?" she asked, her eyes alight with inner fire. How she glowed with the blush of lovemaking upon her, rouging her cheeks, glistening upon her moist skin. For that was what they had been doing . . . making love.

She took a deeper breath. "Don't you smell it?" she prompted.

Gar likewise sniffed the air, taking deep breaths. "Something burns," he said, hesitating. "Not peat, but something similar, I think . . . what?"

"It is the Samhain fires," she said, taking his hand. "Come . . ."

"But that was before, in the Otherworld," Gar said, holding back.

Anya smiled her winsome smile. "There is no such thing as time in the Otherworld, remember?" she said. "It is a parallel world, not a simultaneous one."

"But we have no clothes!" he protested.

Anya giggled. "Believe me, none will notice," she said. "These are drunk with much wine and just as naked as we are, and there are many costumes that have washed up on shore from the shipwreck for us to choose from later."

Still Gar hesitated, trying to grasp the reality of benighted time. In that split second, Anya let his hand go, snatched the sealskin up from the floor of the cave, and ran out through the narrow opening in the rocks to the strand beyond, where indeed the Samhain bonfires had been lit. She was heading straight for the nearest fire.

Moving upon long, corded legs like pumping pistons, Gar sprinted after her. He reached her as she was about to throw the sealskin into the flames and seized her wrist.

"Are you sure, Anya?" he panted. "If you burn that . . ."

"I am sure," she said, her moist eyes catching red-gold glints that matched her hair from the flames. "As long as it exists, it will stand between us. Deep down, you will never believe that I stay of my own free will, and I will never be able to convince you otherwise. Once the fire consumes the sealskin, I am yours, Gar Trivelyan. Help me, my lord, it grows heavy!"

Gar took hold of the sealskin and together they tossed it

into the bonfire flames. A shower of shooting sparks rose up toward the full moon that had risen over Land's End to mark the Samhain feast. All around them revelers were dancing to the plaintive strains of flute and lyre, their voices raised in song.

Taking Gar's hand again, Anya raised it to her lips. "Come, my lord," she said, as they joined the dance. "Rejoice, my love, this is our wedding day!

THUNDERSTRUCK

Devyn Quinn

1

The statue of Herakles stood like a monolith, the epitome of divine masculinity and extraordinary sexual prowess.

Her masterpiece. Perfect in every way.

Danicia Ryan smiled, feeling the corners of her mouth move in an upward arc for the first time in months. The marble god reminded her of a mountain. Massive, immovable. A challenge to be conquered.

Mountains were made to be moved. Reaching out, her palms skimmed the ridges of his rippling stomach. A sizzle immediately traveled between her skin and the marble, bringing her hormones to life. *And marble created to be shaped into the form the artist desires.*

With broad shoulders, narrow hips, and well-muscled thighs, the Greek god appeared strong enough to throw down a skyscraper. Posed in defiance of heaven and earth, his head was thrown back, a tangle of windblown hair whipping his face and shoulders. Legs parted, his left arm lifted toward the sky, fingers half-clenched as if reaching up to grab bolts of lightning. His right reached out, hand open, fingers spread, reaching for the lover just out of his reach. Veins bulged over rippling muscles, giving a heightened sense of realism to his straining naked figure.

Dani's hands continued to explore, touching every hard curve of his sinewy torso. The marble glowed with an unearthly, almost iridescent sheen.

Excitement mingled with attraction filled her. "I created you." A tremor went through her. Sensations of sexual arousal left every nerve raw and exposed. The flood of emotions threatened to turn her limbs to liquid. "You belong to me."

Outside, thunder from the night's squall rolled across the earth. Somehow she had the feeling mighty Zeus approved the hard-given birth of his greatest son. She could easily imagine the power of the furious rainstorm stirring under the surface of the stone beneath her hands—born not only of the earth, but of sky and heaven, too.

Filled to the brim with accomplishment, she drew a shuddering breath. She'd created a work that would span not just decades, but centuries. When she'd first seen this piece as a solid block of marble, she couldn't imagine this day would ever arrive. Yet time and her diligence had paid off.

Herakles was finished.

Dani shifted her weight, trying to ease the ache building deep inside. Sensually, slowly, her fingers moved over his form. Her palms explored his bare chest, moving down the column of his abdomen, then lower, toward the penis nestled in a shock of delicately wrought curls. The fullness in his cock hinted of arousal. One could almost imagine the beat of a pulse under his pale faux flesh.

Stroking a hand over one smooth thigh, Dani laid her cheek against his broad chest, between his flat male nipples. Nipples so perfectly formed that she could barely restrain herself from tracing one hard nub with her tongue. She closed her eyes. A sudden mental picture flashed across her mind's screen. Easy to envision powerful hands catching her, dragging her against a straining erection.

Desire surged through her like a rising wave. Heat trickled between her thighs. Heavy awareness pulsed though her veins, an enchanting accompaniment to the steady throb emanating throughout the stone. She felt as if her whole body were attuned to some mysterious frequency issuing from inside the statue. Sensual awareness pulsed thickly around her. The sensations sent blood pounding through her temples.

It felt right they were together. Natural.

Muscles weakening, her heart fluttered. All rational thoughts fled. Chills of desire raised the fine hairs at the back of her neck. The erotic sensation traveled through her stomach, straight to her clit. A liquid trickle followed the delicious twinge of need. The thought of an erect cock made her mouth go bone dry.

She pressed harder against the stone, taut nipples compacting against masculine solidity. Wanton need enveloped her, intensifying the sweetest of pains. She closed her eyes, submerging herself in the sensations. Her thighs pressed against his, a desperate attempt to alleviate the ache. A needy moan escaped her lips.

"God, yes . . ."

A voice tinged with just the slightest hint of an English accent broke in from behind. "Have I caught you at an inconvenient time?"

Reality set in, shattering her fantasy. The images of two naked bodies locked in rapturous joy fled. "Damn it."

Dani regretfully untangled herself from the strong figure. Taking a deep breath, she abandoned the wide platform the statue stood on, navigating down the small set of steps propped against the wide base.

Jack Wilde, her longtime friend and patron, stood at the threshold of her studio. "Okay for me to come in?" His eyebrows rose in a devilish tilt. "Or would you two like to be alone?"

Aw, shit. Busted as a desperate pervert.

Shaking with unfulfilled sexual energy, Dani forced a smile. She'd been so engrossed up in wanting her dream god to make love to her that she wasn't thinking clearly at all. "You've snuck up on me, Jack. I wasn't expecting you until Monday."

Jack tossed off lingering droplets of rain along with his expensive coat. The gusty storm winds outside had restyled his thick mop of silvery hair, giving him an impish air. "I couldn't wait one more minute to see it. When you told me he was done, I had to come right over."

Dani sighed. She knew he'd been dying for a peek. She never let anyone see a piece until it was finished. Might as well get that crucial first examination over with.

Stopping a few feet away from the statue, Jack placed his hands on his hips. His gaze swept head to foot, then back again. "So this is my expensive block of Grecian marble."

Dani pressed a hand against her nervous stomach to quiet her nerves. "You know damn well it is—or was." Unveiling a new work was like stripping herself naked for flagellation. Everything in her soul was revealed. Other than the rain beating against the windowpanes, there wasn't a sound in the studio.

Silence stretched on, stretching her nerves along with it.

"Well?"

Jack practically sparked with excitement. "My God, this is one of the most impressive pieces of sculpture I've ever seen."

Suddenly awash in feelings she couldn't explain, Dani stammered, "You like him?"

The flash of straight white teeth revealed boyish dimples on either side of Jack's mouth. "He's absolutely *fucklicious*." He gave her a quick hug. "I don't blame you one bit for pawing all over him. You capture the male physique so beautifully, my dear. I'd just love to have a bite out of that nice round ass."

Fucklicious. Jack Wilde's stamp of approval on any man he deemed attractive enough to sleep with.

Control returned. The muscles in Dani's gut thankfully unclenched. "Back off, buddy." She grinned. "I had him first."

Jack grinned and playfully eyed the statue, giving ample study to the arresting cock. "Your hands have been over every inch, I'm sure."

Heat crept up into Dani's cheeks. "Just being thorough in my work."

He laughed. "He's the best you've ever done."

Reeling in the aftermath of his praise, Dani felt her lips curl into a satisfied smile. "Then you're pleased with your investment?"

Jack Wilde nodded. "When I saw this piece of raw marble in Athens, I knew there was only one sculptor who would know how to bring out its true form." Their gazes caught and held. "You have succeeded brilliantly." He clapped his hands in delight. "Bravo."

"Thank you." A pause. "I needed to hear that."

"You've certainly earned the praise." Jack walked around the statue, examining it again from all angles. "The realism is amazing. Looks like he's going to step down from that pedestal any second now."

God, I wish he would.

"So tell me the identity of your inspiration. Surely he is a great man."

A sexy beast with bronzed skin and compelling eyes flashed across Dani's mind-screen. Nipples peaking under the silky material of her bra, her inner muscles contracted with raw lust. The dampness between her thighs increased.

"Not a man. A god."

"Fabulous!" Jack pressed his hands together as if about to have a heavenly consultation. "Greek or Roman?"

"Greek, of course. It's Herakles."

Jack chuckled. "An absolutely astonishing interpretation in the style of the old masters." He pressed a hand to his chest. "My heart is about to burst with excitement. I knew you would do something wonderful, but not this fabulous! Allow me to say your talent for sculpture is unmatched in this present day. Marble is certainly your medium. It's like the stone speaks through you."

Dani couldn't help smiling. That was Jack. Laying it on with a trowel. "The stone spoke for itself," she answered honestly. "When you told me the block came from the same quarry that most likely gave birth to some of the greatest sculptures in Greek history, how could I not be inspired to create a god?"

"And fabulously so. Were he alive, your Herakles would personify the Greek ideal of a pure and perfect beauty." Jack turned around to study her, admiration in his gaze. "I really didn't think you'd be able to finish it on schedule after Lucien—" Realizing his slip, he cut off his words.

The first unpleasant shock of the evening.

Spine stiffening, Dani cut a sharp look at her friend. Mention of Lucien struck like a slap across the face. Pleasure at her accomplishment vanished. Emotion tightened her throat, threatening to squeeze off her air.

A thousand conflicting feelings converged in the intersection of her mind, threatening to jam up in a jumbled wreck. The elation and passion of her work mashed against the anguish and hurt of losing her husband to another woman. She'd been so busy sculpting her dream man that she hadn't even noticed the one she'd married slipping away until it was too late.

Thoughts churning in her mind, Dani rubbed her temples with the tips of her fingers. *I made my choice and Lucien made his.* The pain of her husband's rejection hadn't killed her. If nothing else, it had only driven her all the harder to succeed.

But it didn't lessen the hurt one little bit.

"I'm sorry," Jack started to say. "I shouldn't have mentioned Lucien. Tonight's your triumph."

Swallowing hard, Dani sighed. "Marble doesn't lie to me, Jack." The words grated out between her teeth. "Marble doesn't fuck my assistant. And marble certainly doesn't tell me it's walking out right when I'm in the middle of creating my most important piece." No, marble had never deceived her. What she'd found in its heart had always been true.

In it she'd place her fragile trust. In it she would find solace. Through it she would rebuild her fragmented psyche.

Jack reached out, brushing her wayward bangs off her forehead. "I've always thought Lucien was a rat bastard." His palm settled on her cheek, warm and reassuring. "He wasn't good enough for you, honey."

Hungering for the touch of real male flesh, Dani covered her friend's hand with hers. "Thanks, Jack." She swallowed, attempting to tamp down the need simmering under her skin. She hadn't had sex in over a year. Desperation practically dripped off her.

But there wasn't the slightest hint of desire in Jack Wilde's gaze. Only concern for a friend. All she'd ever be to him was a friend. Women didn't turn him on.

"If there's anything I can do—" he started to say.

Dani suddenly became aware he'd spoken. Her mind jerked back from half-finished thoughts. She gulped a quick breath. Sexual tension congealed, threatening to clog every artery in her body and smother her. Her knees trembled, threatening collapse. She didn't need sympathy. She needed a hard cock.

Too damn bad she was shit out of luck.

Letting his hand go, she stepped away from him and forced a smile. "I'm all right, Jack." The lie slipped out easily.

No reason to worry him. Again.

2

Attempting to quell the erotic energy threatening to overload her body's circuits, Dani walked around her studio. She stopped in front of a counter spanning the entire face of one far wall. All her tools were set out in neat rows, silent for the first time in years.

Jack caught her melancholy. "Everything okay, Danicia?"

No. Everything wasn't. "Yeah." Heart pounding, her head ached. "I'm fine."

Right. Define fine, she thought. *Fucked-up. Insecure. Neurotic. Emotional.* Yep. Definitely fit her to a "T."

Dani left the counter behind, the tools untouched. Her steps carried her back to the center of her studio. To her brilliant stone god. Herakles drew her like a magnet. Lit by a set of overhead lights, no inch of him was spared from viewing.

A subtle tremor shimmied through her when she recalled the raw carnal force she always felt emanating from it. Just the thought of touching the statue again made her senses hum. "I can't believe he's finished. It seems like I just started yesterday."

Jack gave a wry smile, half in sympathy, half in relief. "You've put in a long and hard commitment." Art was his passion. He revered those with talent, nurturing the fragile vision—and emotions—of those who could create what he himself could not.

Dani was shaking all over, and her jaw tightened. Helplessly, numbly, she stood in the shadow of Herakles and trembled. Finishing a piece always left her feeling let down, like a deflated balloon. "This one's wrung me dry. I think it's taken more than sweat out of me. He took my soul."

Jack moved to soothe her. "Of course he did. You say that every time you complete a piece. Your last show was excellent, but this will be superb."

Dani frowned. She didn't feel like being mollycoddled. "Don't rush me, Jack. I'm not quite ready for the public to see him just yet."

He waved a hand. "I know, I know. But the excitement of a new piece from Danicia Ryan just overwhelms me."

Dani had to restrain herself from rolling her eyes. "He'll be ready to go soon," she promised. "I just want to keep him to myself a little bit longer."

Jack waggled a disapproving finger. "Not much longer, my dear. I'm coming Monday with camera in hand to get the photos for the brochures. I'm sure *Modern Art Magazine* will want to cover this, too, so I'll give them a call to let them know we're getting ready to unveil your newest piece."

Dani sighed. Jack Wilde was the only man she knew who could get an erection looking at a fine piece of art. Back when she was a starving artist, and too broke to make the rent, Jack had stepped up with an offer to show her work at his gallery. His patronage, as well as his open checkbook, had given Dani her launch as a serious artist. Her sculptures had been displayed in such places as the Smithsonian and the Museum of Modern Art. Collectors all over the world vied to own one of her original pieces.

"You're incorrigible."

Jack tsked, waving a single finger. "Excited," he corrected. "Since you've worked like a demon, why don't you let me take you to dinner? To celebrate." He checked his watch. "If I call Anthony's now, I can still get a table."

Dani demurred, glancing down at her torn faded blue coveralls over a T-shirt. As usual, Jack was elegantly dressed, outfitted in a charcoal suit and white shirt undone at the collar, no tie. She looked like a rag hag, maybe dressed well enough to wash his Porsche. Remaking herself into something presentable to the public eye would take at least two hours.

"Do you mind if I decline? I'm tired and the only thing I want right now is a long hot shower and a few glasses of wine."

Mother hen kicked in. "Agreed. Rest is what you need. I could whip up something here." Jack gave her a hard look. "Assuming the cupboards aren't bare."

She shook her head. "Nothing. Thanks. I couldn't possibly eat right now."

He tsked again. "You have to remember to nourish your body, Dani." He admonished her like she was a naughty child. "No more neglecting yourself. The stone will last forever. The artist but a brief time."

Dani grimaced, grumbling, "Your concern touches me. I think."

Jack checked his watch again. "I can still get us in. In an hour we could be digging into a wonderful orange-glazed duck."

She begged off. "Some other time, please." She rubbed at her temples again to add emphasis to her words. "Right now I'd just like the chance to rest." What she really wanted was a little male companionship. Preferably in naked and sweaty positions.

Jack sighed in defeat. "I understand. Too soon the spotlight will be on you again. Two years is a long time between shows, but the wait was worth it." He waggled thick silver brows suggestively. "One look at your virile naked god and eyebrows will raise. Not to mention the price he'll fetch on the market." Hand rising, he spread two fingers apart. "I'm going to ask two million, Dani."

Tension knotted her shoulders at the mention of such an unbelievable amount. She gave him a long disbelieving look. Surely he couldn't be serious? Two. Million. Dollars. Even after the gallery fees, a substantial chunk of that would be hers.

A shudder rippled though her when she realized the implications. She could only stare, wondering if she'd heard right. "You must be kidding?"

His nostrils flared with glee. "No, babe. We're going to go for the big dollars."

Dani swallowed hard. This was a turn she hadn't expected. "I didn't think I could command that high of a fee."

"You've earned it," he assured her. "Michelangelo himself could not have sculpted a finer piece. It took him four years to do his *David*. That you did your Herakles in twenty-four months is a feat I don't think even he could match."

Mind still reeling from the figure he'd dropped so casually, she cleared her throat. "I did have a more cooperative patron. And I didn't have to stop and paint the Sistine Chapel, either."

Jack chuckled in agreement. "True." A final check of his gold Rolex. "Sure you don't want a night out? We'll eat good food, drink too much wine and pass out from the joy of being alive."

She nodded. She didn't feel very joyous or even glad to be alive. Mostly empty. "I'm sure."

Jack pecked her cheek. "Have it your way if you must."

"I must."

"So be it." With a wink and a whistle, he playfully pretended to take a picture with an imaginary camera. "Good-bye gorgeous. Soon you're going to be a star."

Dani winced. *Damn.* Soon, too soon, her Herakles would be

taken away. Of course the piece had to be sold. Jack Wilde fully expected to recover his investment. More important, her own bank account badly needed replenishing. Lucien had done his best to drain it dry before he left. Not to mention the fact that she'd soon be paying a divorce lawyer.

Jack practically waltzed across the studio and reclaimed his raincoat. He shrugged it on. "I'll see you both Monday."

He gave a final wave before departing. Back to the whirl of an active social life.

Envy jabbed. *No doubt he'll have company in his bed tonight.* A long sigh escaped her. *Alone again. On a Friday night.*

Grappling with disappointment and a loneliness that stung, Dani considered going upstairs, but to what? An empty apartment, and an emptier bed?

No thanks.

She lingered, reluctant to abandon her beautiful work to a dark studio. The statue seemed to beckon, calling her back. Come Monday he would belong to the world. Her work—her masterpiece—would no longer be her own.

Dani climbed back onto the pedestal. She wanted to touch her Herakles again. Feel his hardness under her hands. Just one more time. Before he left her, forever.

Cool stone warmed under her hands. Earlier sensations returned, triple strength. The pulse beating beneath the marble seemed to synchronize with the rhythm of her heart. The perfect tempo, ascending toward the highest peak of pleasure two beings could share.

Dani closed her eyes. Her nipples peaked. Erotic images bombarded her from all sides. Desire evidenced itself in the insistent pulse between her legs. Drawn deeper into a twofold link she was barely aware of, she felt the surge of actual response.

Her body, demanding now, insisted on completion. The

stone under her hands felt wholly pliant, wholly yielding. "I wish you were real."

A deafening crash of thunder interrupted at the exact moment the words left her lips. A hard gust of wind smacked the walls outside. The lights flickered, weakening, then plunged into darkness. Some untapped psi-force inside her made instant connection. Burrowing down to the roots of her brain, reality was destroyed. The barriers between the fact and fantasy crumbled.

Eyes adjusting to the unexpected darkness, Dani blinked. Faint currents of color swirled and pulsed, a cascade of electric sensation pouring through her. Pressure throbbed behind her eyes, threatening to blast her skull to pieces.

Dani screamed. The electricity building around her stabbed harder. Lava-hot spikes dug through her skin.

Without warning, a flash of liquid flame seared the stone. Vibrations inside the block intensified. A cataract of effervescence shimmered around it. The pressure grew around her.

With blinding force, the energy all of a sudden blasted outward. The explosion sent Dani reeling backward. Fighting to keep her balance, she stumbled off the pedestal, landing smack on her ass. Her senses whirled from the mystical energy radiating around the statue.

And her own skin. A soft sensual glow surrounded her.

"Holy shit." Too shocked to be frightened, she examined her illuminated flesh. "I'm lit up like a fucking Christmas tree."

Thunder cracked again. Louder. Fiercer. The walls around her and the floor beneath trembled from the force.

Dazed by the unfamiliar sensations flooding every fiber of her being, Dani didn't move. She could only watch as particles of energy dissolved, then reformed, the stone melting like wax under hungry flames. Blazing tension vibrated and the glimmering figure of Herakles erupted into glorious animation.

Silence gripped, a strange waiting stillness. Even the storm outside had quieted, its force seemingly drained away. The supernatural glimmer enveloping Herakles flared bright a final time, then faded into a muted glow. Though the rest of the room seemed blurry and far away, Dani saw him perfectly.

Every naked inch.

3

Jaw dropping in astonishment, Dani couldn't believe what had happened right before her eyes. She just stared. And stared some more.

The visitor wore not a stitch of clothing. Disheveled hair the color of spun gold brushed his shoulders. A straight nose, fine mouth, and strong jaw completed his face. His presence lent the room an otherworldly spellbinding aura. One word described everything about him.

Magnificent.

Dani gulped as though the air was an alien substance. In her struggle to breathe, blood pounded in her veins, dizzying her. Perspiration dotted her brow. Liquid fire trickled down her spine. Carnal hunger throbbed between her trembling legs.

An intense stare bore holes right through her. Strangely hued, his eyes were a pure amethyst shade as startling as it was striking. Every inch of her was visually examined in an intimate manner. Approval parted his lips. A brief flash of straight white teeth followed.

Dani tried to swallow past the lump forming in her throat.

Stomach tightening, her spine stiffened. A ghost? Nonsense. Clearly she'd gone quite mad. Her breakdown must have driven her over the edge. She was hallucinating. Strangely she felt no real fear. Only wonder.

What the hell is going on?

"How did you get here?" The question tumbled over her lips.

"How does any god move, but as he wishes?" Every inch of him rippled sinew and muscle. Tight, hard, and lean, he padded toward her with a predatory grace. His bare feet made nary a sound.

His answer sounded so reasonable that it actually made sense, in a funny sort of way.

Tipping her head back, Dani's heart skipped a beat. She caught her breath because just looking at him threatened to snatch the oxygen from her lungs. "Herakles?"

His smile dazzled. The air sizzled around him with erotic tension. "In the flesh."

Trembling, she climbed to her knees. "I don't believe this."

A suggestive smile curved his lips. His hand drifted toward his groin. "I could make a believer out of you." A sly grin followed the twinkle in his eye. His fingers brushed his cock, stirring it from its sleep.

His bold move shot through her like a jolt of electricity. Every hair at the nape of her neck prickled with acute awareness. Accepting this situation might be easier than she'd expected. When push came to shove, she wasn't a woman to turn down a hearty fuck.

Especially when her dream god was doing the fucking.

Hot breath rasped across her parted lips. "I wish you would."

"No easier done than said." Flexing into sinuous motion, Herakles bent and caught her around the waist, lifting her as if she weighed ounces. The heat emanating from his hands scorched bare skin. "Not much to you."

Dani looked down and gasped. Somehow her clothing had melted away. "I'm naked," she started to say.

A booming masculine laugh filled her ears. Huge hands settled on her hips. "Which is just how I wanted you."

Hardly a small woman and certainly not a weak one, Dani felt dwarfed by his massive girth. If he'd chosen to pick her up and tie her in a knot, she would have no choice but to bend.

He pulled her closer. Her erect nipples grazed his chest. His thighs brushed hers.

Dani savored his strong hold, the warmth emanating from his very masculine body. His flesh felt warm and hard beneath her hands. She couldn't help but notice that her skin emanated a soft pinkish shade. His own rich hue nearly matched his eyes. "I don't know how this is happening . . ."

His hands felt strong and sure on her skin. Spreading like molten lava, his surging power seemed to pour straight into her veins. "What do you think is happening?"

She swallowed hard, moistening dry lips. "I don't know." Her voice throbbed with huskiness.

He touched her cheek with his fingertips. "A god exists when you believe." His words resonated in her ears, silky and deep as a night ocean.

Believe.

A shiver of anticipation shimmied down her spine. Somehow a connection had been made, drawing their two worlds together like a magnetic force. He could be her salvation, she thought with utter certainty. Pull her out of her gray dim world and into an existence bursting with color and vitality . . .

Herakles traced his fingers down her cheek, stroking the smooth curve of one shoulder. "Long have I waited for a woman who breathes in stone." His hand curved around her neck, fingers softly teasing her bare nape. Head dipping, he lowered his mouth to hers. The forceful passion of his kiss sent a wave of electricity shimmering through her.

Locked in place, Dani found herself incapable of motion. Not that she wanted to break away, leave his warm embrace. She parted her lips, allowing his tongue to sweep in and claim her. A honeyed dreaminess spread through her limbs as their kiss deepened. She had never known that something as simple as a kiss could be so bluntly intimate. It had taken little effort on his part to overwhelm and conquer her.

Huge palms cupped her ass. Strong hips moved against hers. The intensity of his body's heat seemed to fuse his length to hers, settling into the center of her soul in a personal and intimate way. His bold, aggressive move was staggering. Electric currents rippled through her, rendering her aware of nothing but sheer sensation.

"Your body is as hungry as your hands." Strong hands cupped and stroked. His mouth softly brushed eager lips with a promise. "It will be a pleasure to feed such an appetite."

Before Dani could form a coherent reply, Herakles lifted her into his arms. He bore her down onto a small bed tucked away in a corner of her studio. Many a night she'd collapsed onto it, too tired from the day's work to make it upstairs to bed.

A hand-sewn quilt spread over its face. Faded, patched many times over, but still attractive in a familiar sort of way. A little nest of nurturing warmth, it also provided a soft haven for bare skin.

Herakles stretched his lean frame against hers. Light blond hair covered his arms and legs. His abdomen rippled, hard and solid as cobbled stones. His jutting cock eagerly prodded her thigh. His gaze caught and held hers. "Do not be afraid," he said softly. "I will not force you."

Pressed against his full length, her nerve endings tingled. Eagerly. "I'm not afraid," she breathed, trembling with need.

"May I touch you?"

Dani shuddered at his size. "Yes," she replied in a hoarse whisper that conveyed both need and eagerness.

Propped on one elbow to support his weight, Herakles slid the palm of his hand over her smooth belly. Trailing his fingers across her breasts, he circled a dusky nipple. "You are as perfect as the stone you work." Head dipping, his lips captured one nipple, sucking it deep.

Her breath cut off sharply at the delicious sensation. His tongue circled the hard tip with a deliberate slowness. "Oh, yes . . ." She moaned, almost exploding from the pleasure. Heated sensations radiated through her, making her wet and ready all over again.

After a moment, he moved to her other breast and slicked the tip of his tongue over it. He took it greedily, brazenly into his mouth, suckling hard.

Trembling beneath the sensual assault of his lips, she moaned again. Body hot and throbbing, her mind whirled. Breathless with anticipation, the final shreds of control slipped through her fingers.

No matter. His long hair filled her hands now. She tugged his head up for another kiss, unable to bear the ache of lust any longer. "I've needed this," she gasped when their lips parted.

Nibbling at her bottom lip, Herakles smiled. "I know. I've felt that need."

Lust kicked up another notch. Sparks of pleasure exploded like a string of firecrackers. Quaking with raw passion, a sound between a moan and a whimper escaped her. "Whatever you do," she gasped between breaths. "Don't stop."

A wicked smile taunted. "As if I could."

Answering her hunger with more kisses, Herakles caressed his way down her narrow abdomen. His lips left no curve, peak or valley untouched. His tongue explored her navel as though to drink of fine nectar within its depth. Moving lower, he parted her legs and settled between her thighs. His fingers brushed through the clipped hair covering her mons. Damp with cream, her sex beckoned.

"What are you doing?" Letting out a soft whoosh of air, Dani gasped out a laugh and squirmed in delight. She had to control herself from coming right on the spot.

Thumb and forefinger parted her silken folds. Her clit peeked out of its shielding hood, a distended pebble of pulsing flesh. The invitation to taste was extended. "You have a hungry cunt," he murmured. "One needing much care and tending."

Biting back a whimper, Dani thrust her hips upward. "So tend away." How he had come to be here, why he'd come to her she didn't know. At the moment logic didn't apply, nor did she care to examine it.

Caught in the moment she only wanted to soar.

Herakles grinned broadly. "Fortunately my hunger well matches your own." He leaned forward. Warm lips closed around her. He circled the hard little bud.

Welcoming the madness that engulfed her, Dani gave herself to the teasing flicks. His mouth was all over her. Abdominal muscles clenching, her hips bucked upward. "Please," she begged, anxious to be filled. "I need to feel you inside me."

Delving into her, Herakles sank two thick fingers to the knuckle. Creamy inner muscles welcomed him with a tight grip.

Dani pressed her hips against his hand. A soft hungry sound broke from her mouth. The first onslaught of orgasm teased, coming just within her reach. Tremors commenced in small waves, lapping at her toes. Her heart tripped a little, missed a beat, and then settled back into rhythm.

Exquisite, but hardly what she truly craved. Hot breath, ragged inhaling. A sheen of perspiration slicked her hungry skin. Brain-twisting need tormented. The unbearable throb deepened.

"Please . . ." Close to the edge of losing control, a delicate quiver moved the muscles across her flat abdomen. "Make me come . . ."

Herakles laughed, a sexy throaty sound. "You give yourself no time to enjoy." His fingers slipped deeper. His thumb worked the tight bundle of nerves he'd exposed. Promising her. Driving her even wilder. "The reward will be greater if you take it slowly." Head dipping, his mouth claimed her.

Dani moaned again, enjoying the feel of his masterful touch. Her fingers tangled in his thick hair, guiding him, holding him. Her thighs trembled around his head. Hot breath rasped between parted lips, matching the beat of blood though her veins.

He feasted at her snatch, his lips dancing slow circles around her clit. His tongue suddenly stabbed deep.

A tiny shudder ran through her. Sensitive flesh pulsed.

Another stab.

A bigger, more intense shudder. Tight muscles began to relax. The torture enticed.

Barely clinging to her self-control, Dani closed her eyes, immersing herself in nothing but pure erotic sensation. She writhed, trying to accommodate every impression at once.

Herakles licked again and the frayed leash holding her desire snapped.

Swamped under by sheer lust, a heated tickle spread through Dani's abdomen as the inferno building inside went supernova. Her orgasm transformed into a dynamic force of space-twisting power; lightning flared and flashed above her. Red-hot fire lashed out. The vibrant force scorched her veins, sweet release flooding every inch of her.

Her low moan turned into a scream of delight under the restless sweep of a tyrant climax. The earth spun on its axis, taking and reshaping her senses into entirely new shapes.

Minutes passed before the surge of her inner convulsions faded away. She lay limp and sweaty, utterly spent. *God almighty,* she thought through her daze. *That was wonderful!*

In no hurry to end her delightful torment, Herakles rose to his knees. Penis in hand, he bought his fist up to the large bulbous head, then back down. Heavy-lidded eyes cast a spell on her as they held hers captive. "I've waited a long time to claim you as mine."

Dazed by the aftermath of her mind-blowing climax, Dani hungrily licked her lips. Stretched out on her back, her legs were spread wide open. "I've waited a long time to be *claimed*."

He lifted an inquiring brow. An iniquitous smile lit his gaze. "Is that so?"

She giggled in happy surrender. "You bet your sweet ass."

Herakles chuckled. "Mine isn't the ass that's sweet." He stretched over her, resting his weight on his elbows and forearms. Hips settling between her parted thighs, his erect cock rested atop the soft curve of her belly. He lowered his mouth to hers.

Dani tasted the spicy musk of her own cream. Hot excitement flooded her all over again. His kiss, an act of possession, swept her up in its force.

His mouth moved from hers. His eyes burned with desire as one huge hand palmed a breast, shaping the erect peak with thick fingers. Her nipples were pink and swollen. "Should I make you beg for it?"

Her hands were on his shoulders, nails digging into his skin. Her body was melting beneath his. No way in hell she'd let him stop now. She couldn't. "Making your creator beg wouldn't be fair or fitting."

Groaning out his own anticipation, Herakles lifted his weight off her. One strong hand guided his cock until the round hard tip found her sex. He pressed the wide crown between her swollen lips, parting her slick labia. Hot steel caressed silk. "Then you shall have every last inch you desire," he promised through a soft growl.

Anxious to be filled, Dani shifted her hips, and spread wide, preparing to take him to the hilt. Heat racked her body. *God, yes . . .*

As Herakles prepared to slide in, the storm outside kicked up with a vengeance. Eerily silent a moment ago, thunder now snapped the air apart with a tremendous earth-quaking force. Darkened bulbs flickered, dimmed, then caught as the electricity surged back.

Herakles roared out in anguished astonishment. Melting away under a brilliant flare of energy, he vanished like a mirage in the desert.

Distressed by the theft of her pleasure, Dani reached out, desperate to pull him back. But the light sucking him into its core was so blinding that she had to cover her eyes. A strangled nonsensical cry broke from her throat, searing her vocal cords.

Not now, damn it!

4

For an instant nothing existed but the brilliant white light, its flares keeping time with her heart. An enormous thrust of power made her head reel. Then the glare receded, allowing Dani to focus.

Dani blinked and her vision cleared. Much to her surprise she wasn't spread out naked on her studio bed ready to be taken. She wasn't even anywhere within touching distance of Herakles. No, not at all. She still stood in the shadow of the great statue, just as she had been when Jack had departed.

She hadn't moved one goddamned inch.

Brow furrowing in confusion, Dani shook her head. Just a minute ago, she'd been making passionate love to her virile god. The next moment—

"Not."

Nothing had happened.

Except another of the strange spells that seemed to have overtaken her lately. Once again her fantasies had galloped off with her senses.

Having lovingly shaped every inch of the statue, how could she not entertain a few scenarios—starring herself and the most delicious male she'd ever created? She'd easily envisioned him as a living, breathing being a thousand times before. But he'd never before appeared as such a Technicolor reality.

Dani ran a hand up her bare arm. Easy to remember his touch dancing over her skin, his scent in his nostrils, his body spread out beside hers.

Tonight she'd wished him alive.

Aching with unfulfilled desire, a lump rose in her throat as the familiar proverb of pointless desires filtered through her mind. "If wishes were horses, then beggars would ride."

She became conscious that she was cold and shivering. The storm outside rattled the walls around her, a great howling screaming wind driving the terrible storm.

Dani tensed, her flesh seeming to crawl on her bones. Pressure banged behind her eyes, knocking at her temples with an alarming strength. For the first time in days she was conscious of the deathly weariness, the terrible depletion of nervous energy that had fueled her strenuous work for so long.

Stress.

She looked up at her Herakles, now and forever only cold inanimate stone. Finishing the statue had consumed every hour of every day for months. She'd barely taken time to eat, much less sleep. Even when Lucien had walked out the door, there was no time to think or feel. Just work.

Now that Herakles was finished, she teetered on the edge of collapse. She needed rest, to relax a bit.

Locking the outside doors to her studio, she shut off the lights. Alas, Herakles wouldn't be going upstairs with her tonight.

Ascending the stairs to the second-floor apartment, Dani couldn't help remembering how much Lucien had hated the place, a two-story barn with a downstairs studio spacious enough to move and position the massive blocks of marble she worked with. The second floor had been completely gutted, rebuilt into a three-bedroom, two-bath apartment.

Passing through the foyer with its huge flying staircase and Palladian windows, Dani walked into the living room. Her apartment was decorated with a comfortable mix of modern and period furniture. The walls were covered with thick wallpaper in a rich creamy shade. Original artwork added to the charm of the room, marvelously blending with the decor.

Windows on the south and west sides of the room offered breathtaking views. Her studio sat on seven acres of land, surrounded by ancient trees; sugar maples, white pine, and black walnut. The space around the place was wide and unending, the sky overhead blotted out not by outrageously tall buildings, but by clouds of cotton candy surrounding the tops of snow-capped peaks. During the day, the landscape outside was brilliant with spring colors. Country living, just the way she liked it, quiet and peaceful. Hartford was barely twenty minutes away, New York a two-hour commute.

Dani looked around and sighed. Nothing was out of its place. The whip of the wind on the walls around her gave the place an empty, eerie feeling, like a tomb. Nine months ago, Lucien had packed up and moved out. He'd taken only personal possessions, credit cards, and Allison, the cute young assistant Dani had hired to keep house and run errands. Allison had kept the home fires burning. A little bit too well.

The sharp lash of self-flagellation cut through the soft tissue of her brain. The bitch had also been keeping Lucien's bed warm on nights when Dani had collapsed in her studio bed, too exhausted to make her way up upstairs.

Her gaze drifted to her desk. In the top drawer were two tickets for the surprise vacation she'd had Allison book as a fourth-anniversary present for Lucien. Round-trip tickets to Greece for a month of sun, sand, and—she'd hoped—lots of steamy sex with her model-hot husband.

"How ironic the bitch stole my husband and my vacation." True. All true. Lucien and his conniving little backstabber were presently on vacation in, yep, Crete.

A black veil settled over her eyes, blotting out her vision. She felt her body going numb, swaying. Her stomach rolled. She swallowed, clenching her jaw, trying to fight off the sickness threatening to overtake her. She pressed the heel of her hand to her forehead hard, as if she feared her skull would crack and spill out her brains.

"Damn, damn, damn," she cursed. "Not now."

Dani lowered her hand and took several fortifying breaths of air. That helped clear her vision, steady her balance. The dark spells usually signaled the beginning of the headaches that had begun plaguing her almost a year ago. She would be all right and then, bam, the pain would arrive, usually in her left temple. When the pain was bearable, she could chase it away with an over-the-counter headache medication. When it was bad, no amount of painkillers could dull the agony.

Stress, she thought dully. *It's the stress again.*

The stress of success. The stress of an unfaithful spouse.

Whispering shadows in her mind, too many voices chiming in her ears. The ifs, the buts, the whys, and why nots all eating away at her psyche, as surely as the acid in her gut ate away the lining of her stomach.

Dani drew in a deep breath, fighting the headache back. *Not tonight*, she silently pleaded. *Please, not tonight.* Her hands curled into fists. "I should have brained the fucker with a hammer." The cheating bastard was having the time of his life. "And I'm having a nervous breakdown."

She sighed. She was feeling sorry for herself and she knew it.

This wasn't the time or place to delve into deep self-analyses of what had gone wrong with her marriage. That would come naturally, now that she was alone and had time to think. Then, she could mentally beat herself senseless. She was good at slashing herself to pieces with bitter memories of failure.

Dani lowered her hands. "Relax," she murmured. A long weekend stretched ahead. She could eat as much as she wanted, drink wine, laze in front of the television, and watch all the trashy movies she wanted. She'd earned the break.

First, a hot bath. Then a glass of wine.

Her bedroom featured plush Oriental rugs, a crewelwork canopy-covered, queen-size, pencil-post bed, and a full private bath with shower and a huge tub. With its soft hues, the room was utterly feminine.

She stripped off her clothes, discarding them in a pile.

Naked, she stretched, running her fingers through her shoulder-length hair. A shadow moved behind her and she turned, catching sight of her reflection in the mirror. Her gaze ranged over her nude body. Strong shoulders ruled under the tilt of a determined chin. Her breasts were small, but firm and round. Her arms and torso were sleekly muscled from years of vigorous work with mallet and chisel. Trimmed short and neat, a blond thatch of pubic hair covered her Venus mound.

Dani frowned. Her reflection frowned, too. God, when had she gotten so pale and thin? The missed meals and sleepless nights told shamelessly on her. So much for living on coffee and painkillers. She couldn't remember the last time she'd sat down to a decent meal.

Shaking her head, she flipped on the light in the bathroom. She sat on the edge of the tub, regulating the water temperature, watching as the water slowly inched higher. Once she turned off the taps, she stepped into the warmth of the bath, slowly sinking into its depth. The back of her head braced against the cool porcelain rim. She closed her eyes and enjoyed the blissful relaxation the water brought her abused body.

I'm thirty-seven and it feels like I'm seventy-three.

She lifted her eyelids and drowsily regarded the steam rising from the water. Pieces of the strange fantasy she'd had reared up to taunt her. The thought made her tremble with expectation, with need, with the memory of the pleasure he'd almost given her. Driven to the height of orgasm but hardly allowed to peak, she was a mass of raw, frustrated nerves.

Dani pushed the memories away, refusing to let anything daunt her immediate sense of well-being. She sank lower into the water, stopping when it reached her chin. But the images persisted on, lingering, playing through her mind like a vividly colored carousel.

If she closed her eyes she could easily recall the feel of Herakles pressing his hard male length against her softer one, how his hands had caressed her.

Wanting to recapture the moment, her hands slipped under the water. She sucked in a deep breath as her palms brushed lightly over her breasts. Soft pink nipples tightened, then peaked. With a soft moan, she lightly pinched the hard tips. That sensation alone was enough to bring her blood to a hot maddening boil all over again.

Remembering the sensation of his tongue laving every inch of her breasts, Dani pinched harder. Deep inside her core, sensation coiled into a tight hard fist as the cream of her arousal mingled with the warm water.

Stiffening with frustration, she tracked a hand over her flat belly. Then lower, between her legs. Experienced fingers parted the soft petals of her labia. Hot breath scorched her lips as she stroked a single fingertip against her clit. Sheer erotic ferocity sent her simmering lust skidding out of control. In one wildly sensual moment she was no longer in the bathtub, but back in bed.

With Herakles.

Losing herself in the pleasure, Dani let the fantasy take full control of her mind and body.

She easily imagined her otherworldly lover shifting his weight to plant tiny kisses down her neck before his lips found and encircled a waiting nipple. She could almost hear him whispering in that sexy voice of his, urging her thighs to open so his hips could fill the void.

Dani moaned softly, biting the pillow of her lower lip. She wanted to feel the heat of a man's cock entering her slick warmth. Only Herakles wasn't here to fill the emptiness. She'd have to take matters—and her satisfaction—into her own hands.

Needing something, anything, Dani slid two fingers into her sex, pressing her palm against her pulsing clit. Overwhelmed by her raw sexual appetite, arousal crept toward blazing hot temperatures. Her hips trembled in a flurry bordering on desperation. Short ragged gasps underscored her soft moans. Not wanting to come too quickly, she slowed her pace, teasing the hooded organ between her legs with long, slow strokes.

Just when she was certain she could reach no higher plane of rapture, orgasm rippled through her. Lust seared her senses, a red-hot sizzle of pure liquid fire. A violent burst of glittering stars exploded behind her eyes.

She cried out in the throes of magnificent carnal pleasure.

Then it was over, as quickly as it had begun.

Her mouth quirked down in a frown. *That was nice, but definitely not enough.* Not by a long shot. Tonight most definitely called for BOB. A little vibrator fun might help take some of the edge off her nerves.

The cold water around her dragged her out of her thoughts. Dani quickly soaped her body, then rinsed off the bubbles. At least the tension had lessened, the stiffness leaving her neck and shoulders.

Wrapping a towel around her waist, she let the tub drain.

She grabbed a hand towel, wiping her face. Wiping the steam off the vanity mirror, she grimaced at the sight of herself. The deepening of crows-feet at the corners of her eyes and the strands of silver weaving in at her temples weren't a welcome sight. Forty was just around the corner.

Marrying a man almost a decade younger than herself had been a mistake. She was well settled into her life and career. Lucien . . . Well, he had no career. Unless you counted professional party animal as a vocation. Lucien craved the bright lights of the big city. The cachet of being married to Dani Ryan had quickly worn thin once he realized the isolation that encompassed her life and work. His own career as a photographer had stalled.

Dani grimaced. Not that he'd ever taken anything aside from nude photos of his girlfriend. Which was how she'd busted Lucien's affair open. He hadn't even bothered to hide them well enough not to be found. His message had been clear. He wanted out.

Picking up a comb, she attacked the tangles in her hair. "I'm a fool." She sighed between strokes. "He was too damn young for me. A boy, not a man." He'd done what any gold digger on the prowl would: married an older successful artist who would support him. Perfect pickings. That's what she'd been.

Fresh off her triumph of her *Four Seasons*—four gloriously nude males depicting spring, summer, fall, and winter—she'd been exhausted, at loose ends with herself. The crash that followed the completion of a new work never failed to haunt her. Lucien had been her anchor, saving her from drowning in a sea of depression. He made her feel young, beautiful, desirable. Much like the nude males she sculpted from stone, he seemed perfect in every way. Only he was real, alive. And, for a time, he'd been hers.

Their story didn't have a happy ending. Once again, she was alone.

Hard to take a man made of stone to bed.

Dani dropped the comb, covering her eyes with her hands. Tears hovered, ready to fall. The emptiness was there again. She could feel it, gnawing her up inside.

"No, no, no," she admonished herself. "It's just the black dog again." Black dog, indeed. The hound was biting hard today. "I just need to take a little time to pamper me."

Taking off her contacts, she slipped a pair of simple black-rimmed glasses on. The specs made her look like the artistic nerd she was. She hated the glasses, refused to be seen in them, but her contact lenses felt like ground glass on her eyeballs. She wasn't supposed to be wearing them more than eight hours anyway. She'd already exceeded that limit by about a week. She could see well enough to get from point A to point B, but without corrective lenses her world was a blur.

Mouth positively rancid from a diet of black coffee and gummy bears, she brushed her teeth, gladly chasing away the nasty film with a liberal dose of mouthwash.

While she took care of the necessities of keeping a body together, Dani deliberately kept her eyes away from her wrists. Yes, she knew the scars were there, knew that she would wear them for the rest of her life.

What she'd done was stupid. Though she didn't want to, she replayed the scenes in her head; pushing the rewind button and watching the events spool out across her mind's screen.

After Lucien left, she'd gotten drunk, wasn't thinking of the repercussions when she picked up the sharp chisel. In a moment of bitter depression, she'd tried to end her life.

She hadn't succeeded.

Dani felt her chest tighten. Her heart felt like lead. She didn't know exactly why she'd done it. She was in pain, needing oblivion, escape.

Jack had found her, drifting in and out of consciousness, covered in blood. The ER docs had to stitch her back together.

She'd spent nearly a month in the hospital, precious time ticking away. All she wanted then was to stop. Stop thinking. Stop breathing. Stop being. To be stone would be perfect. Immobile. Immovable. Incapable of feeling hurt, jealously, and betrayal. The night Lucien had left, he'd made a little speech. Belittling her, humbling her. Denigrating and destroying her all in one sweeping arc.

Why had he done it?

Jealousy, perhaps.

Dani walked in rarified air, blessed with a talent that made men gnash their teeth with envy. While many could envision the soul in the stone, few could bring it forth in a realistic and lifelike manner. Her sculptures not only looked real—the figures appeared to breathe, draw air into living lungs.

"Thank God for Jack," she murmured. Visiting her every day without fail, he'd helped lead her back toward the light of sanity. He'd gotten her through the depression. Gotten her back on her feet.

To work.

She knew why. She might be a fool where men were concerned, but she wasn't a fool when it came to her art.

An unfinished Dani Ryan piece would be worthless, the vision unrealized. She suspected that Jack Wilde had already leaked the details of the piece to certain collectors. He wouldn't have named a figure if he didn't have prospective buyers in mind. Having a nervous breakdown had cost her more than money and lost time. It'd cost her self-respect, self-esteem, and almost every other self a human being could possess.

Dani sighed again. Through the last months, she'd known it was time to make some changes in her life or she'd soon be a dead woman. To keep her sanity, she'd had to make some sacrifices. In retrospect, she wondered if she'd made the right choices. When she thought about the decisions she'd made recently, the only thing she felt was totally screwed. Like a small boat adrift on a large ocean, she somehow had to make her way back to land. This time giving up wouldn't be an option.

Feeling human again, she wandered back into the bedroom. Digging out a pair of sweatpants and a t-shirt, she started to dress, then stopped.

"Boring. Unsexy." She tossed the sweats with a snort of disgust.

She opened another drawer, digging out a sheer negligee and a pair of panties that were little more than see-through lace. She hadn't worn the knock-his-eyes-out ensemble since her honeymoon. Amazing how quickly the nice lingerie got tossed aside for the tried and true.

Dani slipped on the lacy confection. The silk whispered against her skin, making her feel soft and feminine. She stepped into the panties, hitching them up her legs and thighs. The lace molded to her hips, barely covering her mound. The thin piece of floss in back settled between her butt cheeks. Much to her relief, the panties still fit. Better yet, her ass didn't droop a bit. To sculpt took hard, brutal labor.

She dug in another drawer. Ah. There it was her favorite toy, unused for months. She switched it on. A nice friendly buzz met her ears. No plain old plastic one for her either. Her dildo had the size and shape of a real penis, one guaranteed to offer lifelike stimulation. The bulbous head tapered gently into a ridged neck and long shaft, complete with expertly contoured testicles.

Not quite the real thing, but it would do in a pinch.

Dani's mind drifted toward her beautiful naked god. Remembering his sleek bronze body, her breath caught in a hitch and her heart fluttered. *Mmm.* She teasingly flicked her tongue around the shaft of the fake penis. "I'd love another taste of that," she murmured. "Wish it had been real."

Too bad Herakles and his lovemaking skills were a figment of her imagination.

Her lips quirked up in a smile. Well, who said a woman couldn't dream a little? A cozy fire, a glass of wine, and some soft music would certainly put her in the mood to fantasize about her immortal lover. Then she could put her favorite toy to work.

Lucien might be out of her life, but someone new, someone exciting, had to be waiting around the corner. Surely she wasn't doomed to be alone forever.

"I'll take a year off," she promised herself. "No work, no stone. Just fun."

5

Leaving her bedroom behind, Dani claimed a chilled bottle of wine from the fridge. No plain wineglass tonight, but one of the good crystal ones. Might as well go all the way and spoil herself rotten.

Drifting back into the living room, she sat bottle and glass down and set to arranging a haven for rest, building a fire in the hearth, and lighting several scented candles. Lush sweet vanilla filled the air as the flames consumed the wicks. Rain beat the roof above her head, flashes of lighting punctuated by rolling peals of thunder lit the room.

Dani spread her favorite comforter on the floor. Several thick lush throw pillows followed. With a little grin she added the dildo.

Nothing more alluring than making love in front of crackling fire. She'd never tried it with Lucien. Somehow she hadn't been able to open up enough and share her fantasies. Not that it mattered. Two years into their marriage he'd stopped sleeping with her.

Reclaiming her bottle and glass, Dani sank down on the floor and poured herself some wine. She drank it down in a single gulp, poured a second, and drank it, too. She hadn't eaten since yesterday and the wine went straight to her head. She just wasn't hungry lately. And, truthfully, she just couldn't face another Lean Cuisine or other frozen bland confection.

Plumping up a pillow, she stretched out on in front of the fire. Nice just to let her thoughts float along with the melodic masterpiece of nature's music. The storm outside resonated with pain and loss, taking its grief out on the earth below.

Eyes half closed, lulled by the wine, the scent of the candles and her own emotional exhaustion, Dani's hand drifted to her left breast. She cupped it, feeling its weight. A little tingle sent shivers up her spine. Through silky material she circled her nipple with the tip of her fingers, enjoying the feel of soft pressure. Liquid warmth spread through her veins and pulsated between her thighs. Aching desire quivered through her.

"Love this." A low sigh escaped her throat. Easy to imagine that her fingers were those of her Greek god, his tongue circling the hard tip. Her free hand slipped down, brushing the curve of her pubic mound. Lifting and bending her legs, she spread them and brushed the fingertips of one hand across the crotch of her panties. Air weighed heavily in her lungs. Her heart raced.

Using only the tips of her fingers and the gentlest pressure, she stroked her clit with soft little flicks. Arousal arrived instantly. Eyes closed, she inhaled again. Tremors of pleasure coursed through her as her fingers gently massaged. She slipped her finger under her panties and rubbed her finger up and down her slit. Her labia were beginning to swell and separate as she thought of what she'd love a man to do to her body. Silky cream drenched her sex. She stroked gently up and down. Her wetness clung to her finger. Soft mewling sounds broke from her lips. Her body shuddered deliciously. Half her finger slipped easily inside. She was primed and so ready to be taken.

Stroking herself was nice, but she needed heavier action. "I bet I know what you'd like, little pussy of mine," she whispered and removed her hand. Flicking on her dildo, she slipped it under her panties and pressed it against her clit.

Dani closed her eyes and threw her head back as the vibrations electrified her sex, sparks of pleasure igniting every nerve in her body. Mind descending into a pleasant fog, her fantasy took on vivid life. She easily imagined Herakles's touch awakening her sexuality, his mouth suckling her breasts, his scent coming directly from heated naked skin.

Growing bolder, Dani stroked with more pressure, feeling the wetness seep up. A moan scratched its way out of her throat. Biting down on her lower lip, she sucked in a breath through her teeth. Spreading her legs wider, she sheathed the pulsating vibrator inside her cunt, rocking her hips harder. Heavy faux balls buzzed against her ass.

She pushed the faux penis deeper, driving the device all the way inside. She groaned and started to move her hips back and forth, thoroughly lost in the sensations of driving the slippery cock in and out. Tension coiled around her swollen clit. Control slipped through her fingers. Lust slipped into the driver's seat and put the pedal to the metal. Close . . . Closer . . . Her body tensed. Orgasm swept her away.

Hell, yeah!

What started as a low moan turned into a scream. Her second climax came swiftly and fiercely, the thunder outside echoing the tremor shaking her senses into a thousand fractured pieces. Gasping from the heated depths of its throes, she felt an irrational need to cry and laugh at the same time. Perhaps she would have if a deep, masculine voice hadn't shocked her senseless.

"Looks like you've started without me." Hands on his slender hips, Herakles stood looking down on her. Lightning flared through the windows, then darkened. His figure remained solidly placed. He was totally nude, and the well-muscled breadth of his shoulders seemed magnified in the firelight's glow. The look on his face was pure delight.

Dani squealed. The dildo went flying. It landed with a clunk on the floor, rolled a bit, then buzzily slipped into silence. A valiant death. Killed in the line of pleasure, serving its owner to the last little shudder.

Scrambling to get her legs beneath her, she clutched a pillow against her breasts and peered guiltily up. Surprise fusing with mortification threatened to incinerate her. How long had he been standing there? Had he seen—

Then she remembered her fantasy.

Must have fallen asleep, she thought dizzily. Dreams never made sense, anyway.

"I was thinking of you," she stammered stupidly. "Of making love to you."

Herakles grinned. "I know. Looks like you were relieving your needs quite nicely."

Heat surfaced in Dani's cheeks, but she refused to break her visual lock with him. A poorly suppressed shudder worked through her. She was conscious of the massive size of his body. Of the masculine sexuality emanating off his skin. And of the hard cock jutting proudly. Oh, he'd seen all right. Seen and wanted.

Dani heaved a breath to calm her racing pulse. "Well you weren't here, so I did it myself."

He dealt her an amused grin and cocked a brow toward the telltale dildo. "Did it do the job?"

Her gaze tracked the expanse of his hard-packed chest, his narrow waist, stopping to linger on his erect shaft. His penis was thickly veined, powerful, arching up toward his lean abdomen. Her mouth watered for a taste.

Take it.

Dani smiled up at him. "What it can do, I have a feeling you can do better."

A sardonic smile twitched on his lips. "You'd be right."

Without thinking about it, Dani climbed to her feet. "Then show me." She stepped up to him. The sheer presence of him overwhelmed. A thrill of sexual awareness raced down her spine.

Herakles reached out, smoothing strands of hair away from her face, running his thumbs over her cheekbones. Her fire-warm skin felt under his fingertips. He was so close, so alluring, so beautiful. Strange sensations flowed through her body, as if slow sensual circles were being drawn around her clit.

Shaken, her breath rattled tremulously. *I'm totally enchanted with this man*, she thought crazily.

But it wasn't possible. He was just a part of her wild imagination. Still, she couldn't ignore the hard knot of desire coiling in her stomach.

Dani hardly cared. What mattered to her was the here and now. She wished her heart would stop pounding before it cut off her breathing altogether. She was all too aware that she was overdressed, even in a negligee. She wanted Herakles to throw her to the floor and fuck her until she screamed out his name.

"I've wanted you since the first day I saw you inside the stone," she whispered, voice going hoarse. "Even then I felt the power inside."

"Your touch has freed me." He leaned toward her and tipped back her head. "For that I owe you everything." His lips covered hers, their kiss a whisper, a gentle meeting of mouths, of tongues. He tasted fresh and ripe, like a newly plucked peach.

Closing her eyes, Dani metaphorically took another step into her fantasy world. Like a rope ladder in the wind, it quivered, but held firm. She cradled his face in her hands, feeling the texture of his stubbly jaw. "I don't know how this can happen, but I don't care."

"I do." He nibbled her lower lip. "I wanted to be with you." His hands moved to her breasts, rubbing gently, squeezing and fondling. He chuckled. "My own wish is my own command."

She drew in a breath, arching her body closer to his. His mouth came down over hers again, his hands sliding around to cup her ass as if to prevent her from escaping him.

Escaping his hold was her last thought. She pressed her mouth back against his, her tongue eagerly entering into the duel. Her arms circled his neck, her fingers delving into his thick long hair to hold him closer.

Everything became jumbled in her mind after that. Somehow, they dropped to the floor, and she was on her back on top of the warm comforter.

On top of her, Herakles had total control, exploring her body with eager hands, trying to taste, lick, bite, and suck every inch of her skin at once. His weight was half on her, one of his thighs nestled between her spread legs, holding them apart. His free hand stroked down her firm belly, reaching for the creamy slit between her legs.

Moaning softly, Dani tilted her hips to allow him free access. "Take me," she breathed. "All of me." Her brain was fogging, but she didn't care. She only knew she wanted to make love to this beautiful spirit. Whether it made any sense or not, she didn't care. She was only thinking of the here and now.

Herakles smiled with an arousing intensity that set her heart afire. "With pleasure."

He pinned Dani's hands on each side of her and lowered his head. She gasped when his mouth closed over her breast, dampening the thin material of her negligee over her bead-hard nipple. Breathless little sounds escaped her lips as he teased the tip.

A quiver ran through her. Her mouth was swollen and red from his fierce kisses, her wits clouded with desire. Her fingers bit into his shoulders. She wanted him. The air surrounding them was charged with electricity. There was a compelling rightness about being in his arms, a rightness she hadn't known with any other man.

Dani wrapped her arms around his neck and pulled him closer. Her gaze settled on his amethyst eyes. "Don't be gentle," she whispered.

When Herakles unwound her arms from about his neck, she feared he was going to leave. Instead, he helped her out of her negligee. "I take what I need from my women." Herakles kissed her hard. Almost brutally, his hungry lips plundered hers.

Dani pressed herself to him again, relishing the hardness of his body against her bare skin, and the cock straining to be sheathed. He kissed her long and hard, like a man who had been locked away alone too long. By the time he ended the second kiss, she was caught up in the rapture of fierce desire and luscious expectation.

The caresses of his strong hands felt heavenly on her feverish skin. He explored her body with the experience of a god knowledgeable in prolonging a woman's pleasure until it bordered on torture.

His fingertips swiped at her nipple. Dani dragged in a sharp breath, blazing darts of pleasure causing her skin to prickle. Herakles teasingly traced the pink aureole before lowering his head and capturing the rigid tip between his lips. Hot moist breath tickled.

Back arching, Dani panted through her mouth. She moaned, driven by the combination of tranquil warmth and passionate sexual desire pulsing though her core.

Threading her fingers through her lover's hair, Dani lifted

his head, dragging his mouth to hers for a long, slow kiss. The kiss didn't remain soft; their needs were too urgent to be contained. Hard muscular planes, taut muscles, and the feel of naked flesh on naked flesh emanated a heady, enticing scent, the musk of the two sexes in heat.

Using just the tips of her nails, Dani grazed the rippling plane of Herakles's back.

He laughed softly. "Vixen," he teased with a grin. "I'm going to make you climax until every bit of you is wrung out." He sounded absolutely serious.

Dani made a mock scoffing sound. "I'd like to see you try."

Herakles ran a hand along her abdomen, following the skim with his lips. "This is just the beginning." His fingers slipped into the waistband of her panties. The tiny scrap of lace disintegrated, torn off as though made of nothing more than wrapping paper. His big hand slipped between her legs, forcefully parting her thighs. He probed the softness surrounding Dani's clit, dipping into her to wet the tip of a thick finger.

Hovering like a balloon riding a Zephyrus summer's breeze, all Dani could do was feel. The moist sensation of her own juices heated by her lover's touch sent blazing-hot darts of fire straight into her core. The glide of his finger made contact with her clit. Desire rocketed her into a whole new stratosphere.

With a knowing smile, Herakles suckled the sensitive tip of her nipple, the long, slow strokes of his tongue alternating with shorter teasing flicks. At the same time, he eased two fingers inside her sex. Inner muscles contracted, drawing him in.

"Hungry?" he murmured in a sultry tone.

Dani bunched a fist in his long hair, the other clutching at the comforter beneath her body. "Oh, yes. I'm starving."

"Not half so ravenous as a god locked in stone."

Herakles slipped lower, adding the hard pressure of his mouth to Dani's pulsing clit. His fingers sawed in and out of her creamy depth as his talented tongue manipulated her most sensitive flesh.

A small strangled cry escaped Dani's lips. At the same time her hips jerked upward, the beginning of a grinding, rocking motion. Sweeter than it was hurried, more paced than it was furious. With every plunge she felt the rough hardness of his big knuckles. The friction was almost too much to take.

Tremors engulfed her, small waves that gradually became frantic convulsions. The agony was so prolonged, so exquisite that Dani wanted to cry out for harder, faster, more pounding thrusts.

Just as she was about to climax, Herakles slowed the pace.

Overshooting climax like a cartoon character skidding off a cliff, Dani clenched her teeth. "Shit! I just missed coming."

Herakles laughed low in the back of his throat. "You didn't miss it because it hasn't happened yet." He was enjoying taking his time. He thumbed Dani's swollen clit. An intense rush of liquid heat submerged her without warning, a crashing wave totally inescapable.

A hoarse mewl escaped her throat as searing sensations built inside her. She arched her back when an explosion of fire and ice coursed through her, his fingers bringing her to a shuddering climax.

Skin glistening with perspiration, she made a vain attempt to control her breathing when he positioned his body over hers. Cock ready and willing, he entered her with all the strength and sureness of a domineering male. Center to center, male conquering female, he claimed her in the most primal way. Pinning her wrists to the floor above her head, he watched her every expression, her every reaction to his mastery.

Coils of desire tightened Dani's entire being. Feeling every last inch of him, she groaned, half in pleasure, half in surprise. She savored the feeling of his bare stomach pressed against hers. Poised above her, his long hair drifted around his shoulders and face like a silken veil. Fierce and masterful, he was a god in all the glory of control over the weaker mortal.

She loved it. Goosebumps rippled across her skin. Her body vibrated under his with delicious anticipation, held captive by his powerful hands and massive weight. Dani was powerless in his grasp. Even if he were to deliver great pain, she would not have been able to stop him. He could do with her as he wished and she would welcome it.

"Please," she moaned, enjoying the sweetest of tortures. Her stomach was doing flips, trying to keep up with her body's intense need for release. The sensations were so intense that they surged upward and she let out a loud moan. The thunder of her heartbeat was so strong that she almost felt as if she would pass out from the sheer pleasure.

His fingers tightened around her wrists. He moved his hips, giving her a taste of bliss. "Tell me what you want."

Hot breath rasped her lips. "Fuck me," she whispered, voice hoarse with demand. "Until I scream."

He lifted a wicked brow. "Oh, you'll scream."

The god made good on his promise.

Dani's back arched when his strong body revved into fierce motion. His move lifted her hips off the floor, driving his cock in to the hilt. Caught in the grip of sheer lust, she whimpered.

Buried to the balls, the rhythm of his savage thrusts pounded, flesh against flesh. His fucking was hard, brutal, merciless. Forgotten was her pleasure or comfort. His low growls soon matched hers. His cock plundered, claiming every inch.

Wrapping her legs around his waist, Dani locked her ankles at the small of his back and held on for the ride of her life. Climax rose in the pit of her stomach, coiling into a hard tight ball. Lust attacked from a thousand directions at once. Arousal spiraled into another orgasm. Without warning an indescribable and incandescent rapture shattered her senses.

Somehow she freed her bruised wrists. Shocked and thrilled at the same time, she clung to him. Trembling from the sensual overload, her fingers convulsed, her nails digging deeply into his shoulders as her shuddering release stole away what little breath she had left.

Twice more Herakles brought her to a pinnacle of release while he fiercely thrust into her, his engorged cock a searing rod driving itself deeper and deeper.

Unable to hold back as her inner muscles contracted around his cock, Herakles threw back his head and relented to his own pleasure, thrusting and making sounds like a wild stallion. Hot semen jetted when release thundered through him. His shudders were violent, as if the experience delivered an excruciating amount of pain.

Aftershocks still rippling through her body, Dani doubted that she'd ever breathe normally again. When Herakles finally collapsed atop her, panting, his flesh slick with sweat, she nudged him to roll onto his side.

He did so without hesitation. Closing his eyes, he dozed, well sated.

Sitting up, Dani winced at the ache between her thighs. Lucien was good in bed, but not this damn good. She hadn't been so well fucked since . . . Well, she couldn't exactly remember. At least a year. Maybe more.

Pushing loose strands of hair off her sweaty forehead, she glanced over the man laying so contentedly bedside her. A smile curved up one corner of her mouth. Stretched out naked, his bronze skin bathed in the firelight, a soft glow of energy seemed to radiate around him like a magical veil. He was so beautiful it made her throat hurt.

She swallowed, trying to rid herself of the frog that had suddenly jumped up into her throat, blocking her air. A piercing sense of need filled her again. Her fingers itched to explore every inch of his body all over.

6

Dani reached out, running her fingers lightly over the curve of one chiseled bicep. When freeing Herakles from the stone, she'd known exactly the proportions of his figure. As a sculptor her job wasn't to create the god from marble, but to reveal what was already there, waiting to be uncovered.

Feeling her touch, Herakles opened sleepy eyes and blinked. Languid in his glorious nudity, he stretched like a lazy tiger, all sinew and sleek muscle. "I've felt you touch me like that many times before." He smiled and her heart squeezed.

Dani smiled back. "I've always been able to feel the pulse beneath stone. To me, it's something living."

He cocked an inquiring brow. "Then you've always loved stone?"

She nodded. "Since I was a little girl. I have my father's love of stone."

Herakles trailed his fingers over the back of her hand, her arm. "Tell me about this man who taught you so much."

Licking dry lips, she spoke hesitantly. "My mother died when I was very young. My father had no one to look after me, so he often took me to work with him. He was a mason, a bricklayer." She lifted her hands, strong and supple from years of holding a hammer and chisel. "He had big hands, strong hands, the kind that could do a lot of work. He looked rough, like a giant, but a gentle one. In his spare time he carved. He could create beautiful things with his hands, take a piece of nothing and make it live and breathe."

He rolled closer, caressing her bare thigh. His gaze caught and held hers. "Something you learned to do."

Her nerve endings tingled. "Yes. At first dad just handed me the tools to get me out of his hair." A little laugh escaped her. "But when he saw I might have talent he began to take things a little more seriously."

Thinking of her father, the sad ache of melancholy filled her. The poor man had worked his fingers to the bone, putting in a lot of overtime to finance her education as an artist. The art of sculpting wasn't a cheap one. All that extra work laying bricks to pay for her studies in Italy and Greece had killed Dennis Ryan. He died working on a condominium construction project when a 300-pound parapet stone broke off from the building and crushed him.

Herakles sensed her sadness. He sat up, and his fingers skimmed the corner of her mouth. A shower of sparks exploded in her bloodstream. Her body leapt to throbbing readiness in an instant. "Good thing he did teach you or I wouldn't be here at all."

His words forced a breathless laugh. Of course he wouldn't know he was part of her dream.

Assuming she was dreaming.

Sure didn't feel like one, though.

Her eyes scanned his magnificent body. Damn, he sure looked real. And by the ache between her legs, he sure as hell felt real.

Taking a deep breath, she tucked sadness into the box where it belonged, in the past. She wanted—no, needed—to enjoy what she had at hand, right here, right now. That it made no sense didn't bother her.

Why question the illogical? Just enjoy it for what it's worth. Too soon reality would surely intrude.

Using only the tips of her fingers, she traced over his chin, down his neck, to his chest. Her touch was light, sensual. When she could speak, she murmured, "Even in stone I felt your presence." However long his delicious fantasy might last, she wanted to wring every second out of it. Already she felt starved for him, despite the fact that he'd left her sated only a few minutes before.

She wanted more.

Urging him to lay back down, Dani's fingers brushed along his chest. His skin felt smooth, so very warm and alive. "Shall I tell you what it's like to work with stone?"

Blond brows arched mischievously. "Only if you promise an in-depth explanation."

Oh, it would be in depth, all right.

She traced his flat dusky nipples. "The sculptor must work the marble with no animosity, but be accepting of its foibles and follies." She rolled the hard beads between thumb and forefinger. "Stone always works against the artist, resistant to revealing what's in its heart."

Herakles stifled a moan. "And you think I resisted you?" he denied through an interested growl.

Dani twisted his nipples a little harder, then leaned over to soothe the ache with her tongue. "Mmm, yes. To strike it is to violate it. It's not in stone's nature to change." She nipped again, then began to paint a soft trail down his cobbled abdomen with her lips and tongue.

"Sure about that?" By the strain in his voice, his self-control was definitely slipping

She inhaled, enjoying his scent of male musk mingling with the slightly pungent odor of his sex. Skin warm from his heat, the smell of him was potent and forbidden. "I'm positive."

"How positive?"

"This positive." She dipped her head, kissing the soft damp silk of his penis.

Nestled in its thatch of blond curls, Herakles's cock stirred.

With a soft moan, Dani shivered and palmed his sac. She squeezed gently, tumbling the balls inside. Thick and powerful, his cock rose, ruling over his lean abdomen. Awakened, the beast waited eagerly to slake its thirst.

Oh, she desired this man, this god, so deeply that it made her ache inside. Desired his lunging thrusts fulfilling her fierce sexual hunger, even as he stroked away the emptiness and loneliness inside her soul.

Dani dropped a long lick down the ridge of his mushrooming shaft. "The artist has to nurture stone, coax it into taking its true form." Another slow, sinuous lick upward toward the bulbous crown. "Then, and only then, will the stone become rich, warm and living. Stone can never be forced." She squeezed his sac again, adding just enough pressure to his sensitive area to bring pleasure. "Give it the wrong touch and it will shatter."

Herakles groaned and rolled his hips. A yearning needy sound rumbled up from his chest. "Give me another touch like that and I will surely come all over." His cock strained, rigid and corded with thin veins. A moist drop of pre-cum seeped from its head. His fingers found and threaded through her hair, guiding her lower, silently urging her to hurry her torturous journey.

Refusing to stop her caressing, Dani laughed softly. She refused to be hurried. "Patience." She lifted up a little to swirl her tongue in the cup of his belly button.

He growled a low warning through clenched teeth. "In this case, patience is no virtue."

Ah. He could dish out sweet torture, but taking it was another matter entirely.

Dani grasped him firmly. His cock pulsed against her palm. Pure steel encased in warm velvety skin. "Maybe not a virtue but definitely an asset." She playfully flicked over the rosy head, beginning a delicious tease.

He shivered when her soft mouth claimed him again. "Virtue be damned."

Dani took him as deeply as she could without gagging, which in this case wasn't very damn deep given his length. With slow, deliberate circles, she traced the engorged head of his crown with her tongue. He was a big man, his penis more than proportionate to his massive body. And she wanted every last inch stuffed in her.

But first she wanted to taste every last inch, lick him like a kid licked a popsicle on a hot summer's day. He'd given her a lot of pleasure. Only fair that she should return the favor.

Coming up for air, she gave a scrape of teeth guaranteed to send a man into the stratosphere.

Herakles stiffened. "Have a care with those canines, vixen."

Popping his cock out of her mouth, Dani glanced up and gave him a cat-eating-the-canary smile. "I can't hear you." Another bob, more scraping.

Herakles pushed himself up on his elbows. "Damn you, woman! Do you want me to set you over my knee and paddle that luscious ass of yours?"

Dani delivered another series of devastating licks, working her tongue in every nook and cranny around his penis and balls. "Only if I get to sit on your face afterward."

Determined not to give up the upper hand just yet, she fisted his erection. Saliva was her lubricant as she began a slow hand job, jacking him toward climax.

Herakles's head fell back and a strangled sound escaped his throat. "You definitely have the touch that brings stone to life."

Dani smiled. "Thank you." Positions reversed, she was most definitely in control.

He closed his eyes in dreamy languor. "I intend to well re-ward—or punish—your skills," he half gasped, half moaned.

Dani laughed and straddled his legs. Her thighs, spread across him, controlled him with practiced skill. She ground her sex in a circle over his erection, leaving no doubt what she intended to do. "Not until I've had my way with you."

Herakles visibly swallowed. Goosebumps rippled over his golden skin. "Please do."

Dani grinned. Scooting back, she pinned his legs under her butt. Leaning forward, she guided her mouth back down his shaft, beginning her torture all over again. She worshipped him with all the skills of a supplicant paying oral homage at the altar of his manhood.

As if on her command, Herakles started to shake. His balls drew up, the pressure of climax threatening to overwhelm him. Propped up on his elbows, he tilted his head back and closed his eyes as his orgasm built.

Any second now hot semen would jet into her mouth.

Dani wanted to swallow every last drop.

Without missing a beat on him, she spread her legs farther apart and drove her fingers deep inside her dripping depth. Her chest heaved, breasts rising and falling. Her nipples were hard, swollen. She closed her eyes and offered everything she had.

Herakles's rough voice broke through her delicious gaze. "If you think I'm wasting a hard cock to your mouth, think again." Tearing himself away from her clever mouth, he toppled her control with an easy sweep of his powerful legs.

"I wasn't ready—!"

Herakles ignored her. Turning a deaf ear to her words, he grabbed a thick pillow, positioned it, then rolled her on top. From behind Herakles positioned himself between her spread legs. His hard cock filled the crack of her ass. Face on the floor, her ass was propped above her head. She was spread wide open for the taking.

Very funny.

Pushing her weight up on her hands, she got her knees halfway under her. "What are you doing?"

"Just wait," came his answer, delivered in a sensual rumble.

A soft moan escaped her lips when he ran his hands up her rib cage. He cupped her firm breasts with both hands. His fingers found and teased her pebble-hard nipples. They hardened even more under his touch.

Herakles rolled and squeezed her nipples. "That's more like it."

Dani closed her eyes and leaned back against his solid weight. "This is a position I've definitely never tried before."

"Glad you like it," he breathed in her ear.

"I'd like it even more if you did this." Catching one of his hands, she pulled it past her belly, guided it toward her sex.

Realizing her intent, Herakles slipped his hand between her parted thighs. He rubbed his finger over her clit; softly at first, then applying more pressure when a soft whimper broke from her lips. "Is this what you want?"

Her clit sang out in pleasure. She moaned. "Mmm . . . yesss . . ."

Herakles slid his finger through her silken labia. Stroking in and out, slowly at first, then building the momentum.

Gasping as he hit a particularly sensitive spot, Dani felt her vaginal walls clench tightly around his finger.

Herakles pushed his finger deeper. "Mmm. Tight and hot. Just the way I like it." He held her around the waist, supporting her so that she would not fall as he gave her pleasure.

Her laugh caught in her throat. Her body trembled, her inner muscles sucking his finger deeper. It touched the ache inside her core, but didn't quite scratch it. She needed something harder, longer and much bigger. "Glad you're pleased."

"I am. Very much." He slipped his finger out. Big hands settled on her hips, burning hot against her bare skin. His burgeoning cock felt like an iron rod against her ass. She was dying for him to impale her with one sold thrust.

Disappointed, a lusty moan broke from her lips. "Don't stop now."

His cock brushed her labia. "It's about to feel better."

Dani shivered when he pushed the head against her nether-lips, but didn't enter. She whimpered, pushing back against him, trying to entice him to enter her. "Do it now."

"I'm taking my time." One big hand slid up to fondle her breast. Trapping her nipple, he tugged it gently, enjoying the way she writhed. "I want you to squirm."

She growled, tossing back her head. "Oh, God, I'm squirming as fast as I can . . ."

Herakles moved his hand down her stomach until it reached her mound. "Do you know how long I've waited for this?" He slipped a finger between her lips and stroked her weeping slit. Her clit was engorged, poking from between her lips. He rubbed it.

Dani moaned again, shoving her body back against his. Want exploded into need. "Do that again and you might lose a hand."

He kissed the soft curve between her neck and shoulder. "Naughty cunt going to eat me up?"

"I'll fucking well devour you," she promised. "Every last inch."

Bending her slightly forward Herakles glided sensuously into her slick heat. "You asked for it." Sinking to the hilt, he growled out his approval. "You're so damn tight." Without pulling out, he flexed his hips for deeper penetration.

Dani pressed back against him, chiming in with her own moves. Delight seared her inside and out. His cock felt like the rock he'd emerged from, and just as solid. "And you're so damn big." Undulating waves of pleasure warmed the blood in her veins.

Herakles pumped into her slowly, steadily, letting the tension between them build. "I can think of other places much tighter." He gave one firm cheek a playful slap. "A cock sucking is nice." A pinch followed, not painful but firm enough to reveal his intent.

Simmering with fresh frustration, Dani groaned. "I've never had anal sex."

"You should try it once. It's very pleasurable if done right."

She considered. The idea certainly intrigued. An unbidden rush of sexual warmth filled her as she imagined the possibilities. "Okay," she breathed. "But take it slow, please."

"I never fuck an ass with menace." A brief pause. "Unless it's well deserved."

Uh, ho. What the hell had she just gotten herself into?

Thoroughly lubed with her cream, Herakles spread her ass cheeks. His cock nudged against her tight anus. "Relax."

Dani sucked in a sharp breath. "I'm trying."

"Mmm. It is always a pleasure to take a virgin ass." But he drew back with a sigh. "But I don't force a woman who doesn't want it."

Cheeks heating, she shook her head. "I—I've always wanted to." The thought of having ass and cunt filled to the brim turned her on. A lot.

The pressure returned. "Then we will take it slowly." Herakles pressed, entering.

She tightened, resisting.

Herakles laughed softly from behind her. "It hurts more when you're tense." He pushed in a little deeper. "Just open up and let it in."

A surge of electricity jangled every nerve in her body. Dani closed her eyes tight, instinctively pressing back against him, feeling the ring of her anus begin to stretch and open to accommodate his shaft. A chill, half of excitement, half of fear of the unknown, worked its way up her spine.

Something new, she thought, half giddy. *Something exciting. Something she'd never dared try with Lucien.*

Herakles worked his way inside her until his thighs pressed against hers.

Dani glanced back in shock. Holy hell! Was the entire length of his cock up her ass? Amazing! She flexed her ass cheeks, closing around him. Didn't feel bad at all. In fact, it felt pretty damn good.

He pulled out, but not all the way. "Feel good?"

His withdrawal was excruciatingly pleasurable. "Feels good," she agreed.

Herakles slid back in. At the same time, he reached around in front of her. A single finger of exploration easily found her insatiable clit. Pure unadulterated lust took off like a wildfire across a dry prairie, blazing viciously through her. A gasping cry escaped her lips. She bucked against his hips.

One hand working her sex, the other on her hip, he settled down to serious work. The salacious delight attacking her ass warred with the equally lascivious pleasure thrumming through her clit. So much, so fast. Such intense torment was almost too much for one body to bear.

Dani panted, shuddering uncontrollably "Harder. I want to feel every inch." Her breasts joggled wildly each time he penetrated her, stretched her. His size dazzled her senses. Short brutal strokes reached all the way to the back of her throat. The keening tension of orgasm coiled into knots in her groin.

"You will." Shoving his fingers deep inside her sheath, he simultaneously slammed her with a long steady lunge from behind.

Filled to the brim with hard cock, and plundering fingers,

Dani trembled under the blitz of pure erotic sensation. A sound started down in her throat, working its way up as he pounded her from behind, loosening a cry that said she was on fire with passion. Blazing sensations emanated outward from the center of her core.

Sensing her tension, Herakles jacked harder. His hips slammed against hers, the strike of naked skin on skin almost as ferocious as the storm raging outside. "Come for me," he growled. No mercy and no stopping. He was going to run her down like a freight train without brakes.

Dani shuddered when a ferocious explosion sent her into heavenly glory. Wave after wave of pleasure spun through her head. The rush was so intense, so utterly overwhelming that Dani vanished completely into the wonderful abyss of pleasure. Body arching in fierce response, a million sparking rockets seemed to take flight all around her. Every sensation dazzled and awed.

Bellowing like an angry bull, Herakles followed her into the yawning precipice. Hips locked together, their bodies became one when his cock surged inside her. Every muscular inch of him trembled as he filled her with a stream of hot semen.

Dani pressed lips together tightly, struggling to make the sensations last just a moment longer. Climaxing once with a cock inside her was incredible. Climaxing twice, with ass and cunt stuffed, was a fucking miracle.

They collapsed in a heap, arms and legs all tangled. Herakles cuddled her close. Pleasantly sated from their physical exertions, Dani lay in his embrace. Her rear was sore, but not unpleasantly so.

He kissed her sweaty forehead. "Good?"

Dani stretched languorously. "Better than good. Excellent."

His gaze caught hers. "How do you feel?"

She grinned. A no-brainer there. "Stretched, pummeled, and

pounded." Her abandoned wine glass beckoned, still half-full. "And thirsty."

Reaching over him, she scooped up the glass and tipped it gratefully to her mouth. Sweet but lukewarm wine cascaded across her tongue and down her throat, soothing the dry rasp from so many heavy moans and groans. She sighed with satisfaction and drank some more.

Herakles captured her glass before she'd finished its contents. "Don't be a glutton," he said, finishing off the last of the dregs.

Dani crawled over him, reclaiming the bottle she'd earlier left on the coffee table. "Plenty left." She refilled the glass. "And more where that came from in the fridge. I'm well stocked up on the vino."

He took another healthy drink. "Good for thirst, but not for hunger. Something to eat would be most welcome." He licked his lips. "I have a craving for something that will fill me as well as fornication sates me."

Mentally rifling through her fridge and cabinets, Dani silently groaned. What to serve a god? She had nothing suitable and couldn't imagine pawning off her usual staple: a frozen low-cal meal and a container of yoghurt. Feeding a hungry visitor was something she hadn't planned on.

She gulped and racked her mind. "I think I could manage an omelet," she ventured, wondering if she even had eggs in the fridge. Damn. She just never cooked. She'd always paid someone to do the cooking and cleaning so she could work.

He sipped more wine. "Sounds uninspiring."

Oh, great. "So suggest something," she ventured, hoping he wouldn't ask for anything more than a bowl of cereal.

He yawned and stretched. "We'll go to my place."

Dani caught her breath, unsure she'd heard him right. "Your, uh, what?"

His smile broadened. "My place."

"Where is, um, your place?"

"Mount Olympus."

She stared at him, a mass of disbelief. Her dream was taking a strange turn, from unreal to surreal. "You're kidding?"

He climbed to his feet. "Of course not."

She shook his head in confusion. "I can't. You're not real."

"You can," he urged, smiling. "Because here I am a god."

"Inside my dream," she countered.

His smile took on a beatific dimension. "Dreams are a reality within themselves, an astral plane where gods can walk freely and dragons can breathe fire. When you are in the netherworld between waking and sleep, it is all real."

Spooky. Rationalizing a dream while having—a dream.

Logic need not apply, she thought wryly.

He reached for her again. "If you want to come with me, now is that time."

Well, hell. Who wouldn't want to?

Dani lifted her hand. Strong fingers curled around hers. Herakles pulled her to her feet as though she weighed only ounces. "Look behind you now," he urged, "and you will see."

Slowly, as if fearing what she would find when she turned, Dani pivoted on her heel. There, behind her was herself; peacefully stretched out in front of the fire, snoring softly in a wine-induced stupor.

Unable to believe her eyes, she looked down. Yes, there was still a body beneath her. She could see feet, legs, a torso, breasts. She raised his hands, clenching her fists. To her own senses she seemed solid enough.

How can I be here . . . She looked at her sleeping figure. *Yet still undisturbed there?*

For the first time she noticed Herakles wore clothing, however little. A loincloth covered his groin and leather sandals covered his feet. She, on the other hand, was still very much naked.

"Hey, how come I haven't got any clothes on? Shouldn't I be dressed in—" She indicated her nude form. "Something?"

Smirking, Herakles eyed her from head to foot. "Naked is how I like you." His answer was very much tongue in cheek.

Dani put her foot down. "Clothes, or I stay home."

He waved a hand. A loincloth solidified around her hips. "Satisfied?"

"My tits," she prompted. "What do you think of them hanging out?"

He grinned. "I like them very much." Nevertheless, a brief leather binding settled around her chest. Altogether, the outfit looked like some kind of designer bikini. She was still barefoot, but two out of three wasn't bad.

"Now we can go."

Herakles's merry laugh drew her eyes back to him. He spread his arms as if welcoming her. "Come to me."

Drawn to him, Dani took a step forward. Herakles's big figure grew more distant, gesturing, inviting her to follow. What did he really want of her? Dare she follow him?

Herakles gestured again, floating farther away, teasing her to pursue him. Utterly impossible for Dani to resist. She experienced a sense of urgency, of compulsion in his tone. His vanishing figure continued to entice her. Come closer. She found the invitation intriguing. What would she find if he followed? What secrets and mysteries lurked in his world?

Whatever they might be, Dani was determined to find out if she could.

I can do this. Though where the notion came from, she didn't know. It popped into her mind and she knew as surely as the sun rose in the sky that she could, indeed, follow him. It seemed incredible. And even though she knew she must be dreaming, she felt as though she were wide awake. The beating of her heart, the air she drew into her lungs. How could she be asleep, yet so aware at the same time?

I can only find out if I try.

She took a step forward, then another, gliding through the wall as though it didn't exist. Before she knew what had happened she was enveloped in waves of pure white light that dazzled around her in the most alarming manner. The rays clutched at her, drawing her into the depths of no return.

For a moment, she felt as though she were rising, expanding toward the ceiling of her apartment, passing through it to touch a far-flung universe. Her soul fluttered on an invisible breeze, a wraith of energy shimmering as lightly as a snowflake in chilly air.

She sensed a male presence beside her. Herakles. He was with her, guiding her.

Suddenly, Dani's senses shifted and light and sound seemed to fuse, twisting and contorting into an indescribable blending of her pulse and the hot darkness of the sorcerer's heart. The power she was to embrace was a vast one . . . endless . . . eternal.

She panicked, trying to step back, but grasping fingers pulled at her, refusing to let go. She seemed to be traveling at a great speed through a whirling vortex of pure energy.

The end of their travels came as suddenly as they had begun.

7

The white light abruptly faded.

Dazed and confused, fighting to keep her balance amid the dizziness that made her head swim and her knees wobble, Dani blinked. It took only seconds for her to realize she no longer stood in her own living room. No, this arrangement was nowhere near her modern contemporary arrangement and decor. This was ancient. Way more ancient.

And maybe not even in the same universe.

The chamber she found herself in appeared to be carved out of pure crystal.

"*Impossible.*"

To convince herself it was real, Dani reached out, touching the nearest wall. Cool and smooth, it felt very solid beneath her fingertips.

Standing beside her, Herakles grinned down at her. "Very possible." He slid a familiar hand across her shoulder, caressing the nape of her neck. "What do you think?"

Looking every which way, Dani fought to swallow the lump building in her throat. The place was almost too damned awesome for description. The huge multilevel chamber was walled with tall columns supporting a high ceiling. In the exact center of the ceiling was a large circular window that allowed the silvery rays of the sun to bathe the rooms in warm natural illumination. The sun's light bestowed a strange and elusively luminous quality to the chambers. Instead of a bright glare, the crystal somehow reflected shades of soothing hues. Very peaceful and restful.

"It's magnificent," she whispered, as though the sound of her voice would somehow shatter the magnificent illusion.

Pleased, Herakles nodded. "I thought you would like it."

"I do," she breathed. "Very much."

"Good." He urged her toward a long hallway. "If I am not mistaken, a feast is about to begin."

With Herakles in the lead, Dani passed into an enclosed court. A hive of activity met them. Men and women lounged, enjoying the lazy languor of the day.

Dani couldn't help but notice that both sexes were immodestly stripped. Her jaw dropped at the way the people touched and caressed each other, some making outright love.

Her body tensed in familiar remembrance. The thought of Herakles's cock entering her caused a curious sensation in her belly. The muscles inside her vagina rippled and a honey-like warmth spread between her thighs.

Two women greeted them at the entrance. Barefoot, they were dressed in scanty clothing, brief bindings of material around their breasts and waists. Just like hers. Twins, they were very fair with long blond hair, soft doe-brown eyes and full red lips. Both were lithe with full breasts and hips. Smiling with joy, they moved with the careless grace of young lionesses.

Herakles made the introductions with a smile. "Calliope and Clio."

Bowing their heads, they simultaneously made a gesture over their hearts.

"Welcome, brother, from your journeys," Clio greeted in a singsong voice.

"You bring a stranger," Calliope piped in. A mischievous smile split her lips. "Tell us of your newest love."

Herakles laughed. "A goddess herself. One who has cast my image in stone. To her I have promised many rewards."

Another deep bow from the twins.

"An artist of rare talent," Clio said delightedly. "We bid you welcome to our home. It is an honor to serve you this day."

Dani smiled in relief, feeling the butterflies in her stomach settle a little. Uncertain of protocol, she said a simple, "Thank you."

"We've come to be fed." Slipping one huge arm around her waist, Herakles patted her rear with a sly hand. "My appetites are many this day, most yet unsated. Bring food, bring wine." He winked down at Dani. "And bring her when she is ready."

Dani's brows shot up in surprise. What the fuck? Surely he wasn't planning to walk off and leave her. This was her dream, damn it. She was supposed to be the one in control.

Apparently things worked differently on Mount Olympus.

"You're l-leaving me here?" she stammered.

"To be bathed and oiled." He eyed her from head to toe. "After that, we shall feast. On food—and on each other." His grin left nothing to the imagination.

Dani hesitated. Having him in her dream was one thing. Having two strange women enter it was another. Maybe now would be the time to wake up. She pinched her cheek, then gave her face a little slap. Ouch! That hurt. As far as she knew she was an incorporeal being, but one still possessing all the sensations of a corporeal being.

Once again logic didn't seem to apply.

Herakles raised his brows. Everyone looked at her like she'd lost her freaking mind.

She thought about his arrival, their intense lovemaking. The ache between her thighs certainly *felt* real enough.

Dani drew a long breath, then exhaled. "Ho-kay, I guess I'm always up for a swim."

Herakles bent, giving her a kiss and a wink. "It'll be good," he promised. "Very good. Clio and Calliope will treat you well." Secure in his control, Herakles padded off like a lion, king of his jungle. He vanished down yet another long corridor.

Dani watched him go. Her dream had taken a curious turn.

Calliope slipped her hand confidently into Dani's. "Come this way, my lady," she said pertly.

Clio took her other hand. "So that we may prepare you."

Dani went acquiescently with the girls, thinking secretly that she wished she were a man, for the twins were the prettiest creatures she'd ever seen. On more than one occasion she'd entertained ideas of a lesbian affair, but had never had the nerve to follow through. What would it be like to be caressed by a woman? She had no doubt the sisters were most skillful in sexual play. Just thinking of their touch, she felt excitement building, imagining how Calliope would suckle and tease her breasts with her tongue or how Clio would nibble at her clit as she pushed her fingers deep into her sex.

The bath chamber held a large oval of clear shimmering water, a buoyant and effulgent cerulean pool beneath a low arched ceiling of bone-white alabaster and floored with blue-veined white marble. The thick and pungent smoke of woody cinnamon-tinged incense eddied over the water. The light from dozens of dark blue crystals flickered like a thousand eyes upon its calm surface, creating a sense of twilight and the impression that one had stepped into a glorious heaven. The soft music of flutes and other stringed instruments drifted in the air, proficiently played by a trio of nubile young men positioned discreetly nearby.

Walking to the pool, Dani saw the water was crystalline, clean and pure. Stripping off the leather bindings covering her breasts and hips, she gazed into it, searching its depths. Acting as a mirror, the pool reflected back her image. Her reflection mesmerized. Forehead high, eyes evenly spaced, straight nose, full lips. Her eyes were a strange hue; green flecked with gold. Her skin was a pale, milky white.

She stood, trying not to shiver, not from cold but from nerves. Of the three, she stood the tallest.

Calliope sensed her tension. She reached out a soothing hand, stroking Dani's arm in a familiar manner. "Are you ready, to bathe?"

Forcing herself to unclench her teeth and smile, Dani nodded. "Yes, I am. Thank you."

Taking off her own bindings, Calliope guided her down, descending the stairs that led into the pool. The water wasn't deep, going only to her knees. A gentle hand on her shoulder guided her to her knees, bringing the water to the height of her breasts. Warm currents vibrated around her.

Clio hovered nearby, holding small silver bowls. When she passed them to Calliope, Dani caught the scent of chamomile and mint. Familiar enough, almost too much so. Her very own brand of shampoo, one that nourished and highlighted blond hair.

Calliope wet her hair, washing it with long mesmerizing strokes of her fingers.

Head dropping back, Dani closed her eyes, relishing the pleasure of a tingling scalp. "God, that feels so good."

"I'm glad you are pleased. You will be as sweet as a baby's kiss when we are done with you." Calliope dunked her head under the water.

Dani came up spluttering and laughing. "I'd much rather have Herakles's kisses."

Without a word, Calliope reached out, palming and cupping the weight of Dani's bare breast. "I see why he finds you so pleasing," she murmured.

Dani felt her nipples hardening with excitement. Hot breath rasped her lips.

Calliope's tongue snaked out and circled the delicate bud experimentally. "I, too, know your deepest fantasies." She suckled softly at the little nubbin, teasing it with soft nips, then drawing on it with sexually charged intent. Her free hand rose, caressing Dani's other breast.

Dani felt a tremor in her stomach. A shiver of anticipation traveled through her, ushering in that familiar heat of desire. As the sensations of arousal spread through her, her clit began to pulse, to ache with the need to be stroked. Her thighs were taut, the water between her legs sensuously mixing with the liquid warmth flowing from her hungry sex. The muscles deep inside her vagina contracted, waiting for penetration.

Kissing the hollow between Dani's breasts, Calliope lifted her head, flashing a wicked grin. "Do you enjoy my touch?"

Skin flushing, Dani's skin suddenly felt too tight to fit over her bones. "Yes."

Calliope's hand slid down her belly, fingers sliding between Dani's legs. Her fingers found the soft petals jealously guarding the tender jewel.

Using only the tip of her finger, she caressed Dani's clit, whispering, "Let me please you before my brother takes you away from me." Her finger flicked at the tender tip in a slow but deliberate motion.

Dani could moan her reply. She bit her lip and shuddered when Calliope slowly penetrated her sex.

"Careful," she warned Calliope between gritted teeth. "I might come right now." In a bold move, her lips covered Calliope's, emitting a breathy little moan as her hands clenched a handful of Calliope's soft hair.

Dani pulled her close, inhaling her clean scent. As a sculptor she loved the soft curves and round plains of a woman's body. She'd often wanted to explore alternate sexualities. Now she had that chance.

Calliope nibbled at her lips, licking them as though they were as succulent as sun-warmed honey. "I hope you do." She grinned, delighted.

Dani panted through her mouth, back arching. It was her turn to moan aloud with pleasure. A combination of tranquil warmth and passionate sexual need pulsed throughout her body.

Calliope's finger slipped in and out of Dani's clenching sex. At the same time her tongue laved a jutting nipple.

Dani's hips rocked motion. The friction was almost too much to take. A series of tiny quakes engulfed her, small waves that gradually became frantic convulsions. The agony was so prolonged, so exquisite that she wanted to cry out for faster, deeper, more penetrating thrusts.

An intense rush of liquid heat submerged her without warning, a tidal wave totally beyond her control. Trembling uncontrollably, her hands dug into Calliope's shoulders. She screamed out as the hard crash of climax swamped her.

The two women remained locked together for a moment, the water lapping at their skin. Calliope's fingers slid from Dani's sex. She gave Dani a quick kiss. "You are well pleased, I hope."

Body shuddering with gratification, Dani drew a breath into thoroughly scorched lungs. "Very pleased," she panted. Legs shaking, she let Calliope lead her from the pool.

Clio came forward with a thick linen towel to pat the water from her skin. She smiled. "My turn to attend you."

Dani nearly swooned. She didn't know if she could take much more.

Kneeling, Clio began at Dani's feet and made her way up. An exquisite and sensual feeling to be pampered in such a luxurious way. A soft sigh escaped her parted lips. "This is heaven," she sighed.

Clio discarded the damp towel. "You are our brother's chosen. To please you is to please him." She took Dani's hand and led her toward a low stone bench. "Sit, please."

Another woman briefly flitted in, offering a silver chalice perched on a tray. "It is our pleasure to serve," she said with a bow.

Dani took a sip from the chalice, rolling the rich burgundy wine over her tongue before swallowing. Ah. Just what she needed. She took a larger sip, and then another until the cup was emptied. Thirsty, she didn't protest when the cup was filled a second, then a third time.

Kneeling, Clio dipped her hand into a small jar and rubbed scented oil into Dani's skin.

Calliope circled behind her, a pick in her hand to untangle the snarls from Dani's wet hair. "Perhaps when you are choosing your attendants, you will remember us." She worked one section at a time until not a tangle was to be found.

Dani smiled agreeably, head spinning a bit from the potent wine. She couldn't remember the last time she'd eaten a meal. She felt dazed, dizzied, weightless, as if she floating in a pleasant haze. "I didn't know I was going to be staying that long."

Clio worked her hands up Dani's legs, spreading her thighs so that her hooded clit was exposed. "You could stay forever."

Dani sighed and sipped more wine. "I wish."

"Wishes can come true," Calliope hinted coyly.

Clio placed a light kiss on the inside of Dani's leg. A thrill went through her from her fingertips to her toes. "Just dream." She continued to spread the oil, her strong hands massaging each and every tense muscle that came under her exploring fingers.

After her skin was oiled and her hair arranged in damp curls, the twins offered up a final gift, something Dani immediately recognized from her own studies of ancient Greece, a chiton. A kind of tunic fashioned from two rectangles of fabric, it fastened together along the shoulder and arms, then belted at the waist.

Dani danced a quick twirl, enjoying the feel of the silky material brushing against her skin. She might as well have been naked, though. The sheer design hid nothing, but enhanced everything.

"So this is dressing to eat dinner?"

The girls giggled and rolled their eyes. "Only if you are to be dessert," Clio warned with a grin.

8

The twins led Dani down another hallway and drew back a curtain to admit her into yet another antechamber, one of the inner private courts. One entire wall was a great window looking out over a breathtaking view of wide lawns, perfectly groomed gardens of exotic blooms and marble fountains. Physical perfection, beauty, and talent were not only expected, but demanded.

Goblet in hand, Herakles reclined on a low backless couch. Overspread with an abundance of thick furs and soft pillows, the lounge looked wide enough to accommodate several occupants. A wooden bench-type table sat beside it. The spread of food laid out upon it was magnificent.

Seeing her, he grinned. "Ah, my goddess has arrived." He sipped his wine. "I had thought my sisters had nabbed you to keep for themselves."

Entranced by his cheeky grin, Dani felt heat creep into her cheeks. Trying to be diplomatic, she cleared her throat. "The twins certainly entertained me well."

Herakles laughed and tossed off a saucy wink. "Knowing Clio and Calliope, they entertained you in the most salacious ways." Stretched out in leisure, he was a magnificent carnal beast.

A magnificently *naked* carnal beast. He clearly didn't spend much time clothed.

Dani blushed hotter, sure her cheeks were fire-engine red. Joining him on the lounge, she felt overdressed. "Most salaciously," she agreed.

"All of which has added to your appetite, I hope." Herakles scooted over to make room, guiding her over his body so she faced the food. He handed her a goblet filled almost to the brim.

Accepting the cup, Dani sat up and crossed her legs, lotus style. "Definitely." She drank down a healthy swallow of wine. Rich and potent it rolled down her throat like the rarest of nectars. "I'm starving."

Rolling over on his side, Herakles propped himself up on one elbow, and tucked his body against hers so that her rear was planted firmly against his groin. "Then you will not be disappointed." The heat radiating from his cock promised her dessert would certainly be sweet.

But that was for later.

Stomach growling, Dani eyed the food. She couldn't remember the last time she'd had a decent meal, especially one so mouth-wateringly scrumptious. Silver platters were loaded to the brim with delicacies. A loaf of dark bread, wedges of smooth yellow cheese and olives were joined by bowls of plump grapes, slices of succulent melon and, heaven be praised, juicy strawberries.

"Looks good to me."

Herakles reached out and selected a grape. He popped it into his mouth. "The best to be had."

Dani picked up a knife, slicing off a hunk of crusty bread. Still warm from the ovens that had produced it, the heavenly scent of stone-ground barley. She added a piece of cheese, fashioning an impromptu sandwich. The bread was crusty, chewy with a delicious nutty flavor. It tasted wonderful with the wine to wash it down.

The food disappeared, devoured by two hungry people.

Watching her stuff her face, Herakles's lips parted into a mischievous grin. "You eat like you fuck," he teased.

Swallowing her last bite, Dani took a deep drink of wine. A warm glow settled in her belly. "Is that good?"

"An appetite for the pleasures of life is always good."

Dani patted her stomach. "I'm stuffed, but those strawberries look so damn tasty."

Herakles sat up and reached for a berry. He guided it to her mouth. "Try just one." His eyes never left her lips.

Dani leaned forward and bit into the juicy fruit. She closed her eyes, chewing slowly to savor all the flavors. "It's delicious."

"Not half so much as you are." There was a suggestive rumble behind his words.

She opened her eyes to find Herakles staring at her. The intensity in his gaze sent a shiver down her spine, renewing her need and anticipation all over again. She smiled. "I could use another."

He claimed another berry. This time he teased her by squeezing it so the juice would dribble on her lips. A few drops missed, dribbling down her chin.

She laughed. "Goodness, you missed."

Herakles leaned forward. "I didn't miss." His tongue gently traced her top lip, swiping away the droplets before his mouth covered hers.

Dani couldn't resist letting momentum take over. He tasted of yeasty bread and fragrant cheese, not altogether unpleasant. She leaned in closer, succumbing to desire. Her whole body tingled, breasts swelling into tight peaks that longed for his lips to suckle them.

Herakles nuzzled her neck, his hot moist breath tickling her skin. He traced slow circles around the hard little bead poking through her chiton, even as he grasped an earlobe gently between his teeth and tugged. "You taste as good as you look."

Dani gasped as erotic sensations traveled through her stomach, echoing the liquid trickle between her thighs. Waves of longing crashed through her, intensifying the sweetest of pains.

Herakles caressed the curve under her chin. "I want you all over again."

A wicked imp landed on her shoulder, whispering naughty things in her ear. She was definitely ready to begin exploring. The imp cackled with delicious glee when she tipped back her head and opened herself up.

She smiled her challenge. "Then take me all over again. Any way you want."

A wicked brow cocked. His hand snaked between revealing folds of sheer material. Thick fingers searched for and found her left nipple. He rolled and tugged at the erect nubbin. "I can think of many ways I'd like to take you."

Dani let out of whoosh of breath. All rational thoughts fled her mind. All she was aware of was the slow circles going around the sensitive pink areola. Her skin rippled in anticipation, the way a cat's does when awakened from its sleep. "I think you're doing that now." Their bodies were rigid with need; sexual tension crackled in the air around them.

Herakles urged her back on the soft furs. "I'm trying." Experienced male hands began to caress her arms, shoulders, and breasts. Heart beating, chest rising and falling with each breath, the musky smell of their flesh tickled her nostrils.

She closed her eyes, determined to welcome every sensation.

"Oh, my," she gasped through trembling lips when Herakles brushed the soft hollow of her throat with his lips. She was still dizzied by the lingering effects of the wine, and her world began to spin in slow motion. She was hardly conscious of a strong hand over her Venus mound, sifting through the silky material and parting her legs.

His mouth covered one nipple, drawing the hard tip deeply into his mouth. At the same time, thick fingers moved slowly against the folds around her clit, the small bud pulsing as he massaged it sensuously. Each time he flicked his fingers over the little button, her heart fluttered, her insides tightened, and a flash of pure heat surged through her. A flood of creamy juices spilled from her body.

Whimpering, Dani squirmed with delightful agony. Her skin felt luminous, glowing, and vibrant. With each beat of her heart, the blood pulsing through her veins, her passion grew heated—verging on the point of desperation.

It was one thing to be caressed by a woman's hand, quite another to be touched by a man. The instinct of a female seeking—no, needing—a male was never stronger in her than it was now. She luxuriated in his touch, in the hard cock pressed so intimately against her. The heated length of his erection lay along her hip, searing her with the carnal nudges of steel encased in skin.

Without a second thought, Dani moved her own hand toward his body, feeling for and then finding his erection. Fingers wrapping around his shaft, she gently jacked up and down its length. Sheer male power radiated from his cock. "God, you feel so good," she murmured.

His mouth captured hers again, beginning the tongue-tangling all over again. She closed her eyes, imagining his body on top of hers, his hips between her spread legs as he positioned his body to enter hers. There would be no hesitation. His thrust inside her would be swift and sure.

Herakles groaned. "Harder. It's not made out of glass."

Dani laughed low in her throat. "Any harder and I'll pull it off."

His gaze lit up with delight. "I don't think I could take that kind of excitement." He treated her to a sexy grin. "As for the touching—" His palm slid down over her flat belly. The glide of his fingers against her most sensitive flesh sent red-hot darts of flame though her every nerve ending.

"My God," she gasped. "That feels wonderful."

Dani melted when he began long slow strokes followed by the short teasing flicks of his fingers. Without her hardly knowing, she spread her legs wider, cursing the confines of her skirt. Her hips bucked upward.

Herakles knew her needs without asking. After all, he was a god. He slipped two fingers inside her. Her vagina rippled around his fingers. His thumb expertly worked her clit. The sensations of his hard digit against her softness made her crave something harder, driving her over the edge into an abyss of pure pleasure.

Caught on the edge of a moan, Dani shuddered. Her stomach muscles clenched as she cried out. Her cunt squeezed his fingers and held them.

His compelling gaze strayed to hers. "I love to hear you whimper," he teased.

Grinding her hips against his fingers as he thrust, she fought to get her words out between moans. "Damn you. Don't stop now." He'd ignited a burning lust inside her, and she wasn't going to be satisfied until she felt his cock ramming into her.

Herakles suddenly pulled his hand away, tracing his creamed fingers across her mouth. "To damn a god is blasphemy . . ."

Dani tasted her own sweet fragrance. She licked her lips. "I'll take the damnation if it'll get you to hurry up and fuck me."

His eyes widened in fake shock. "So a double fuck with an ass-reaming wasn't enough?"

Frustrated, she wound her fingers through his luxuriously thick hair, ridiculously resplendent with curls most women would envy. "Not by a long shot, buster." Face-to-face, she flicked her tongue against his upper lip.

Chuckling at her bravado, his hands moved to her breasts, cupping and squeezing them. "You're insatiable."

Throat tight with tension and need, Dani whimpered, wanting him to penetrate her. He was holding off, torturing her. She felt dizzy from her awareness of him, from her over-responsiveness to him. Even now she was completely unable to control her body's physical compulsion for intimacy with him, unable to control the soft melting sensations within her soul.

"Then please do," she invited with a grin. "You've fed me. Now it's time to fuck me."

He pretended exasperation. "Women. So damned demanding."

She grinned up at him. "Got a complaint? Take it up with management."

"With the owner of such a delectable pussy?" Rolling over onto his back, Herakles pulled her up over his body to straddle his hips. Gripping his penis in one hand, he stroked it a couple of times, then guided its swollen purple crown against her slit.

"I certainly intend to have an—" He impaled her with a quick thrust. "In-depth discussion."

In depth? Indeed.

Dani's reply vanished, morphing into a long moan. His cock penetrated deep, stretching her every which way. And then some. The tightening of muscles, the tensing of nerves was a wonderful sensation. Stunned and surprised, she let herself go with the moment.

He gazed up at her. "Ah, now I know what will make a woman speechless."

Firmly seated, Dani leaned forward, giving him access to her breasts. Her clit was swollen, poking between her lips to rub against the base of his erection.

Oh, yes. Just right.

"I won't be quiet for long." She gyrated her hips in a long slow motion. "A girl just has to scream when she's got a cock like this shoved inside her."

"Scream away." Guiding her through long slow strokes, Herakles set into motion a relentless friction that was both pleasurable and excruciating. They were coming together, the completion of a destiny both had been waiting for, but yet were unaware of.

Dani's fingers dug into his shoulders. As she pushed back to meet his thrusts, a tiny frisson of sensation coiled through her. "That's a hell of a lot of cock you have there." She welcomed the ache.

Herakles grinned and thrust his hips upward, impaling her like a moth on a pin. "There's a lot more where that came from."

In retaliation, she raked her nails down his musclebound arms. Inner muscles tight, she lifted her hips, then sank back down with a body-shuddering slam. His eyes glazed as he savored the feel of her hips driving down on top of him.

One hand moved to her breast, squeezing, teasing the taut nipple. "I enjoy seeing a woman claim her pleasure."

Dani shuddered violently, her lips pressed together as she struggled to make the sensations last just a moment longer. "Glad you're entertained," she gritted.

She whimpered, faltered, then lost control of the pace, shock then pleasure turning her moans into primeval guttural cries. Red-hot pressure imploded in her belly, running like rivers of fire from the tip of her head to her toes. Her body shook violently, her moans mingling with his.

Herakles drove his cock into her a final time, then came hard. His huge body shuddered under her. Spurt after spurt of hot cum filled her.

Dani collapsed on top of him, trailing wet kisses along his neck and shoulder as she tried to catch her breath. For a long moment there was silence. Willpower alone slowed her breathing.

After a long moment she lifted herself up, looking into his eyes. Probing inside, she found an ache beneath her breastbone. She focused on it, searching. In a stunning moment, she realized that he completed her, made her a whole woman.

I don't want this night to end.

But she didn't want to think of that.

"I can't believe I'm still here," she whispered, kissing him again. "It's just a dream, I know, but I don't want to wake up."

Giving her a lazy smile, Herakles reached up, placing a single finger against her lips. "Then don't," he murmured in a sated voice. "Just lay here and rest."

She shook her head. "It'll all go away. I'll wake up and you'll be gone."

"I'll always be here," he promised. "Whether waking or sleeping, you'll know when I am near."

"Promise me that."

"Promise."

Laying her head against his strong shoulder, Dani sighed. If she listened hard enough she could almost hear the pulse of blood through his veins, the whisper of breath entering and leaving his body. His featherlight stroke trailed up and down her back, calming, soothing.

Lulled by food, wine, and good sex, she felt as if she were floating on air, her body buoyant, her mind untrammeled. "If wishes were horses," she murmured. "I'd have you forever." She closed her eyes, only meaning to doze for a few minutes.

In no time at all, Dani fell fast asleep.

9

Dani came back to consciousness with a shuddering jerk, dumping the last of her wine across her breasts as the glass she'd held precariously balanced in sleep escaped her lax fingers. The squishy sensation of liquid seeping over the front of her negligee snapped her eyes open. Awareness of her surroundings began to register.

"Shit," she muttered, knocking the glass aside. It rolled across the comforter. She must have fallen asleep, though she didn't remember dozing off. She hadn't really had that much to drink, just a few glasses of wine; enough to relax, not enough to get doddering drunk. Still she felt like hell, her body stiff from spending too many hours in one uncomfortable position.

Leaning forward, she cradled her head in her hands. She struggled to find her memory. Full awareness came slowly as images of Herakles drifted up to the forefront of her brain. The dream had seemed so real that she was half inclined to believe it had really happened.

Face it, Dani, you're alone and very damn frustrated.

She sat still through several long minutes, trying to sort

through the pieces lingering in her mind. It was so vivid, so real, that she would have sworn she'd really stepped out of her body and visited Mount Olympus.

Realizing she sat in a sodden negligee, she pushed herself off the floor, struggling to get up. She'd slept the night away and was more exhausted than ever.

"You're out of shape." She huffed, making her way to her bedroom. One step at a time. In the bathroom she twisted the cap off a small bottle of aspirin and popped two into her mouth, washing them down with a swig of water.

Yes, indeed. A quiet disintegration. Should have it printed on a T-shirt so she wouldn't forget it. Jesus, how she hated herself, her life, the brain in her head that was coiled too tightly. A ticking time bomb. Only instead of blowing up, she would simply wind down, and then there would be nothing.

She groaned and shook her head. She was in a strange mood, one hard to explain. She supposed it was a touch of depression, that slow erosion of acid eating through her psyche. Once again the faceless black specter was descending in her mind, beating its evil black wings. She wished she'd died when she'd tried to end her life. Maybe she would have if she'd gotten serious and done the job right.

Going insane, she mused, must feel like being dipped in honey. At first it was wonderful, but the deeper one became immersed, the more smothering the sensations became.

"Yeah." She grimaced at the bleary-eyed woman in the mirror and rubbed her face. "This killing time is going to get me. Can't last much longer." A sound that was half a laugh broke from her throat. It might have been a sob for all she knew.

Stripping off her gown and panties, she stepped into the shower and turned the right tap on to full blast. Cold water drenched her, giving her a shock. The best way to wake up, send the nasty shakes running.

When she could stand no more of the cold, she turned on

the hot tap and adjusted the water to a decent temperature. She washed off the stench of sticky wine and her own sour sweat. At least she felt human again.

Dani stayed in the shower until the water ran cold. Throwing on a pair of faded jeans and a T-shirt, she combed her hair and slicked it up into a ponytail. Hardly chic, but who cared?

The kitchen was her destination. Sexy dreams or not, she was positively ravenous. Too late for breakfast, too early for dinner, she settled on a cup of coffee and a cinnamon roll heated in the microwave. Not the healthiest diet, but who the hell cared? She gobbled down the sweet and helped herself to a second cup of pure caffeine. The sugar rush went straight to her head.

Cleaning up the living room, she noticed the batteries in her dildo had gone completely dead. The twinge between her thighs reminded her it had gotten quite a workout last night. Back into the drawer it went. Her negligee went into the hamper. So much for relaxing. All she felt was stiff and sore. Every muscle in her body ached.

No sign of the night's storm lingered in the early afternoon sky. The day was bright and clear. The sun twinkled in the sky, the promise of a new beginning in its warmth. A careworn world had been washed clean.

A new beginning? Maybe.

She could only take things one day at a time. She'd let her art isolate her. No longer. After twenty years in the business, it was time to seek new avenues. She thought about the two tickets in her desk. Why not grab Jack and take the damn vacation? They could both sunbathe on the beach and ogle sexy Mediterranean men.

Cup in hand, she drifted down into her studio. Flipping on the overhead lights, her gaze settled on Herakles. The statue stood as she'd left it, immobile and unmoving.

Dani sighed. Last night she'd wished him alive. "Well, Herk," she said, giving his massive figure a nod. "I guess not even a god can break out of stone."

She didn't recall becoming aware of the presence. It was suddenly just there. At first, she didn't see anything. Rather, she felt it. The presence was not in any one spot in the room, but something gradually surrounding her, like the air she breathed. It wasn't frightening or menacing. She just had the uncanny impression that something was about to happen.

The buzzing of the doorbell shattered her strange feeling.

Her brow wrinkled in annoyance. Who the hell could that be? She wasn't expecting anyone.

Fumbling with the latch, she pulled the heavy door open. Jack Wilde stood, waiting.

"About time," he said. "I've been ringing you for the last ten minutes."

Dani sipped lukewarm coffee. "Wasn't expecting company, Jack. You said Monday. Today's Saturday."

Jack waved a hand. "I know," he said chirpily. "But we've got the chance for a full spread in *Modern Art* magazine, and I just had to grab it. I've got one of their photographers with me. Nick just happened to be in town. I ran into him at dinner last night and told him everything about—"

Dani gritted her teeth and cut him off. "Here? Now? Shit! I wasn't ready to show him . . ."

Jack cut her off. "No worries. Nick's just here to get a few shots of Herakles to e-mail off to his editors. It's close, but we're thinking we can get a sneak peek into next month's issue. Later we'll iron out the interview details."

"You just couldn't wait, could you?"

Jack's smile was disingenuous. "Nope." He turned, motioning to the man still sitting in his car. "Nick? Over here," he called.

The stranger got out of the car and joined them. Rays from

the midday sun touched his hair, subtly highlighting the golden-brown shade. Worn in a long shaggy style, his hair brushed his shoulders. The closer he got, the better he looked, a model perfect example of the male sex. Almost too handsome to be a living, breathing man. A white Oxford, unbuttoned at the neck, crisp slacks, and tan boots outfitted his masculine frame.

Dani's breath caught in a hitch and heavy awareness pulsed through her veins. In that moment she would have sworn her Herakles had stepped down from his pedestal, so striking was the resemblance.

She blinked. *Impossible.*

She looked again. *Possible.* The resemblance was almost too close to be mere coincidence.

In danger of sensual overload so early in the day, Dani drew a deep breath to still the tremors of awareness flowing through her veins. No man had ever affected her in such a purely physical way.

Beaming like a proud papa, Jack Wilde happily made the introductions. "Danicia, meet Nikandros Makricosta. Nick, this is the fabulously talented and beautiful woman I was telling you about."

Stepping forward, Nikandros Makricosta smiled. Straight white teeth flashed against darkly tanned skin. "Sorry to disturb you, but Jack insisted." He looked her over her from head to foot, obviously taking in every inch. His gaze, steady on her face, slipped to her breasts, then lower, inching toward her hips. He was confident in his appraisal, his penetrating eyes unblinking in his examination.

Stomach clenching, Dani couldn't imagine what sparked his interest. She looked like something the cat puked up. He, however, looked perfect in every way. His eyes crinkled at the corners. Strands of pure silver threaded his temples. He was old enough to know better, but young enough to try.

Hmm, later thirties or early forties. Just the right age for her.

Mouth going bone dry, she managed a shaky smile and offered her hand. "It's still nice to meet you, Mister Makricosta."

His hand came out. Another devastating smile followed. "The pleasure is all mine. I've been an admirer of your work for quite a few years."

A charge of static electricity buzzed straight to the center of her heart. His skin was warm, his touch possessive and confident. "Thank you."

Her guest clearly felt the same thing. "Call me Nick, please." he said in his low sexy voice. "I told Jack we should leave you alone, but he insisted."

"That's Jack," she quipped, feigning nonchalance. "Always wanting things yesterday.

Eyes twinkling with mischief, his gaze raked over her again in an intimate way, a way that said he knew every inch of her. "You must excuse me for being rude, but I have the strangest feeling that I *know* you."

As he spoke, an invisible current pulsed between them. Time stood still. The outside world with all its cares and troubles seemed to drop away. Everything morphed into a weird and distant blur. For a moment only the two of them existed.

A familiar voice whispered in her mind: *Wishes can come true when you believe.*

Dani smiled in total agreement. "I think we've met before," she murmured softly. "In fact I'm sure of it."

Somehow, her wish had been granted. No other explanation could possibly make sense. It didn't matter, though.

She had her Herakles.

In living, breathing flesh.

Compelling and extraordinarily sensual . . .
Don't miss Dawn Thompson's LORD OF THE DEEP,
available now from Aprhodisia.

1

The Isle of Mists, in the Eastern Archipelago,
Principalities of Arcus

Meg saw the seals from her window, their silvery coats rippling as they thrashed out of the sea and collected along the shore. She'd seen them sunning themselves on the rocks by day and had watched them frolic in the dusky darkness from that dingy salt-streaked window in her loft chamber many times since her exile to the island. But not like tonight, with their slick coats gleaming in the moonlight. Full and round, the summer moon left a silvery trail in the dark water that pointed like an arrow toward the creatures frolicking along the strand, lighting them as bright as day. Meg's breath caught in her throat. Behind, the high-curling combers crashing on the shore took on the ghostly shape of prancing white horses—pure illusion that disappeared the instant their churning hooves touched sand. In the foaming surf left behind, the seals began to shed their skins, revealing their perfect male and female nakedness. Meg gasped. It was magical.

Her heartbeat began to quicken. She inched nearer to the window until her hot breath fogged the glass. The nights were still cool beside the sea—too cool for cavorting naked in the moonlight. And where had the seals gone? These were humans, dark-haired, graceful men and women with skin like alabaster, moving with the undulant motion of the sea they'd sprung from in all their unabashed glory. They seemed to be gathering the skins they'd shed, bringing them higher toward the berm and out of the backwash.

Mesmerized, Meg stared as the mating began.

One among the men was clearly their leader. His dark wet hair, crimped like tangled strands of seaweed, waved nearly to his broad shoulders. Meg followed the moonbeam that illuminated him, followed the shadows collecting along the knife-straight indentation of his spine, defining the dimples above his buttocks and the crease that separated those firm round cheeks. The woman in his arms had twined herself around him like a climbing vine, her head bent back beneath his gaze, her long dark hair spread about her like a living veil.

All around them others had paired off, coupling, engaging in a ritualistic orgy of the senses beneath the rising moon, but Meg's eyes were riveted to their leader. Who could they be? Certainly not locals. No one on the island looked like these, like *him*, much less behaved in such a fashion. She would have noticed.

Meg wiped the condensation away from the windowpane with a trembling hand. What she was seeing sent white-hot fingers of liquid fire racing through her belly and thighs, and riveting chills loose along her spine. It was well past midnight, and the peat fire in the kitchen hearth below had dwindled to embers. Oddly, it wasn't the physical cold that griped her then, hardening her nipples beneath the thin lawn night smock and undermining her balance so severely she gripped the window ledge. Her skin was on fire beneath the gown. It was her finest. She'd worked the delicate blackwork embroidery on it herself.

It would have seen her to the marriage bed if circumstances had been different—if she hadn't been openly accused of being a witch on the mainland and been banished to the Isle of Mists for protection, for honing her inherent skills, and for mentoring by the shamans. But none of that mattered now while the raging heat was building at the epicenter of her sex—calling her hand there to soothe and calm engorged flesh through the butter-soft lawn . . . at least that is how it started.

She inched the gown up along her leg and thigh and walked her fingertips through the silky golden hair curling between, gliding them along the barrier of her virgin skin, slick and wet with arousal. She glanced below. But for her termagant aunt, who had long since retired, she was alone in the thatched roof cottage. It would be a sennight before her uncle returned from the mainland, where he'd gone to buy new nets and eel pots, and to collect the herbs her aunt needed for her simples and tisanes. Nothing but beach grass grew on the Isle of Mists.

Meg glanced about. Who was there to see? No one, and she loosened the drawstring that closed the smock and freed her aching breasts to the cool dampness that clung stubbornly to the upper regions of the dreary little cottage, foul weather and fair.

Eyes riveted to the strand, Meg watched the leader of the strange congregation roll his woman's nipples between his fingers. They were turned sideways, and she could see his thick, curved sex reaching toward her middle. Still wet from the sea they'd come from, their skin shone in the moonlight, gleaming as the skins they'd shed had gleamed. They were standing ankle deep in the crashing surf that spun yards of gossamer spindrift into the night. Meg stifled a moan as she watched the woman's hand grip the leader's sex, gliding back and forth along the rigid shaft from thick base to hooded tip. Something pinged deep inside her watching him respond . . . something urgent and unstoppable.

Her breath had fogged the pane again, and she wiped it away

in a wider swath this time. Her breasts were nearly touching it. Only the narrow windowsill kept them from pressing up against the glass, but who could see her in the darkened loft? No one, and she began rolling one tall hardened nipple between her thumb and forefinger, then sweeping the pebbled areola in slow concentric circles, teasing but not touching the aching bud, just as the creature on the beach had done to the woman in his arms.

Excruciating ecstasy.

While the others were mating fiercely all along the strand, the leader had driven his woman to her knees in the lacy surf. The tide was rising, and the water surged around him at mid-calf, breaking over the woman, creaming over her naked skin, over the seaweed and sand she knelt on as she took his turgid member into her mouth to the root.

Meg licked her lips expectantly in anticipation of such magnificence entering her mouth, responding to the caress of her tongue. She closed her eyes, imagining the feel and smell and taste of him, like sea salt bursting over her palate. This was one of the gifts that had branded her a witch.

When Meg opened her eyes again, her posture clenched. Had he turned? Yes! He seemed to be looking straight at her. It was almost as if he'd read her thoughts, as if he knew she was there all the while and had staged the torrid exhibition for her eyes alone to view. She couldn't see his face—it was steeped in shadow—but yes, there was triumph in his stance and victory in the posturing that took back his sex from the woman's mouth. His eyes were riveting as he dropped to his knees, spread the woman's legs wide to the rushing surf, and entered her in one slow, tantalizing thrust, like a sword being sheathed to the hilt, as the waves surged and crashed and swirled around them.

Still his shadowy gaze relentlessly held Meg's. For all her extraordinary powers of perception, she could not plumb the depths of that look as he took the woman to the rhythm of the waves lapping at them, laving them to the meter of his thrusts, like some giant beast with a thousand tongues. She watched the mystical surf horses trample them, watched the woman beneath him shudder to a rigid climax as the rising tide washed over her—watched the sand ebb away beneath the beautiful creature's buttocks as the sea sucked it back from the shore. All the while he watched her. It was as if she were the woman beneath him, writhing with pleasure in the frothy sea.

Captivated, Meg met the leader's silver-eyed gaze. She could almost feel the undulations as he hammered his thick, hard shaft into the woman, reaching his own climax. Meg groaned in spite of herself as he threw back his head and cried out when he came.

She should move away from the window . . . But why? He couldn't see what she was doing to herself in the deep darkness of the cottage loft . . . Could he? All at once it didn't matter. A hot lava flow of sweet sensation riddled her sex with pinpricks of exquisite agony. It was almost as if *he* were stroking her nipples and palpating the swollen nub at the top of her weeping vulva as she rubbed herself, slowly at first, then fiercely, until the thickening bud hardened like stone. She probed herself deeper. She could almost stretch the barrier skin and slip her finger inside, riding the silk of her wetness—as wet as the surging combers lapping relentlessly at the lovers on the beach. A firestorm of spasmodic contractions took her then, freeing the moan in her throat. It felt as if her bones were melting. Shutting her eyes, she shed the last remnants of modest restraint and leaned into her release.

The voyeuristic element of the experience heightened the orgasm, and it was some time before her hands gripped the windowsill again instead of tender flesh, and her gaze fell upon the strand below once more. But the silvery expanse of rockbound shoreline edged in seaweed stretching north and south as far as the eye could see was vacant. The strange revelers were gone!

Meg tugged the night shift back over her flushed breasts, though they ached for more stroking, and let the hem of the gown slide down her legs, hiding the palpitating flesh of her sex. Her whole body throbbed like a pulse beat, and she seized the thrumming mound between her thighs savagely through the gown in a vain attempt to quiet its tremors and made a clean sweep through the condensation on the window again. Nothing moved outside but the combers crashing on the strand. But for the echo of the surf sighing into the night, reverberating through her sex to the rhythm of fresh longing, all else was still.

No. She hadn't imagined it. The naked revelers mating on the beach had been real—as real as the seals that frequented the coast. Selkies? Could the shape-shifter legends be true? She'd heard little else since she came to the island.

Meg didn't stop to collect her mantle. Maybe the cool night air would cure the fever in her flesh. Hoisting up the hem of her night smock, she climbed down the loft ladder, tiptoed through the kitchen without making a sound, and stepped out onto the damp drifted sand that always seemed to collect about the door-sill. Nothing moved but the prancing white horses in the surf that drove it landward. Waterhorses? She'd heard that legend, too: innocent-looking creatures that lured any who would mount them to a watery death. Real or imaginary, it didn't matter. The people she'd just seen there having sex were real enough, and she meant to prove it.

The hard, damp sand was cold beneath her bare feet as she padded over the shallow dune toward the shoreline. The phantom horses had disappeared from the waves crashing on the strand, as had every trace that anyone had walked that way recently. There wasn't a footprint in sight, and the sealskins Meg had watched them drag to higher ground were nowhere to be seen, either.

Having reached the ragged edge of the surf, Meg turned and looked back at the cottage beyond, paying particular attention to her loft window. Yes, it was close, but there was no way anyone could have seen her watching from her darkened chamber. Then why was she so uneasy? It wasn't the first time she'd touched herself in the dark, and it wouldn't be the last, but it had been the best, and there was something very intimate about it. The man who had aroused her seemed somehow familiar, and yet she knew they'd never met. Still, he had turned toward that window and flaunted himself as if he knew she had been watching, exhibiting his magnificent erection in what appeared to be a sex act staged solely for her benefit. Moist heat rushed at her loins, ripping through her belly and thighs with the memory.

Meg scooped up some of the icy water and bathed the aching flesh between her thighs. She plowed through the lacy surf where the lovers had performed—to the very spot where the mysterious selkie leader had spent his seed—and tried to order the mixed emotions riddling her. Absorbed in thought, she failed to feel the vibration beneath her feet until the horse was nearly upon her. It reared back on its hind legs, forefeet pawing the air, its long tail sweeping the sand. A *real* horse this time, no illusion. Meg cried out as recognition struck. There was a rider on its back. He was naked and aroused. It was *him*, with neither bridle nor reins to control the beast, and nothing but a silvery sealskin underneath him.

He seemed quite comfortable in the altogether, as if it was the most natural thing in the world to sit a horse bareback, naked in the moonlight. She gasped. The horse had become quite docile, attempting to nuzzle her with its sleek white nose as it pranced to a standstill. She didn't want to look at the man on its back, but she couldn't help herself. He was a beguiling presence. As mesmerizing as he was from a distance, he was a hundred times more so at close range. Now she could see what the shadows had denied her earlier. His eyes, the color of mercury, were dark and penetrating, and slightly slanted. Somehow, she knew they would be. And his hair, while waving at a length to tease his shoulders in front, was longer in back and worn in a queue, tied with what appeared to be a piece of beach grass. How had she not noticed that before? But how could she have when he'd made such a display of himself face forward? Besides, her focus was hardly upon his hair.

Her attention shifted to the horse. At first she'd thought its mane and tail were black, but upon close inspection, she saw that they were white as snow, so tangled with seaweed they appeared black at first glance. But wait . . . What had she heard about white horses whose mane and tail collected seaweed? A waterhorse! The phantom creature of legend that seduced its victims to mount and be carried off to drown in the sea . . . But that was preposterous. Nevertheless, when its master reached out his hand toward her, she spun on her heels and raced back toward the cottage.

His laughter followed her, throaty and deep. Like an echo from the depths of the sea itself, it crashed over her just as the waves crashed over the shore. The sound pierced through her like a lightning bolt. The prancing waterhorse beneath him whinnied and clamped ferocious-looking teeth into the hem of her night shift, giving a tug that brought her to ground. She landed hard on her bottom, and the selkie laughed again as she cried out. Plucking her up as easily as if she were a broom straw, he settled her in front of him astride.

"You cannot escape me, Megaleen," he crooned in her ear. "You have summoned me, and I have come. You have no idea what it is that you have conjured—what delicious agonies you have unleashed by invoking me." His breath was moist and warm; it smelled of salt and the mysteries of the Otherworldly sea that had spawned him. "Hold on!" he charged, turning the horse toward the strand.

"Hold on to what?" Meg shrilled. "He has no bridle—no reins!"

Again his sultry voice resonating in her ear sent shivers of pleasure thrumming through her body. "Take hold of his mane," he whispered.

His voice alone was a seduction. He was holding her about the middle. Her shift had been hiked up around her waist when he settled her astride, and she could feel the thick bulk of his shaft throbbing against her buttocks, riding up and down along the cleft between the cheeks of her ass. The damp sealskin that stretched over the animal's back like a saddle blanket underneath her felt cool against Meg's naked thighs, but it could not quench the fever in her skin or douse the flames gnawing at the very core of her sex. The friction the waterhorse's motion created forced the wet sealskin fur deeper into her fissure, triggering another orgasm. Her breath caught as it riddled her body with waves of achy heat. She rubbed against the seal pelt, undulating to the rhythm of the horse's gait until every last wave had ebbed away, like ripples in a stream when a pebble breaks the water's surface.

In one motion, the selkie raised the night shift over her head and tossed it into the water. Reaching for it as he tore it away, Meg lost her balance. His strong hands spanning her waist prevented her from falling. Their touch seared her like firebrands, raising the fine hairs at the nape of her neck. The horse had plunged into the surf. It was heading toward the open sea, parting the unreal phantom horses galloping toward shore.

Salt spray pelted her skin, hardening her nipples. Spindrift dressed her hair with tiny spangles. The horse had plunged in past the breakers to the withers. Terrified, Meg screamed as the animal broke through the waves and sank to its muscular neck.

"Hold on!" he commanded.

"I cannot," Meg cried. "His mane . . . It is slippery with sea-weed."

All at once, he lifted her into the air and set her down facing him, gathering her against his hard, muscular body, his engorged sex heaving against her belly. How strong he was! "Then hold on to me," he said.

"W-who are you?" Meg murmured.

"I am called Simeon . . . amongst other things," he replied. "But that hardly signifies. . . ." Heat crackled in his voice. Something pinged in her sex at the sound of it.

He swooped down, looming over her. For a split second, she thought he was going to kiss her. She could almost taste the salt on his lips, in his mouth, on the tongue she glimpsed parting his teeth . . . But no. Fisting his hand in the back of her waist-length sun-painted hair, he blew his steamy breath into her nostrils as the horse's head disappeared beneath the surface of the sea.

Meg's last conscious thought before sinking beneath the waves in the selkie's arms was that she was being seduced to her death; another orgasm testified to that. Weren't you supposed to come before you die? Wasn't it supposed to be an orgasm like no other, like the orgasm riddling her now?

The scent that ghosted through her nostrils as she drew her last breath of air was his scent, salty, laced with the mysteries of the deep, threaded through with the sweet musky aroma of ambergris.

2

Meg groaned awake and opened her eyes to eerie green darkness. The sound of rushing water echoed nearby. She tried to raise herself, but her limbs felt weightless, as if she were floating. But she wasn't floating. Something was holding her down. She waved her arms about in the water . . . *water!* She was immersed in water. But it couldn't be. How was she breathing?

Frantically, she groped her body. She was naked. Where had her night smock gone? Oh yes, the selkie lord had flung it into the sea. But he couldn't have. That was just a dream . . . Wasn't it?

Something snaked its way between her legs, and she cried out. How strange her voice sounded under water. Why didn't she choke on it when it rushed into her mouth? Why hadn't she drowned?

She swatted at whatever was groping her thighs and cried out again when it probed the V of golden hair curling between, parting her nether lips. This was no eel . . . no creature of the deep, and sea vegetation did not move with the deftness of fingers. She shot her hand out and gripped a wrist . . . a man's wrist . . . *his* wrist!

His warm mouth covered her scream.

In spite of herself, Meg groaned as his pointed tongue plunged in and out of her mouth, filling her the way his penis had filled the woman on the beach. It felt like hot silk, moving with the same ebb and flow of the sea. She was dead; she had to be. She had drowned and this was the entrance to the Netherworld the elders spoke of, the purification by water the dead must endure that the shamans held in such high regard. But if that were so, why had he entered it with her, this enigmatic lord of the selkies?

Reason returning, she fought the human tether he had become. "Let me go!" she cried, slapping at his arms and kicking her feet. "Take me back. I will be missed. There will be reprisals. My aunt Adelia and my uncle Olwyn are shamans. They are mentoring me in the Witching Way. I am to become a priestess of the Isle of Mists! Take me back, I say, and no harm will befall you!" Why was the water so murky? Why couldn't she see?

He slipped one arm around her waist, threaded the other between her legs, and stroked her buttocks. "Every man, woman, and child on the Isle of Mists practices shamanism," he said. "They are nothing to me. You are in my world now, Megaleen, and here I am Simeon, Lord of the Deep. You summoned me, remember?"

"When did I do that?" Meg snapped at him. "How? I never summoned you. This is some wicked nightmare—some vicious trick of my subconscious mind. I will awake in my loft, in my bed of feather quilts, and you will be what you really are . . . a wet dream; a figment of my imagination . . ."

A deep gravely laugh lived in Simeon's throat. It resonated through Meg's body, sending little tingling shockwaves along her spine. She stiffened in his arms as his deft fingers traced the cleft between her buttocks. Her quick intake of breath rang in her ears as the finger slid lower, ever so lightly flitting over the taut pucker of her anus, then moved on to explore her virgin skin. The finger traveled higher, reaching for the tiny bud at the top of her vulva. Rolling it between his fingers, he pressed down upon her nether lips until he had exposed the hardened erection to his tongue, and he laved it until she cried out in excruciating ecstasy.

Meg gripped his shoulders. She should struggle—push him away. She could not. Instead, she threaded her fingers through his long wavy hair. Carried on the underwater current, it flowed about him like strands of silk. It was beyond bearing. Never had she dreamed such ecstasy existed. As if they had a will of their own, her hands fisted in that cool dark silk and held his head against the tender spot he nipped and laved and sucked until her body shuddered to a riveting climax.

The moan that left her throat echoed through the underwater labyrinth, through her body—through her very soul.

"This is only the beginning," Simeon murmured in her ear.

Taken with a sudden wave of remorse, Meg stiffened in the arms that pulled her closer. "I did not summon you!" she got out. Her voice was no more than a hoarse whisper. "Take me back! I beg you . . . Take me back to the Isle. . . ."

His deep throaty laugh shot her through with gooseflesh. She had heard tales of the selkies' hypnotic power over women, of their prowess in the art of seduction. What else had she heard about them? Why couldn't she remember? Why couldn't she think? There was more to the legend, so much more . . . But his hands were exploring her body again, playing with her nipples, just as he had played with the nipples of the woman on the strand—rolling them between his thumbs and forefingers, making them hard and tall for his lips to suck on, first one and then the other.

"Did you not come to the strand . . . and watch the seals sunning themselves on the rocks?" he said between tugs upon her aching buds, meanwhile laving the pebbled areolas mercilessly. He was going to drive her mad. *Please the Powers, let this be a dream!* she prayed.

"The seals, yes," she said. "Many times, but I don't see how—"

"Did you not lament your lot, little fledgling witch? Did you not wish the kind of love your situation denies you, for you know no priestess of the Isle can marry, Megaleen?"

"I-in my secret heart, perhaps, but that does not mean—"

"Did your condemnation as a witch not make an end to your betrothal on the mainland?" Simeon interrupted. "You are not simpleminded. You know a witch of the Isle's mystery—her very power—lies in her maidenhead, in the taking of it by the shaman high priest in her right of initiation. . . ."

Meg had all but forgotten about that, and cold chills riddled her as she remembered what fate she'd resigned herself to when she escaped to the Isle of Mists. These traditions were eons old, rooted in the mists of time that gave birth to the Isle and created the mystical priestesses who ruled it.

Simeon's sultry voice cut into her thoughts. "Was that not the reason you were whisked away from your marriage bed before the conjugal quilts were laid out upon it?"

Meg gasped. "How could you know that?" she cried.

"We selkies are perceptive entities," he responded. His hands were everywhere, flitting over her skin, exploring every orifice, every crevice and fissure. It was as if he was memorizing every contour of her body with hands that knew just how to touch, to arouse, to tantalize in ways not even she had fantasized in her wildest dreams, waking or sleeping.

Whatever sea plant she was lying upon was as soft as satin, caressing her in places he could not reach since his hands were occupied elsewhere seeking out her pleasure zones. The broad, flat ribbonlike growth swaying in the water seemed an extension of him, as alive as he was and of like mind with his advances. How far did control of his water world extend, this Lord of the Deep?